Live your truth!
Mary Perrine

The Lies They Told

by

Mary Perrine

The Lies They Told

Cover photo taken by Penny Langguth Thorkildson.

DEDICATION

To anyone who has ever felt marginalized
by the people who should love them the most.
Believe in yourself.
You are enough.

ACKNOWLEDGMENTS

A huge thank to Sean Bloomfield and Colton Witte at 10,000 Lakes Publishing for continuing to believe in my dreams as much as I do. Their support is priceless.

As always, thank you to my Beta-Readers: Bridget Christianson, DeeAnn Eickhoff, Barb McMahon, Ruth Novack, Cheryl Meld, and Linda O'Neil. Your skillful editing, suggestions, insight, and refining polished this story. Thank you to Bobbie Knutson for answering my desperate plea for help with the book blurb. An enormous thank you to Penny Thorkildson for the beautiful cover photo! Also, thank you to Beth Lynne at BZ Hercules. She critiques with an honest and beautiful heart. You are all wonderful friends.

Infinite gratitude goes to Tim Johnson and Curt Graff who were invaluable in my research. They were my go-to guys when I had insurance and law questions. I can't tell you how much time they saved me. I am so grateful to have had their wise counsel as I was penning this book. Thank you!

And, as always, a special thank you to my husband, Mitch, for being my first and last reader before it goes to the publisher. He is my best friend and critic—in a good way. He also holds me up when I begin to hit the wall. Without his love and support, I wouldn't be writing.

I love and appreciate every one of you so much. Thank you for all you do for me.

TABLE OF CONTENTS

CHAPTER 1 1

CHAPTER 2 17

CHAPTER 3 30

CHAPTER 4 36

CHAPTER 5 40

CHAPTER 6 53

CHAPTER 7 60

CHAPTER 8 66

CHAPTER 9 74

CHAPTER 10 84

CHAPTER 11 92

CHAPTER 12 101

CHAPTER 13 105

CHAPTER 14 113

CHAPTER 15 130

CHAPTER 16 139

CHAPTER 17 143

CHAPTER 18 151

CHAPTER 19 164

CHAPTER 20 175

CHAPTER 21 187

CHAPTER 22 194

CHAPTER 23 205

CHAPTER 24 221

CHAPTER 25 235

CHAPTER 26 244

CHAPTER 27 252

CHAPTER 28 259

CHAPTER 29 268

CHAPTER 30 279

CHAPTER 31 285

CHAPTER 32 296

CHAPTER 33 306

CHAPTER 34 315

CHAPTER 35 319

CHAPTER 36 327

CHAPTER 37 331

CHAPTER 38 336

CHAPTER 39 342

EPILOGUE 347

CHAPTER 1

Jane Hart

No one saw me until the day I disappeared. I had always been right in front of them; they just didn't notice. I was invisible to nearly everyone I knew. At least that's the way it always felt. But on that day, the day I went missing, people couldn't stop seeing me.

Maybe everyone in the world felt as I did. Perhaps social media had turned us into people who felt and saw ourselves for less than we were—made us doubt our value. Was that possible? But then I remembered. The way they treated me wasn't the way they treated everyone else. For forty-seven years, they had treated me as if I didn't exist; I was a nobody, completely unseen—until that day.

The local stations ran stories about my disappearance at the beginning of every newscast. Social media exploded with photos and posts. You couldn't scroll through Facebook, Instagram, or Twitter without seeing my face multiple times a day; even people who didn't know me shared the posts, spreading the message across the country. Old YouTube videos from my work resurfaced. Photos had been clipped from the videos asking if anyone had seen Jane Hart, the missing woman from Cedar Point, Minnesota. KCLM Radio invited my ex-colleagues, neighbors, and friends to call in with leads, stories, and information—no matter how small or insignificant. And believe me, they would have been insignificant since no one bothered to treat me the way I treated them.

I was everywhere in Cedar Point, and yet, I was nowhere. I was so close, they could have felt my breath, but they still didn't see me past their insecurities or their obsessions with themselves. I was with them, standing among them, but their blindness to anyone else made it nearly impossible to focus on me. Oh, they tried, but doing something because it looks good to others and doing it because it's the right thing to do are two entirely different beasts.

After nearly sixty hours of the local police unearthing the clues so carefully laid out for them, the search turned in a new direction. Were they searching for the Jane Hart who was still breathing life or the one who was silenced by death?

***

On the third day, near nightfall, people poured into the town square, leaving the comfort of their couches and homes in the small town of Cedar Point to help in the search. Police cars lined the main street; red and blue lights blindingly flashed shards of light into the crowd from both ends of the block. Local officers, as well as those from neighboring towns, directed traffic onto the side streets where cars had been abandoned at odd angles. Heavy bags loaded with search gear dangled from their shoulders or hung across their backs as they made their way to the center of the square. Neighbor greeted neighbor with nothing more than a nod or a smile. Being there was for their benefit, not mine.

A sharp whistle dulled the drone of the group of nearly three hundred but did not silence it. I knew every person there: colleagues whom I had worked with for the past twenty-five years before I retired a few months earlier, Pastor Gray and other parishioners from Holy Cross Lutheran Church where I attended services, acquaintances from the hospital where I had recently begun volunteering one day a week, the woman from the floral shop—the only person who knew my secret penchant for anonymously sending flowers to locals who needed an extra pick-me-up, neighbors to whom I dropped off gifts, meals, treats, and flowers—but who never reciprocated—and people claiming me as their Facebook friend, but never inviting me to their homes or calling me on the phone.

Old John Henry, a recently arrived drifter, who everyone knew had a nose for free food, strolled the edge of the crowd near the provisions station. A dark blue sweater riddled with holes, covered by an oversized ratty suit jacket, worn cargo pants with a surfeit of pockets, and a pair of my husband's old running shoes were his choice of clothing today and every day. His sudden appearance in town a few weeks back had not surprised any of the locals. Cedar Point was located on a main highway, which made it a common location for the homeless or drifters to rest before moving to warmer destinations for the winter. A filthy, tattered pillowcase filled with John Henry's worldly belongings never left his hand. When he first arrived, I gave him money and delivered food to him on multiple occasions. I repeatedly tried to take him to the On Again, Off Again thrift shop, but he always politely refused.

The owners of Knuckle Sandwiches and Just Desserts Bakery had set out trays of mini-sandwiches and bite-size sweets. Fresh Thyme Market, the local grocer, pulled in a pick-up filled with cases of cold water and soda. The tailgate had been left open for the thirsty search party. As John Henry passed in front of the tables, he helped himself to one of each item. The elderly woman who monitored the food wrapped up a second sandwich and handed it to him. He acknowledged her kindness with a sideways grin before tucking the food into his pillowcase and moving near the edge of the crowd.

My family—if you could call them that—was there as well. Doug and Viv, my parents, had driven down from their home in Duluth, on Lake Superior. It was the first time I had seen them together since I left home nearly thirty years before. I would have recognized my mother's *perfection* anywhere. No one, except Viv, would arrive for a search in heels, dress slacks, and a designer coat. My father was now gray, both in hair and skin color. He didn't stand as tall as he once had; he was slightly hunched over and walked with a cane. He appeared to be unsteady on his feet, but when he tried to hold my mother's arm for support, she pushed his hand away.

My identical twin sisters, Laurel and Lily, arrived a short time later with their husbands in tow—dressed in what I assumed to be their *Thursday* matching outfits: designer jeans, silky blouses, pink sweaters draped over their shoulders, pink plaid canvas deck shoes and, of course, pink leather Coach purses tucked in the crook of their elbows, held like they were on a shopping trip. Their clothes weren't identical, but they were close enough to ensure it was part of their joint shopping ensemble. Lily and Laurel looked more alike today than they ever had with their straight blonde shoulder-length hair, highlighted with ultra-blonde streaks in nearly the same places.

Their husbands appeared to be cut from the same cloth. But while they looked alike—the same haircut and similar dress, they weren't twins. They had just been sucked into my sisters' childish game of *samesies*—a game they played growing up, one that excluded everyone else, including me—their younger sister.

My sons, Luke and Cole, both introverts except with their closest friends, hid in the shadows to avoid the free-flowing hugs and meaningless comments the locals felt obliged to deliver. They both looked so frightened. I wanted nothing more than to save them from this fiasco, but I couldn't.

Sean, my husband—and I use that word loosely for a variety of reasons—worked the crowd: shaking hands, touching shoulders, even hugging people he had grown to dislike over the years. He thanked each person for coming, patting their hand as if it was a celebration, all the while displaying his million-dollar smile of expensive, brilliantly white teeth he had to have done during law school. He spoke in complete sentences, unlike the grunts and silence he reserved for me.

He was incredibly handsome; I had to give him that. His jet-black hair, strong jawline, square chin, and slightly hollowed cheeks made him the catch of the season twenty-six years ago. The problem was that Sean knew he was incredibly good-looking. It wasn't until after we married that I realized he was in love with himself much more than he was with me.

On the morning we met, I just happened to cut through the pre-law building to get to my class. It was pouring, and I looked and felt like a drowned rat. My hair and clothes were soaked, and my shoes squeaked as I traipsed down the hallway. For some unknown reason, it was that morning that Sean decided he was ready to settle down, take a wife, and raise a family. It could have been anyone else he set his eyes on, but it was me he bumped into. I spent almost twenty-five of our twenty-six years together wishing I had braved the rain that morning, wishing I had never set eyes on the likes of Sean Hart.

Sean was impulsive. If he suddenly decided he wanted or needed something, it had to happen right then and there. There was no waiting, no thinking about it, no discussion. It was a done deal. He pursued me for one month, making me feel like the luckiest girl in the entire world. The day after graduation, we went down to the courthouse and pledged our love before the Justice of the Peace. The judge's assistant and a man waiting to file a complaint against his neighbor's dog became witnesses by default. I don't know their names. I just wish none of us had been at the courthouse that morning.

We had spent the last two years of our marriage in what Sean referred to as *divorce negotiations*. Most of those *discussions* started civilly but often ended with me being hurled to the floor, spit on, kicked, or desperately struggling to peel his hands and fingers from my mouth and nose. Through the years, I became an expert at hiding bruises and other marks he left on me—both physical and emotional.

Why didn't I leave? It sounds simple, doesn't it? As simple as *Why didn't you make the bed?* or *Why didn't you buy groceries?* Why didn't I pack a bag, walk out the door, and never look back? Sean was always at work, at a sporting event, in a bar, or somewhere else he would not divulge. There were plenty of missed opportunities to pack and leave. But it just wasn't that easy. I was terrified of losing the things he held over me. He controlled every aspect of my life, from our household to the boys' affection. Besides the money I had hidden away, I had nothing and no one to support me: no family, no close friends, no colleagues. Simply put, I felt abandoned, alone, and helpless. No one could save me from the mess I was in.

I retired not by choice but because Sean forced me to do so. When I reached twenty-five years at Hallman and Carter, most as the Director of the Human Services Department, he wanted me done. Not for any reason other than his insecurities. On a rare evening out, a night that revolved around Sean's law firm, he thought the owner's son and my boss, Drew Carter, had paid a little too much attention to me. It was completely innocent. While Sean played the room, Drew and I talked about work, but Sean didn't see it that way. In his mind, I cheated on him, fraternized with someone who couldn't help him climb his way to partner at his firm. He saw me as worthless that night.

I paid for it when we got home after midnight. The argument started in the car and didn't end until I escaped out of the bathroom window and slept in an unlocked boathouse on the shore of Cedar Point Lake. I returned home later the next day to find Sean waiting to punish me for my indiscretion of the previous night. After a week of absences due to the *flu*, I returned to work in long-sleeved blouses and a new hairstyle— one that covered the bald spot and yellowed bruising on my forehead.

A month later, exactly two weeks before I could retire from Hallman and Carter with my full pension, Sean called Drew Carter and gave him my two-week notice. Then, he mailed a letter he typed and forced me to sign—if I wanted to continue to live. I was furious. He had crossed the line, and I was willing to fight for what was right. The drama went from zero to sixty in a matter of seconds. In a fit of rage, he threw a Waterford crystal vase at me. I ducked, but it shattered when it hit the marble fireplace. It would have been better had the vase hit me because missing me sent him into a rage worse than I had ever seen. He snapped. Sean grabbed a large piece of glass from the broken vase and chased me through the house, trapping me in a corner. He grabbed me in a chokehold; the crook of his elbow pressed against my windpipe as I struggled to breathe. Holding the glass to one side of my face, he lightly ran the point down my cheek before moving it toward my neck. I tried to turn to the side so I could draw a breath. As I dug my nails into his forearm, he squeezed harder. Finally, as everything began to fade to black, I stomped on the top of his foot with the heel of my boot. Instead of letting go, he threw me to the floor. I kicked at him, trying to get away, but he lay on top of me, pinning my arms against my chest, and stared into my eyes with his blank death stare. Again, he lifted the piece of glass for me to see before he methodically reached down and shoved it into my thigh. The more I reacted, the more he smiled. He stood up, kicked me in the head, and screamed at me to clean up the mess. He spun on his heels and walked away. It was like a release for him; once he was through hurting me, it was over—until the next time.

I sobbed silently and quietly writhed in pain, pressing my hand over the long cut to suppress the bleeding. I was afraid if he heard me, the cycle would begin again, and I wasn't sure I could defend myself from another attack so soon.

I carefully pulled the glass from my leg. I needed stitches, probably a dozen or more, but over the years, I had become

Mary Perrine

accustomed to taking care of my own injuries, protecting Sean's dirty little secret. The cut bubbled and stung; I held my breath for several seconds. Finally, I dried the gap and pulled it together, sealing it the best I could with skin glue before stretching butterfly strips across the cut to hold the two sides together. Then I covered it with several large sterile pads before I cleaned up the rest of Sean's mess.

It made no sense to me why Sean insisted I retire. I was sure he wanted out of our marriage as much as I did. But as I lay in Cole's twin bed that night, with my throbbing leg propped up on two pillows and an ice pack over the wound, it became perfectly clear. Sean didn't want me, but he didn't want anyone else to have me either. I was positive he'd kill me before he'd let that happen.

***

On the night the first search party formed, I stood in the middle of the town square surrounded by three hundred people. I saw every one of them, but not one of them saw me. No one noticed me. No one attempted to speak to me. Yet there I was. Sometimes, people can look right at you and never really see you when you have lived your life invisibly—not because of anything you have done, but because others have put you in that situation. This gathering of my *family and friends*—for me— proved that point. I meant nothing to anyone. They were here for me, but I honestly didn't matter to any of them.

It's ironic how my disappearance brought the town together.

10

It was the most newsworthy event to ever happen in Cedar Point—a city that could have been used as the background for the movie *Groundhog Day*. Nothing ever changed. Watches could be set by who was parked at Pauline's Café at any particular time, the order in which folks entered the church, or the moment one of the patrol cars turned down any street. It was like living in Mayberry but on a bigger scale. The town drunk's name wasn't Otis—it was Frank—and none of the four deputies were named Barney.

For a town bordering on nearly 7,000 people, something exciting should have happened from time to time, but there was nothing: no carnivals, no celebrations—nothing.

A second whistle, this time low and hollow, cut through the evening air. People quieted as they inched closer to the gazebo, standing shoulder to shoulder, holding hands—neighbors, colleagues, and people who considered me their *friend*. The unusually warm September day had quickly faded into a cool, damp evening around sunset, forcing many to retrieve jackets and heavy sweatshirts from their bags. Then, much like the parting of the Red Sea, the crowd split down the middle, creating a path for Sean and the boys to move toward the platform. A sea of whispers filled the air and hung above the crowd as if in large speech bubbles—a few mentioned me, but most were about *that poor handsome man*.

Sean was clearly in his element; he loved the attention and slowly turned in a circle to soak it in. The boys hung their heads, hiding from the attention, the prying eyes of the crowd. I tipped my head and pulled the bill of my baseball cap down to keep from meeting Sean's eyes.

"First, thank you for coming." A portable microphone sat on a wobbly makeshift podium. Brian Enderly, the Chief of Police, bent the microphone forward and then back again. He towered above the mic; for it to capture his voice, he had to lean forward. The position looked tremendously uncomfortable. Camera lights flashed in his face, and he blinked several times to clear his vision as he looked into the crowd. The media shoved microphones on extended arms in his direction, forcing him to block one that narrowly missed his face. "As you all know, Jane…ah," he stumbled, "Mrs. Jane Hart is missing. The last time she was seen was Tuesday morning around 5:30 a.m. when her husband left for the gym before going to work." Brian looked at Sean. I couldn't believe Sean had the audacity to turn and wave to the crowd.

Brian adjusted his hat with both hands; he tugged it down over his short brown hair. It was very apparent he was hiding his frustration. He hated Sean nearly as much as I did. "When Sean returned home around ten o'clock Tuesday night, his wife was missing. According to Mr. Hart, her cell phone and purse were located in their entry. Her black Armada was still parked in the garage. We've had a search team at their house for the last two days and a second group of detectives following other leads. Lake searches are also underway. None of Mrs. Hart's credit cards have been used, and there has been no activity on any of their bank accounts."

The air was crisp; the excitement of the crowd added to the chill. I almost got caught up in it myself until I remembered it was me everyone was searching for. There hadn't been a missing person case in the town since John Bauer accidentally locked himself in his cellar nearly three decades before. Most Cedar Point crimes fell under one of three categories: parking tickets, loitering, or noise violations. Other than the sheer number of people in the town, there was no reason to employ a sheriff and four deputies.

Brian looked up toward the darkened sky above the throng of searchers. I could tell he was uncomfortable in the spotlight. He scanned the crowd as he loudly cleared his throat without turning away from the hot mic. "Evidence suggests there was a struggle. I can't go into details, but we are certain Mrs. Hart did not leave on her own accord."

Hearing him refer to me as Mrs. Hart felt so wrong. Brian Enderly had known me his entire life. We went to elementary and high school together; we even dated for several months before we graduated. We had planned out our entire life together after college, but Brian insisted on returning to Cedar Point afterward, and I wanted to get as far away from this town as I possibly could. But you see how well that worked.

"Our goal is to reunite Mrs. Hart with her family. As I said, we have a group of officers working on other leads, but we have to consider the possibility that..." he took a deep breath and blurted out his next sentence, "we may be looking for a body." The crowd inhaled, sucking away the air I needed to breathe. I coughed, but no one noticed. A high-pitched wail suddenly rose from the back of the crowd. People turned to watch my sisters sobbing uncontrollably. Those closest to them circled around and offered words of support. But I knew their outburst was all for show. The last time I had spoken to either of them was almost two years before—a month after Grandma Betty died. Both before and after, there had been silence.

"Please," Brian called into the microphone. "Please, friends! Please, we need to focus on finding Ja... Mrs. Hart." Several officers, both from Cedar Point and the neighboring communities, climbed up the back of the platform and stood slightly behind Brian. "So here's how this is going to work. Based on where you are currently standing, I'll divide you into teams." A few individuals *linebackered* their way through the crowd to join up with friends. "Your officer will give you specific directions about where and how to search." I watched him suck in a deep breath and blow it out; the microphone caught the gust and started to squeal. Brian stepped back and waited for it to quiet before dividing the crowd. Whenever Brian got frustrated, you knew. His frustration was etched deeply into his face. His breathing grew deeper, and he forcefully exhaled.

As the searchers shifted to their part of the square for further instructions, I wandered toward the edge of one group, keeping enough distance for no one to see me. I stood in the shadows of a massive elm tree and tilted my chin toward the ground. Peering over the top of a pair of dark lens glasses, I watched Sean climb the steps and stand in front of Brian.

"Where do you want me to go?" he asked. "And just so you know, we're not staying at that shithole motel you put us up at for the last two nights." Leave it to Sean to care about his accommodations while I'm missing.

I could tell Brian wanted to choke him. I saw his jaw tighten. "Take Jane's family and go over to the Moonlight. Nancy's expecting all of you. I'll send word when I know more. But don't expect to hear from me until morning." Brian turned toward the boys. "Cole and Luke, you can head on home to your place tonight, if you wish, but there's plenty of room at the Moonlight if you'd rather stay there." He looked at the large group of Harts and the Sterlings. "I'll want to talk to all of you at some point in the next couple of days. So don't plan on leaving town. Understand?"

The boys were gone before Brian finished. I watched them head toward the main drag. I wanted nothing more than to follow, but I couldn't put them in danger.

"I need to go home and pick up..." Sean started to tell Brian.

Brian held up his hand. "Not gonna happen, Sean. My team hasn't finished over there. And even then, it could be several days before we let you back in."

"Oh, you've got to be kidding!" Sean kicked the railing with the tip of his Danner hiking boots. "My wife's missing, and I can't go home to get clothes?"

"You heard me, Sean. You step one foot on your property and I'll have your ass in jail so fast, you won't see it coming." Brian walked toward the back steps of the gazebo. But before descending, he spun around. "You know what burns my ass, Sean? If my wife were missing, I'd be a hell of a lot more worried about *her* than having clean clothes or where I spent the night." Sean lurched at Brian but stopped at Brian's first word. "IF...you lay your hands on me, Sean, you'll spend the night in jail instead of at the Moonlight. Got it?"

Way to go, Brian! I thought.

Then I walked out of the city park for the last time.

CHAPTER 2

Jane Hart

Being invisible is soul-crushing. It is a loneliness that squeezes so tightly across your chest at times you can't breathe. That was how I was treated for my entire life: alone, unnoticed, unappreciated—at least to the people who should have mattered the most to me. I was born into invisibility; I was raised with it. And for some inexplicable reason, it has continued throughout my entire life. It is not something I would wish on my worst enemy—not even Viv, my mother.

For years, I had nightmares about running down a hill, trailed by a gigantic steel ball. No matter which way I turned, the metal ball followed. When I grew too tired to run anymore, I tried to push back to keep it from destroying me, but I could never change its trajectory. I would always lose control and it would run me down.

That nightmare was a metaphor for my life.

***

Cedar Point is where I was born and raised—if you can call it that. Let's be clear. I wasn't an *oops baby*. I was more of a *dammit*.

My father worked as a pharmacist at Holder Drug, about a half dozen blocks from our house. Shortly after I was born, he purchased it from Charlie Holder. My dad owned the pharmacy until about four years ago when he and my mother suddenly sold their house in Cedar Point and the business before moving to their *cabin* on the shore of Lake Superior in Duluth. I found their place on Google Earth one day during my lunch break. It's *not* a cabin; it's a mansion.

I hadn't spoken to my parents since the day I left home. I had no idea they had even left town until the new owner of their house tracked me down and demanded I come and get my boxes out of her yard.

That afternoon, for the first time since the day I left home thirty years before, I drove down Meadow Street. I spent a lifetime avoiding that street. I wiped my sweaty hands on the front of my jeans as I weaved my Armada along the winding road. The house looked just as pretentious as it had when I was a child. Nestled in the center of a double lot, it was surrounded by an overabundance of mature trees and massive flower gardens tended to by a master gardener my mother hired. The yard was fenced in on all four sides by a tall picket fence. At my mother's insistence, an electronic gate had been installed across the driveway to, quoting my mother, *"keep the riff-raff out."* It was obvious she included me in that group. When I was younger, to appease my mother, my father brokered a deal with the owner of a seedy music store a couple of blocks away—to park my car in his lot in exchange for free drugs. It was an illegal arrangement, but it kept my heap of junk out of their pristine yard, and it kept my mother happy. Her happiness seemed to be my father's life-long goal.

I parked at the end of the driveway, got out, and pressed the buzzer at the gate. The same deep chimes of my childhood rang out, announcing my arrival. I waited for someone to answer. A woman's voice came through the speaker, and I introduced myself. "The boxes are right behind you," she grumbled. "Didn't you see them?" Two boxes had been stacked in the corner of the driveway. I thanked her and turned away. *Of course, the new owners would be just as ostentatious as my parents*, I thought. Why would I believe anything different? When I reached the sidewalk, I heard the click of the speaker. "I don't ever expect to see you here again. Your mother told me all about you."

I turned toward the gate; my curiosity had gotten the better of me. "What exactly did my mother say?" I asked.

"Don't be so naïve," she barked. "She told me the entire town knows about you." I heard the speaker click off. My mother had brainwashed yet another new Cedar Point resident.

It no longer mattered. My parents weren't residents here any longer. I no longer had to live in fear of running into them.

I picked up the first of the two boxes. It was filled with posters that had been torn from the walls of my bedroom, literally ripped down. Why, of all the things my parents could have returned, did she choose to return these? I walked over to the woman's garbage can; the front edge was carefully placed parallel to the street, precisely as my mother would have insisted the help do. I overturned the box into the bin. At the very top of the heap of posters was my diary. It had disappeared the day I left home. My innermost thoughts had been locked away in those pages. I reached into the can and retrieved the book. The lock had been broken, and the pages were thick from moisture that had somehow found its way into the book. I opened it and leafed through it. Someone else's writing appeared over the top of my words. In her beautiful script handwriting, my mother had refuted nearly every statement I made; criticizing, complaining, and correcting my feelings— based on her accounts. I closed the cover and walked toward my car and dropped the book through the open passenger's window before returning for the second box.

Multiple layers of wide, clear box tape had been used to seal the box. It was light in weight and appeared to hold almost nothing at all. I picked at the tape on the edge of the box until I was able to pull it back and break the flaps free. I reached in and lifted a gray box with a lid. My baby book was inside. I paged through it, but it was devoid of a single pen stroke. The words *Plain Jane* had been gouged deeply into the cover. Burning with rage, I opened the trash bin and threw the book and the box inside. My mother had found one more way of making me feel less than nothing.

***

Viv was the town librarian. My grandmother told me she

had taken the job shortly after I was born, around the same time my father bought the pharmacy. For as long as I can remember, my mother threw herself into the pages of books and other people's stories, separating herself as far from mine as possible. I was convinced she was trying to eradicate my existence—if not physically, then mentally and emotionally.

I was born into what was supposed to be the perfect family, *the Sterlings.* We were the envy of the entire town—until the moment jealousy turned to disbelief and sympathy. That was years before I was born. By the time I arrived, the perfect family had begun to crumble; it was held together by a single thread.

My sisters were identical twins. Laurel and Lily were a perfectly matched set: blonde and adorable. From the time my mother was a girl, she had dreamed of having a boy and a girl, but identical twins garnered her attention beyond anything she could have imagined. And so, the perfect family came into existence. And Laurel and Lily could do no wrong.

Two years later, Viv gave birth to my brother, Jordan Joseph Sterling. Like me, JJ, as he was nicknamed, was a surprise baby. But that didn't matter; my mother finally had her boy. And even though JJ put an extra burden on their finances, my mother couldn't have been happier. They were the perfect family—until tragedy struck.

Grandma Betty always said JJ was incredibly curious. He was a watcher. Everything JJ learned was by studying the world around him. He could do and understand things other four-year-old children could not. My mother would take him to restaurants and stores, making him demonstrate his knowledge and abilities to impress others. My father would often place bets with people in his store about what JJ could or couldn't do. He bragged to anyone who would listen to stories about his brilliant son.

When JJ was small, my grandmother lived next door, in the same house my father had grown up in. She was the *self-proclaimed* neighborhood snoop, and she took great pride in it. Grandma Betty knew what was happening in everyone's house, sometimes before they did. Because her kitchen window faced the street, she knew who had flowers delivered and who had parcels dropped at their front door. Grandma was aware of who came home later than expected and who missed a day of work. She knew everything—except on *that* day.

It was a beautiful spring morning near the end of the school year, and for the first time since my grandfather's death, my grandma went to the backyard to salvage what remained of her gardens. It was weeding time for both her garden and her grief. She believed it was time for a fresh start.

My mom had gone upstairs for a quick rinse-off before taking JJ to preschool. Before she went, she again warned him about the dangers of leaving the house, but JJ's curiosity got the better of him. On the way to the kitchen, Mom's car keys, hanging with several other sets on the keyboard in the entryway, grabbed his attention. He crawled onto the bench and pulled them from the hook. The entire board fell from the wall and onto the tile floor with a clatter. JJ grabbed the set of keys he wanted and kicked the rest of them under the bench, along with the board. He pushed the screen door open and headed toward her new Volvo station wagon. He tugged the door open and hoisted himself into the driver's seat, adjusting the mirror as he had seen her do every morning before preschool. He had no idea what it should reflect, so he tilted it so low, it had to have shown only his face. The engine sprang to life as he put the key in and turned it. He pulled the gear shift toward him and put it into R. He knew that meant *reverse*. The station wagon rapidly rolled backward down the steep driveway and into the street. Too short to press the brakes and steer the car, he did what he had learned from my father when riding his bike in an unsafe situation—*abandon ship*. He flipped the door open and jumped, but the door swung back toward him and knocked him to the ground. He fell to the concrete and rolled under the car. It was his bloodcurdling scream that brought everyone running.

In all my years at home, no one ever spoke of JJ or his accident. It wasn't until I was 14 that I read the entire report. I discovered it in my father's desk during one of the weeks when they left me home alone. There had been no funeral, no gravesite, nothing to commemorate JJ's life. It was as if he had never existed. Grandma Betty was the one who told me the story. She was the only person who was ever honest with me, the only person I trusted.

Joy left the house with JJ that day. It didn't walk out; it ran. Mother self-medicated with alcohol, and Father helped himself to an array of pills from the pharmacy: little yellow ones to keep him going during the day and small green ones to help him fall asleep at night. In between, he drank whatever my mother hadn't.

During that year, my mother disappeared nearly every day. She'd slip out in the early morning before my father woke and would often not return until long after he was asleep. She would be gone for days on end. When my father asked her where she had been, she told him she just needed time.

Lily and Laurel nearly lived at Grandma Betty's for several months. She had to be strong enough for everyone. But a year later, still broken from a second death so close to that of her husband, she sold her house and moved across the country, settling in Nevada with her sister Evelyn.

By the first anniversary of JJ's accident, things slowly began to improve. Life took on a new normal. My mother pushed my father to take the twins to Disney World for their seventh birthday. This trip was more than just a birthday celebration; it was supposed to be a beginning, but my mother lived in an alternate reality, and she had ulterior motives. Less than nine months later, their new normal came to a screeching halt.

Yes, I was a *dammit* baby. It was evident to everyone from the moment my mother told my father they were expecting again. I wasn't part of their big perfect plan; I wasn't JJ. My parents didn't want me; that was clear.

On the day I was born, my mother walked out of the hospital without me, less than ten hours after giving birth. My father, afraid such an act would tarnish their shiny reputations, returned her to the hospital, claiming postpartum depression. For my entire childhood, my mother freely tossed out the phrase, "I should never have gone back for you!" It was clear she blamed my father for making her return, and even more, she blamed me for being born.

My given name is Jane Sterling. That's it—no middle name. Grandma told me the nurse asked about a middle name, but my mother simply replied, "None. She's such a homely thing. My twins were both so beautiful. This one is just so...so plain. *Plain Jane* fits her well, don't you think?" My mother called me Plain Jane until the day I moved away. It was how she introduced me and how she referred to me when speaking to or about me.

My earliest memories are of watching my parents and sisters load the car with suitcases and drive away. Because my grandmother had moved nearly fifteen hundred miles away, a sour-faced, wrinkly old woman was my only companion until they returned in what I came to know as *many sleeps later*. This happened several times a year, not always to Disney, but each time they returned, I knew they had been on a grand adventure, one of which I was never a part.

My parents' graduation from parenthood coincided with my

sisters' graduation from high school. I was almost nine. From that day forward, I lived in survival mode—eating meals of peanut butter and jelly sandwiches alone, usually in my room with old issues of *Teen Beat* magazine I swiped from the shrines once known as my sisters' bedrooms. By the time I was twelve, my parents had begun abandoning me for up to a week at a time. The old woman no longer came to stay with me. I didn't dare mention it to anyone because I knew what would happen. Bobby Conyers, a boy in my class, was sent to a foster home. His life was *not* any better in his new home than it had been with his abusive mother.

By junior high, my father began referring to me as Plain Jane as well. After a lengthy conversation with the cosmetic counter woman in his store, he selected multiple packages of make-up, insisting my mother teach me how to accentuate my greenish-blue eyes—the only thing he found acceptable about me. "At least if people look at your eyes, it might draw attention away from the rest of your face and that Brillo Pad on your head." This was the discussion on my 13th birthday. There was no cake or gifts—except for the stack of make-up my father dumped on the table. It was his way of making me less of a pariah in their perfect family.

At 17, I walked onto the stage of my high school auditorium and gave a ten-minute Valedictorian speech. The topic was about being true to yourself, not letting anyone else determine your self-worth. An hour later, I walked into my house, still in my cap and gown. My father was in his den and my mother was under an umbrella next to the pool, paging through a decorating magazine. I stood near each of them, hoping they would say something, but neither of them even looked up. They had not attended my graduation. There were no pictures, cake, or celebration.

I stood in the bathroom with my grandma's 35mm camera and took a picture of myself in the mirror. Then I changed into a t-shirt and pair of shorts and packed four cardboard boxes. Two held clothes, all of which I purchased myself, because *why would we spend money on someone who doesn't appreciate anything we give her?* One of the boxes was filled with awards and memorabilia from school—the only place I remotely felt I belonged. The last was loaded with odds and ends: my camera, tape recorder, an alarm clock, hangers, notebooks, etc. I searched for my diary, but after ten minutes, I gave up.

I retrieved my tan 1986 Chevy Chevette with the woodgrain panel sides from the shady record shop parking lot two blocks away, opened the gate using the code 613, my sisters' birthday, and drove up the long driveway. I loaded the four boxes into the back and slammed the hatch shut, hoping the noise would draw some attention, but I got nothing.

From the time I was 14, I had worked multiple jobs and saved every penny to buy that car, fill it with gas, and pay the insurance. It was Brian Enderly who taught me how to change the oil and keep it running.

Through my packing and departure, Doug and Viv, as they insisted I call them when I turned 16, never uttered a word. My mother remained on the deck, and my father, as always, was glued to the TV in his den. After the last box was loaded, I walked into the house just to see if they might say something, but I knew better. The silence was deafening. I could hear the kitchen clock ticking so loudly that I wanted to rip it off the wall. I turned on the tap and let the water run. I filled one of my mother's favorite glasses with cold water and carried it out to the car, setting it into a cupholder. Then I slid into the worn tan and brown plaid seat and stared at the house for what felt like an eternity. It wasn't my home; it had never been my home. So why did it hurt so much to leave? It made no sense. Anywhere I went, anything that happened from then on had to be better than what took place within those walls.

Finally, I backed down the driveway and through the open gate. I backed onto the street and shifted into drive, but just before I hit the gas, my father called through the gate speaker telling me to wait. I didn't get out of my car. Hope filled my chest, and I held my breath in anticipation. *Would he tell me he loved me? Would he apologize for the way they treated me?* I wondered.

When Doug reached my car, he stuck a ten-thousand-dollar check through the open window. I didn't understand. I couldn't even lift my arm to grab on to it. "Take it," he barked. I snatched the check from his hand before he changed his mind. He cleared his throat and more gently said, "Have a good life, Jane." He turned to walk away but spun around and leaned into my window. "Say nothing to Viv about this money. Understand?" I nodded.

He held my eyes for just a few seconds before returning to the house; for the first time ever, I saw a gentleness on his face, a caring I had never witnessed before. Tears spilled over and ran down my cheeks as I drove away. Those were the first positive words my father had ever said to me. It was the first time I ever felt like he saw me as his daughter.

CHAPTER 3

It was almost 10:30 p.m. when Brian jabbed a tack through photos of Doug and Viv, securing them to the investigation board. Some hotshot young deputy sent over by the sheriff's department in Alexandria had told him that no one used investigation boards anymore; they used software to track information. Brian almost shot him on the spot. He hated computers, but he hated smart-ass 22-year-olds more.

He connected the Sterlings with a short red string; then, he ran a second string from them to the approximate location of their Lake Superior home on the map. He picked up his coffee cup and took a sip, anticipating heat on his tongue; instead, his coffee was lukewarm. He spit it back into the cup and dropped it on his desk harder than intended. The contents sloshed over the top. Without looking, he swiped his hand across the puddle, sending the liquid airborne.

He stared at the board. Something didn't add up. What was he missing? *Who* was he missing?

Brian knew too well that three days without a sighting of Jane was too long. There were too few leads, and no one was talking. Jeff Porter, his head deputy, had nothing to report after the night's search. Brian knew he had to get people out searching during the daylight, but, that was nearly impossible in a blue-collar town like Cedar Point.

Brian walked out of his office and into the breakroom. He dumped the contents of his cup down the drain before pouring the last drizzle from the pot into his mug. "Sonofabitch!" he bellowed, slamming the decanter down on the counter. He snapped off the brewer and pulled the fridge door open. Silently, he bitched out his assistant, Mauri, for stocking Pepsi instead of Coke. He grumbled as he popped the top and poured it into a clean cup he had snatched from the open shelf. Maybe he could convince himself it would be enough to keep him going. It was going to be one of those nights when he'd see daylight before sleep would come.

An earsplitting cacophony of shattering glass, followed by a thud, sent his cup flying. A sticky mess sprayed across two walls. "What the hell?" he shouted. Instinctively, he pulled his gun from his holster and leaned against the wall outside his office door. He flipped off the lights in the breakroom and stood in the dark; a beam of light bled across the lobby floor.

He was the only one in the station—or at least he thought he was. Holding his gun in both hands, pointed outward, he peered around the doorframe and into his office. The window near his desk was shattered, and a large rock lay on the floor near the bulletin board. Brian snapped off his office lights and stood in the dark, searching for movement behind the station. About twenty yards away, he saw someone dressed in black, wearing a white mask. After taking a theatrical bow, the culprit raced into the woods behind the station.

Brian shoved his gun into his holster. His night just got infinitely longer.

After closing the blinds, Brian turned his lights back on. He tugged a pair of rubber gloves on before beginning his investigation. His oversized hands nearly stretched them past their limit. First, he measured the distance between the window and the rock and the height of the break before noting the thickness of the glass. Next, he snapped photos of the window and the rock before turning it over. Printed in large black letters was a two-word warning: *Stop looking!* He drew in a sharp breath and held it much longer than he should have. Someone did not want him to find Jane.

The glass shop was closed, but he knew the owner, Jack, would take care of the window before daylight. While he awaited his arrival, he printed the pictures of the rock and added the information to the investigation board. He flipped it around just as his phone rang, announcing Jack's arrival.

Jack removed the broken pieces of glass and boarded up the hole before settling into Brian's chair and placing an order for the new window to be picked up in Alexandria the following morning. Brian would be sleeping at the station tonight—another sleepless night in that old recliner. He pretended it was because of the boarded-up window, but he knew that was a lie; it was because of Jane.

After walking Jack out, Brian flipped the board over. He

added a note about the rock incident. *Suspect ran into the woods.* That alone eliminated Doug and Viv from tossing the rock; they were too old and frail to run. But it didn't absolve them of Jane's disappearance. He added a note to three other suspect photos: *runner*—Sean Hart, Lily Blake, and Laurel Scanlon. *Who didn't want him to find Jane—or her body? Was it one of these people, or was it someone else?*

Brian opened his laptop and typed in his password: JS73*LvU!. Over the years, he had used different variations of this password, but it always was about Jane. Even when he dated Ella Connors, his password was still a tribute to the only woman, besides his mother, he had ever loved.

The printer jammed as he tried to print out the photos of Jane's sisters. After a few choice words and what amounted to a knee to the plastic "groin" of the machine, the photos emerged. He cut them and hung them on the board before returning to his computer.

Unread emails populated his inbox. He scanned the subject lines, deleted several, and began to work his way down the list. Several were from lonely people who had nothing better to do than fabricate false leads. He had worked with these people before; nothing had ever panned out. Playing good cop with these armchair detectives wasn't something he could afford time to do—not with Jane missing.

Earlier in the evening, Mauri had shown him a Facebook page that had been started by one of the parishioners at Jane's church. It was called *Bring Jane Hart Home*. Brian hated social media. He despised the political posts that seemed to bring the crazies out of the woodwork, but even worse were the family photos, reminders of what he had missed out on, pining away for the one woman he could never have. But as much as he didn't like it, the one thing he had learned over the years was that criminals often showcased their crimes on multiple platforms. They were more often than not narcissists who liked to brag about their accomplishments.

He loaded his Facebook account and typed *Bring Jane Hart Home* into the search bar. Almost instantly, Jane stared back at him. Her eyes pierced his soul, touching something inside of him no one else ever had. Emotion filled his chest, and his eyes welled with tears. Quickly, he scrolled down to the messages, removing her face from his view. It upset him to know she was missing and he hadn't found her.

Some of the posts were incredibly disgusting. It couldn't have hurt Brian more had he been clubbed with a two-by-four. The horrible things people said about Jane, *his Jane*, cut him to the quick. After scrolling through a couple dozen posts, he slammed his laptop shut. *Damn them! Damn every last one of them!* They had no idea who Jane even was. If they did, they would feel her disappearance the same way he did.

Maybe there were posts that held information, maybe there weren't. He'd have Mauri sort them out tomorrow. She was the best sleuth he had.

It was nearly dawn when Brian grabbed a blanket from the supply closet and settled into the recliner. He'd spent more nights in that chair than he would like to admit—not working on cases—just not having Jane to go home to. For thirty years, that had been the only thing he ever wished for.

CHAPTER 4

Chief Enderly, without warning, walked into the Moonlight Inn with his lead deputy, Jeff Porter. Party sounds wafted from the dining room and into the hallway. Brian stopped and pressed a finger to his lips. "Listen," he whispered. "Sounds more like a party than a vigil." Laughter exploded into the hallway. The sound about sent Brian through the roof. It wasn't his lack of sleep that made him despise the Hart and Sterling families; it was that they were complete and utter assholes.

Silence fell like an iron curtain when the two men walked into the room. All eyes were on them. Brian looked around and noted that Cole and Luke had chosen their house over the Moonlight.

"I've got nothing new to share."

"And you call yourself a cop?" Sean nearly knocked his chair over as he jumped up. His shoulders arched backward, and his chin tipped upward in defiance. "My wife's missing, and you have nothing! Rookies!" he yelled. "You're all a bunch of Barney Fifes who can't tell your head from your ass!"

Enderly, who had five inches and nearly fifty pounds of muscle on Sean, took a step toward him. He pointed his finger in Sean's direction. "Sit your sorry ass back down in that chair or I'll do it for you." Sean quickly stepped backward, catching his heel on the leg of the chair before awkwardly falling into the seat.

Brian folded his arms across his chest to keep from *accidentally* grabbing his gun and shooting him. He hated Sean Hart—for multiple reasons.

Enderly loudly cleared his throat. "As I was saying, we've turned up nothing new." He glared at Sean, silently daring him to utter one word. Finally, Sean looked away. "We have to look at every clue, follow up on every possible lead." Brian looked at Doug and Viv. "That includes looking at anyone who has had contact with Jane recently." He studied every person in the room, trying to read them. "At this point...you're all suspects." Panic flooded the dining nook. Brian could almost hear their hearts thudding in their chests. Sean picked up his napkin and wiped the sweat from his forehead. Jane's dad slid his chair away from the table and headed toward the back door of the dining room.

"Going somewhere, Sterling?" Brian asked.

When Doug turned around, his face nearly matched his white polo shirt. His hand was pressed to his chest. "I-I need my nitro pills."

Brian almost felt sorry for him—almost. After all, the man was nearly eighty. Enderly jerked his head toward the door. "Jeff, go with him and make sure he's okay. When he's ready, we'll take him and Viv down to the station for questioning." He wasn't sure it was possible, but Doug looked almost whiter than before. *He knows something*, Enderly thought.

"The rest of you are not to leave the Moonlight—today, tomorrow, or until I tell you that you can leave. Got it?" Silence. No one moved. "Sean? Understand?"

Instead of turning white like his father-in-law's, Sean's face had grown red. "Yeah," he mumbled.

"What?" Brian leaned his ear in Sean's direction. "I didn't hear you."

Sean stared at the table. "Yes," he said louder.

"If you need anything, let Nancy know. She'll make sure you get it."

Enderly picked up a cherry and an apple cinnamon pastry from the buffet table and strutted back down the hallway and out of the Inn. The corners of his mouth turned up as he slid into the squad car and called the station.

"Hey, Boss," Mauri sang into the phone, always a little too cheerful for his liking. "Need something?"

"Why else would I call?" Enderly barked sarcastically into the phone. "Set up the conference room. Make sure the cameras and mics work." He didn't wait for a reply before pressing the end call button. Brian knew he owed her an apology.

He took the last bite of the pastries. A voicemail indicator flashed on the screen of his phone. Somehow, he'd missed the call when he was putting the fear of God into Sean and the Sterlings. He pressed the button and listened to the message. His heart banged against his rib cage and he dropped his head against the headrest. The message was long, but still, he replayed it a second time—and a third. He pressed the pause button when Deputy Porter opened the squad's backdoor and ushered Jane's parents inside.

"You okay, Chief?" Jeff asked when he crawled in. "You don't look so good."

Brian took a deep breath before putting the car in drive. "Hard to say."

CHAPTER 5

Brian hurried into the conference room and closed the door behind him before Mauri could make one of her stupid comments. He wasn't in the mood for her biting remarks. They would have only pissed him off. He pressed his forehead against the cool woodgrain veneer of the door and drew in a long breath, releasing it with such force, it fluttered the edges of the papers in the folder he held under his arm. That was something he had been doing a lot lately—drawing deep breaths that escaped in an explosion. Frustration did that to him. He dropped the folder on the table and checked the equipment. This case was too important to have even one thing go wrong.

"September 22. Interview with Doug and Vivian Sterling, parents..." This breath came out as a sigh, loud enough for the microphone to pick it up. "...of Jane Hart," he said slowly. He paused the recorder and the camera. "Dammit!" He slammed his fist on the table, then grabbed the edge for support.

The door opened enough for Mauri's head to slip through. "Everything okay, boss? I just heard the big one."

"Fine, just frickin' fantastic." Brian winced as he stood. He rubbed his lower back with one hand. *Damn yard work!* "Mauri, have Jeff bring the Sterlings in."

She stepped in and closed the door. "Together? You want

them both? At the same?"

"Yes," Brian barked as he turned back toward the conference table. "Stop questioning me."

Mauri's eyes grew wide as she backstepped toward the door. "Wow! Looks like somebody got up on the wrong side of the recliner this morning." She waited for him to respond but got nothing. "Jack told me about last night." She stopped herself before pulling the door open. "Brian, you know I'm here for you, right? We've been friends for a long time. I would do anything for you." Brian opened his mouth, but nothing escaped. "It's okay. You know I've got your back." Mauri moved toward him and draped her arms around his waist, squeezing, trying to make her fingers touch behind him, but he was nearly three times her size, and no matter how hard she tried, she couldn't make them connect. Finally, he bent over and wrapped his arms around her. "You know as well as I do," she said into the front of his shirt, "when I retire, you have to go too. 'Cuz no one else is going to be able to deal with your crap." She smoothed the front of his shirt with both hands and left the room to deliver his message to Jeff. As angry as Brian was, he couldn't help but smile.

Jeff escorted the Sterlings into the room, brushing by Brian before settling them into their designated seats. Sweat rolled down Brian's back. The walls felt like they were creeping inward. Claustrophobia was another ugly gift his father had given him—drunkenly locking him in the cellar, laughing as

Brian pounded on the metal door, begging for mercy. None had ever been given.

His father repeatedly punished him for his mother's death. His crime? Surviving the car crash that killed the only other person he had ever loved. From that day, at the tender age of seven, to the day he turned eighteen and walked out of the house with a ratty suitcase, there wasn't a day that passed that Brian hadn't wished he had been the one to die that night.

They had left a friend's dinner party early—not by choice. The host *suggested* they leave before things escalated more than they already had. Mack Enderly had never walked away from anything a day in his life, and he couldn't do it that night either. No, he had to make a scene, smashing several wine glasses and shouting that he only came because his wife was too stupid to get herself there and back.

When they finally got outside, Brian's mom raced to the car, climbing into the driver's seat before his dad. But Mack jerked her out and threw her to the ground. "You ain't gonna drive, woman," he shouted at her. "I'm the man!" he said, pounding his chest. His mother limped around the front of the car and pulled the passenger door open. Brian slid onto the bench seat between his parents. He reached for the middle seat belt but only found half of it.

Alcohol permeated the rusted 1968 Ford Bronco. The odor was so strong that Brian started to cough. "Shut the hell up," his father screamed as he elbowed him in the chest. His mother pulled Brian toward her and rolled down her window enough to let in some fresh air. He held her hand as he leaned across her lap, his face aimed at the open window. He was petrified—both of his father's driving and of the punishment that would occur when they got home. For six miles, his father repeatedly jerked the car off the shoulder and back onto the road before it was sucked down into the muck and rolled, ejecting his mother into the ditch and tossing him around the cab.

Four days later, Brian woke up in the hospital connected to machines that amplified the pounding in his head. All he wanted was his mom, but some lady in red shoes told him she had died. He never looked at the woman's face. Instead, he just stared at her shoes and cried until he fell asleep again.

For the next three weeks, he remained in the hospital connected to those same noisy machines. He slept away much of each day, occasionally leaving the room in a wheelchair to attempt walking. The only person who ever visited was the woman in the red shoes. She wore them every day. He was afraid to ask her what would happen to him when he could leave the hospital. Where would he go? He had overheard the nurses saying he would be going home soon. But where was home?

On the day he was supposed to leave, his father appeared in the doorway of his hospital room. His dad had a dark red line across his forehead that Brian had never seen before. Brian was in shock; his dad was alive—and sober. He hoped this would be the beginning of better times, that his father had finally stopped drinking for good. When they arrived home, before his dad even entered the house, he went to the shed and returned with a cardboard box filled with bottles of booze. Brian watched as he pulled a dirty glass from the sink and sat down in the filthy kitchen. "Don't judge me," his father warned. "My wife is dead, and I've been left with a...a seven-year-old burden named Brian."

Brian turned away and hobbled to his bedroom, pushing things out of his path with his crutches. The tip of one crutch caught on his door frame and he fell to the ground. He angrily swung his feet and kicked the door shut, sobbing until he fell asleep on the cold linoleum floor.

From that day forward, there was rarely a week that passed that he wasn't on the receiving end of a willow switch or a leather belt. Physical abuse left marks, reminders that could usually be covered by clothing or hats. But the scars of the emotional abuse ran deeper. There was only one person who could truly understand how that felt. He and Jane shared more than just a friendship growing up—much more.

***

After a few minutes, Brian nodded at Jeff, indicating he was ready to begin. "For the record, I want each of you to state your name—your whole name." Deputy Porter was in charge of recording the interview. The two had been friends since college. Brian trusted him with his life—that was how important this was.

"Umm, Doug...Douglas Joseph Sterling." Doug tucked his hands into his lap to steady them. The shaking didn't stop. Locking his hands together only made his arms and shoulders tremble. Tiny beads of sweat grew on his forehead as he tried everything. "I have Parkinson's," Doug admitted.

Brian nodded toward him. "I understand."

"This is ridiculous!" Viv quipped. "You've both known us for years."

"State your name," Jeff calmly repeated as he pointed to Viv.

"Oh, for Pete's sake! Vivian Ellen Sterling. Are you happy?"

Jeff smirked. "Quite."

Brian looked directly at the camera. "Let it be known Vivian Sterling is a hostile witness."

Viv huffed. "I am not a hostile witness. This is all just so stupid. Our daughter is missing and you're sitting in here digging for something you won't find when you should be out there looking for her."

Brian looked at the Sterlings. "Also, for the record, would you like to have your lawyer present during questioning?"

Viv laughed. "We have nothing to hide. You know that."

"Do you want your attorney present?" Brian asked again.

Doug looked at Viv and then back to Brian. "No."

Brian gave a questioning shrug. "Okay then. When was the last time either of you spoke with Jane?"

The Sterlings stole a sideways glance before Viv spoke. "We haven't spoken to or about her since the day she left for college. Even when she moved back to town with that handsome husband of hers, she wanted nothing to do with us, so we accepted her wishes. We've never even spent time with our grandsons. Can you imagine anyone being that hateful not to let us see our grandchildren?" She tilted her head downward. Clearly, Viv was vying for *best actress*. The only honest statement she'd made was that he and Jeff had known them for years. Which was the reason he knew she was lying.

"So you're saying you haven't spoken to Jane in almost thirty years?" He let that statement settle before moving on. "You both lived in Cedar Point for what, thirty-some years, and you have never spoken? Your paths never crossed? You've never run into each other at the grocery store or in a restaurant?" He didn't blink. "The library—where you work?" He emphasized those last three words. "The post office? The..."

"Yes, of course, we've run into her, but we haven't spoken. Jane's an angry woman. She always turned the other way when I tried to make small talk."

Brian rubbed his aching jaw. *Liar,* he thought. "So, again, for the record, you have never called her and she has never contacted you. Correct?"

Doug pressed his fingers to the center of his chest. "Mr. Sterling, are you all right?" Jeff inquired. "Can I get you something?"

"Maybe some water." Doug swiped at his forehead with the back of his hand. "It's really warm in here."

Jeff retrieved a water bottle from the mini-fridge at the end of the conference room, twisted off the top, and handed it to Jane's father. Other than the initial sloshing over the top when Jeff released it into Doug's trembling hand, he downed it all. He stared at Brian for a few moments before cupping his hand over his wife's. "Viv?" If looks could kill, Doug would have been dead where he sat.

His wife jerked her hand from beneath Doug's quivering one and folded her arms across her chest. "I've already told you: we haven't spoken to her." Viv stood up so unexpectedly, she launched her chair into the wall. "You've wasted enough time playing investigator. We're leaving so you can get out there and find our daughter."

"Sit down," Brian hissed through gritted teeth. "We're not done. I'll let you know when we're done."

Viv didn't move. Jeff retrieved her chair and placed it behind her, inching it forward until her knees buckled and she fell into it. "Well, of all..." she snorted.

"Again, for the record, you have not spoken to Jane since the day she left for college. Is that correct?" Viv nodded her head. Brian closed his eyes, beyond frustrated with two people he didn't trust and liked even less. "You have to respond out loud."

"And again, I will repeat—this is absolutely ridiculous."

47

She glared at Brian, but he won the stare down, and she turned away. "No, we have not spoken to Jane since the day she left for college."

Bingo! Adrenaline shot through Brian's stomach as he smugly opened the manilla folder he had carefully organized. "You're sure?" He waited for her nod; he already had her answer on record. "Because according to phone records, there have been twenty-seven phone calls from your house phone in Duluth to Jane's cell over the past two months—outgoing calls." He let that sink in while he watched them squirm. "Twenty-seven," he stated again. "That means someone from your house had to have called her. Care to explain?"

Red splotches sprouted on Doug's neck and cheeks. He looked at his wife, who jumped in before he could speak.

"That's got to be an error. You know how messed up the phone company is. We have *not* spoken to her."

"That's weird," Brian was grinning on the inside. "On August 4th there was a seventeen-minute call. August 6th, twenty-four minutes. August 9th, thirty-seven minutes." He turned his head to the side. "A thirty-seven-minute call…and yet, *neither* of you spoke to her. "It just seems odd to me that the phone company would make that many errors." He shrugged. "Well, someone must have placed those calls." He looked back down and continued. "August 14th, twenty-three minutes. August 21st, eight…"

Doug shifted in his chair. Brian could see him coming

undone. "Okay," he said. "Stop. I'll tell you everything you want to know. Just give me another water first."

Viv's face turned as white as the Minnesota snow.

***

"Good evening. I am Angela Wellens, and this is the five o'clock KNOW News. Tonight, we want to update a story we brought to you three days ago—about Jane Hart, the missing woman from Cedar Point. While there is nothing new to report, we hoped sharing more about Mrs. Hart might help our viewers recall something they may have seen or heard. For this, we turn to Justin Manuela. Justin?"

"Angela, I am here at Hallman and Carter in Cedar Point, where Mrs. Hart worked for twenty-five years before retiring just months ago. With me, I have two of her colleagues, Elin Fortier and Aly Shandler." Justin positioned himself between the two women.

"What can you tell me about Jane Hart?" He tilted the microphone toward Elin.

She looked directly into the camera. "Well…" An uncomfortable silence filled the air.

Justin quickly shifted the mic to the other woman. "Ms. Shandler?"

"Oh, well, umm. Well, Jane worked here forever. She was, ah, in the company long before Elin and I started at H & C."

"I understand she was your boss. What was she like?" Justin asked.

Another awkward silence landed before Elin spoke. "Well, she was like the head boss. She wasn't exactly our direct boss." She leaned across the front of Justin and looked at Aly. "I guess she was good at what she did. She won awards for it."

"Yes," Aly said. "Lots of awards; she had a whole shelf full of them."

Justin shifted gears, hoping to get the women talking. "As I understand, Mrs. Hart retired a couple of months ago. She seemed awfully young to retire. Was there a reason she left when she did?" He moved the mic toward Elin.

"Well, ah, I guess she had in enough years to get her pension, probably."

The reporter tried to make a save. "Twenty-five years in one place. That must have been one huge retirement party."

The women peeked at one another behind Justin. "Well, to be honest, we, ah, sort of forgot she was retiring. I think everyone did," Aly said sheepishly.

"But in our defense," Elin added, grabbing the mic and tilting it toward herself, "she didn't tell us she was even retiring until two weeks before she left."

The reporter cringed. "Is there anything else you would like people to know about Jane Hart?" he asked.

"We just hope they find her," Aly added.

Justin turned back toward the camera, clearly reeling from the most uncomfortable on-air interview he had ever conducted. "If you have any leads in the disappearance of Jane Hart, please contact your local police. This is Justin Manuela in Cedar Point sending it back to Angela in the studio."

"Justin," Angela inquired, "do either of the women believe Jane would have left on her own?"

Justin repeated the question for the women.

"Well, we thought we knew her, but when she left the office on her last day, she didn't even say goodbye," Elin said. "So, who knows. She's likely to do anything."

Wrinkles formed across the reporter's forehead; his eyebrows dipped into a deep V. Anger seethed through his entire body. He carefully delivered his final message, focusing on keeping his words light. "There you have it, Angela. Even after working together for many years, neither woman feels they knew Jane Hart well enough to know what she might do."

The two women scurried off-camera, giggling about being on TV. Their phones instantly lit up, spreading the news of their *stardom*.

"Thanks, Justin," Angela stated. "And now..."

The camera had barely cut when Justin muttered, "What the hell was that?"

The cameraman slipped the camera from his shoulder. "Hard to imagine you can work with someone for so long and not care enough about them to show a little human decency."

"I'm beginning to see more of that kind of behavior with every story I do." Justin slipped his mic into a velvet sleeve and tucked it into his leather satchel. "People are becoming more and more self-centered all the time. They only see what they want to see—or *who* they want to see."

CHAPTER 6

For the second time in two days, Brian stood on the gazebo platform in the center of the town square. The sun beat down on the crowd, clothed in long pants, long sleeve shirts, and boots. It was too hot for this kind of dress, but the terrain necessitated it, and once the sun fell below the horizon, the cold would move in. The crowd had nearly doubled since the previous night. Word had spread to neighboring towns, and people came to lend their support. Carloads of volunteers descended on Cedar Point hours earlier than the scheduled meeting time. The local shops had been inundated with shoppers for most of the afternoon, killing time until the search was to begin.

Brian turned away and cleared his throat before turning back toward the mic and the same too-short makeshift podium. Deputy Porter whistled three times before the crowd quieted.

"Thank you for helping in today's search and thanks to those of you who searched last night." Brian pulled a piece of paper from his front shirt pocket, rebuttoning it with two broad fingers. He unfolded the single sheet and smoothed it out on the unsteady tabletop. A dozen or so reporters shoved microphones in his direction. A few were attached to long extensions that reached over the others and swung uncontrollably. "Back up," he whispered angrily. His words, caught on the live mic, swirled through the park and into the crowd.

"People, our only goal right now is to find Mrs. Hart and bring her home safely, but because of circumstances I can't yet discuss, we need your help to search areas we don't have the staffing to cover." He swallowed hard. "For those of you who are joining us today, when you get to your search area, you will form a line. Stretch across the space, fingertip to fingertip. Then, as a group, begin walking slowly. Don't just look down, but around you and above you as well. Feel the ground with your feet as you walk. If you find anything, yell for assistance. The line will immediately stop and an officer will come to you. Do you understand?" The crowd's acknowledgment came as silence. "Okay, just like last night, I'll divide you into sections. When I dismiss you, turn away from the gazebo and toward your officer for additional instruction. Are there any questions?"

Someone from close to the gazebo platform spoke first. "Chief Enderly, Mira Anthony, KMZL TV," she introduced herself. "Do you have any new leads? Anything that would make you focus on the areas the searchers will be walking through today?"

Brian despised the media, and everyone knew it. They were one of the most frustrating parts of his job, but today, he needed them. It was critical they keep Jane's face and name in the public's eye for as long as possible. "We have no specific leads at this time. However, we are talking with her family, friends, and colleagues, hoping to gather more information. As for the areas we are searching, there is a different reason for each one."

He was done with questions; he looked back at the crowd. "And this goes without saying, but if any of you have information, no matter how big or how small you believe it is, please call the station. I can't stress that enough. Alright, I'd like to get several hours of searching in before dark." Then, using his hand to gesture, he began splitting the group into search teams.

***

The waiting was excruciating. It was driving him over the edge. He owed it to Jane to be out searching; he wanted to be the one to find her, but he couldn't leave the office. He had to follow up on the message left on his phone earlier in the day. He couldn't trust anyone else—not even Jeff.

He wasn't even sure where to start. The number had been blocked. It didn't mean he couldn't track it down. He would officially have to secure a search warrant to obtain the number, but he wasn't ready to do that—not just yet.

He'd burned a pathway between his desk and the coffee maker, never filling his coffee cup, just picking up the pot as his thoughts roiled. By the umpteenth time he'd walked through the office, it hit him.

It was nearly 4:00 p.m. when he buzzed Mauri.

"Need something, Boss?" She smiled as she poked her head into his doorway.

Brian cleared his throat.

Mauri pointed at him. "Oh-oh. You got something big on your brain, don't you?" She knew him better than he knew himself. "Spill," she told him.

He frowned at her intuition—always irritatingly accurate. "I need you to track down some information for me." He looked at her empty hands. "Did you bring a notepad with you?"

"Where've you been, Boss?" She wagged her cellphone in front of him.

"Whatever," he said.

Within minutes, Mauri was back at her desk, headphones connected to her phone. She was busy listening to and checking off the list of things Brian asked her to find—including *the effing case of Coke.*

Finally, with a fresh cup of coffee in his hand, Brian closed his office door and dropped into his chair. He locked his fingers behind his head and leaned back. From the first time his father abused him, he knew what he wanted to be when he grew up—a cop. Not an officer in just any town; he wanted to work in Cedar Point. At just five years old, he dreamt of the day he could lock his dad away. He could still hear the clang of the steel doors slamming shut—his father inside—the first time, the third, the fifth, the twelfth—and the last. That last time should never have happened. The last one should have come long before—long before Mack Enderly took *another* life. Yet, no matter how hard he tried, Brian couldn't shake his guilt.

Killing his wife hadn't made his father stop drinking; neither had multiple DUIs, sitting in a jail cell for a couple of months, or having his car repossessed for lack of payment. By the time Brian was ten, he knew his father was a lost cause. When he didn't have booze, or a way to get it, his father drank cough syrup, NyQuil, and mouthwash until he could convince someone to bring him a bottle or two.

Mack Enderly couldn't hold down a job. He also couldn't take care of Brian. When there was food, Brian cooked their meals. When the refrigerator was empty, Brian resorted to stealing fruit and vegetables from the townspeople after dark. He dug through garbage bins and dumpsters, searching for scraps of food behind restaurants. In the winter, on his way home from school, he often stole from the grocery store. In the beginning, the stealing didn't bother him, but as time passed, the guilt ate away at him, and he wondered if he was any better than his dad. He was mortified. His mother would have been ashamed of him. So, finally, when Brian turned 14, he got a job at the same grocery store, secretly putting part of his paycheck back into the till each week.

His father never noticed the empty fridge and never asked where the food came from when it appeared. The only thing he seemed to notice was an empty alcohol bottle. Brian would often come home to a shattered bottle and a new hole in the sheetrock. On those nights, he would silently clean up the mess and leave the house, often sleeping in the shed, covered in layers of quilts his mom had handsewn over the years. He would hear his father screaming for him, but he never dared respond.

One spring evening, many years after Brian was hired as a deputy in Cedar Point, in a frantic search for alcohol, his father hotwired an old farm pickup he came across on his walk to town. He drove the heap of junk nearly twenty miles to the next town over—where they wouldn't recognize him as the drunk he was. That day, he sat on a barstool, pouring down one drink after another, waving his welfare money under the bartender's nose. Finally, the owner cut him off, refusing to serve him anything but coffee. His father became belligerent and took a few swings at the staff. The bartender called 911, but while on the phone, his father had disappeared—stealing a second, almost new car. Nearly home, somehow keeping the car out of the ditches, he lost control on a ninety-degree corner and plowed into the home of Clara Jessop—the home where she had raised her family, watched her husband die, and entertained more visitors than anyone else in Cedar Point. Clara took her last breath when the walls of her sanctuary crumbled around her, trapping her beneath the rubble. Brian's dad walked away with nothing more than a few scratches—and a sixty-year sentence for grand larceny and second-degree murder. His drunken father would never see the light of day. For that, Brian was thankful.

Brian was the first officer to arrive at Clara's. He handcuffed his father and shoved him into the backseat of the squad car, slamming the door as his dad begged for a drink, calling him an ungrateful piece of shit.

After the trial, Brian knew he would never see his father again. He had finally won. "Mom," he said that night before he fell into bed, "I did it. I hope you're finally at peace."

It was nearly 6:00 p.m. when Mauri tapped on his door and called, "Headed home now, Boss. Everything you asked for is on my desk." She waited for Brian to answer, but she heard nothing. "Hey, Brian, I know this is hard on you, but you should probably go home early and get a good night's sleep. That old recliner's not the same as a bed."

He didn't hear her leave the building, but the vibration of his office door told him she was gone. As always, she would have locked the door behind her, leaving him alone, isolated with his thoughts.

He was deeply entrenched in other memories when the phone rang with a second message.

CHAPTER 7

Jane Hart

Hallman and Carter is a multi-million-dollar human resources firm. The company contracts with businesses that are too small to have their own HR departments and those who don't want to deal with the organization, recruiting, and training for their employees. Businesses that are part of the H & C family also have access to the company's dynamic legal team.

I was 22 years old and recently married when I landed back in the one place I said I would never return to. Unbeknownst to me, Sean, three years older, and with the ink from the word *passed* barely dry on his bar exam, had applied at a highly respected law firm in Alexandria. He interviewed, got the job, and purchased our house on Lake Cedar without a word to me. At the time, I was so in love with him, or at least the idea of having someone love me, that I didn't care nor question his actions. I kept quiet about my past in Cedar Point, not uttering a word about my parents living in the town. I figured he'd find out soon enough, but he never said one word to me about them or my past.

As soon as we were settled, I threw myself into finding a job. I spent my days writing cover letters and resumes and filling out applications. I applied at a couple dozen businesses within an hour's drive of Cedar Point. I didn't apply at H & C. They were known for hiring only the cream of the crop, and even then, only those with years of experience.

After three weeks of interviewing but getting no offers, I received a call from Drew Carter. He told me he had been given my resume and felt I would be a good fit for Hallman and Carter. I was dumbfounded.

I had known Drew since high school; he was a few years older than me, but in a small town, everyone is connected. It seemed he was too young to oversee the hiring for such a prestigious HR firm, but I didn't want to look a gift-horse in the mouth. I dressed in a navy-blue pantsuit, a white blouse, and my lucky pumps—which hadn't exactly been lucky on my job search so far. As with every other company, I expected to be interviewed by a team of employees, but Drew was the only one present for my interview. It did not go well. I was nervous and overthought every question. My answers often came out muddled and incomplete or rambling. When I left, Drew shook my hand and told me he would call me within the next few days with his answer. I already know what it would be. That was why I was stunned when he called the following day to offer me a job. It seemed too good to be true.

I couldn't believe how fortunate I was to land not just a job but one with the most prestigious human resource firm in the Midwest. Because of the economy, most of the people I graduated with had begun settling for jobs out of their field.

I started in a low-level job. Within three years, I worked my way into a managerial position. I oversaw twenty businesses at a time and had a team of ten people working under me. At 28, I became the youngest director to ever work at H & C. I loved my job—right up until I walked out the door after Sean forced my retirement.

My teams worked hard, and we won numerous awards; some were for my role as a director, but most were earned by my teams. I was so proud of every one of them. I realized, though, how little I meant to the employees of H & C on the day I packed my twenty-five years into a single box and carried it out of my office. A card from Drew had been left on my desk, but other than that, my desk looked the same as it did any other day. On my way to the door, I walked past each employee, but not one person noticed me, asked me about the box I was carrying, or spoke a word. So, with the edge of the box, I pushed the door and stepped outside, away from the building that had been my second home for the past twenty-five years.

When the door closed behind me, and I stood in the stillness of the parking lot, I realized my life there had meant nothing. I was nothing.

The weekly treat from the Perk-Up Coffee House I set on each employee's desk on Monday mornings, the pans of bars I left in the workroom every Wednesday, and even the birthday celebrations or random lunches I paid for, had grown to be commonplace and expected rather than appreciated. My teams saw those things, but they never thought about who was behind them; they never saw me. And so, on the day I left, I felt like an inflated balloon, blown up but not tied, released into the sky. The air felt like it had been sucked out of me. I had been filled with such hope until I heard the doors close. Then that hope sailed away.

I opened the back of my Armada and dropped the box into the car. I drove toward the exit, but at the last minute, I made a quick turn to the left and drove around to the back of the building. I pulled up close to the loading dock, climbed the backstairs, and tossed all twenty-five years into the dumpster. My crystal awards lay among the bags of garbage. I had thrown a lot away lately, but this really hurt.

My heart ached for what was; it longed for what could be—what Sean had taken from me. But it was over. I went home and fell into the role of a *stay-at-home mom* without kids under my roof and an absentee husband who rarely walked through the front door until long after I had fallen asleep—in a different bedroom.

Shortly after I retired, my parents started contacting me several times a week. I was taken aback by the suddenness of their need to talk to me. The calls were strained at best. Usually, it was my mother on the line, but from time to time, my father would call. I could hear Viv feed him words, making sure he asked things the way she wanted him to. At first, I didn't understand, but by the second call, it became crystal clear. My parents needed me. They were nearly penniless; other than their monthly social security checks, they had nothing. Their retirement money and the money from the sale of the pharmacy and their Cedar Point home had disappeared like sand through their fingers. Their extravagant lifestyle had been sucked down into the quicksand of greed. And, of course, they were looking for a handout—from me, the daughter they had ignored, belittled, and turned away from.

I had money put away, a lot of money. As things began to go south with Sean, I opened accounts in several different locations—in small banks in neighboring towns and in large banks in Minneapolis. Early on, I met with a new hire on our legal team who helped me set up investments to protect my assets. Sean had no idea. He was more concerned about his own money. When we married, he insisted we keep our money separate, and that included filing our taxes separately. We were married, shared a house and two sons, but nothing else.

Doug and Viv had no idea how much money I had, but they knew I pulled down a six-figure salary—including a full pension. They also knew Sean was no slouch in the income department either.

Each call contained a large portion of begging, infused with small, broken pieces of insincere apologies. There was no genuine admission of wrongdoing, of being horrible parents, or of treating me like an outsider; there were just words pieced together in what someone else might interpret as an apology, but what I heard was an excuse.

Years ago, I made a deal with myself that if they came to me for anything, I would treat them as they had treated me—as invisible. But being retired, I had time to kill, so, instead of ignoring their calls, I took them—all of them. It became my entertainment. I took great joy in their begging and pleading. I reveled in holding all the cards for once. But no matter what they said or when the call began to drag on, or when I just got tired of listening, I turned them down and hung up, all the while knowing another call was on the horizon.

Then suddenly, as abruptly as they started, they stopped. I assumed Doug and Viv had come up with another ingenious plan to finance their extravagant lifestyle. Honestly, I was thrilled with that; never having to speak to them again was a gift.

But a few weeks later, I received a call from an unknown number. Halfway through, I could barely breathe. I lost my footing and collapsed in a heap on the floor. It was as if my bones had abandoned my body. The hair on my head stood on end, and my arms were covered in goosebumps. I shivered, yet I was sweating. I couldn't move, and I couldn't speak. The room spun around me as I gasped for air. Eventually, the call ended, but I stayed where I was for what felt like hours. The message was like a cryptogram. I didn't understand it, or why anyone would want to hurt me.

CHAPTER 8

ONE MONTH BEFORE JANE DISAPPEARED

Harrison Andrew Carter III, known to his father, friends, and employees as Drew Carter, prepped to leave his office. For him, the day had dragged on well past 5:00 p.m. when everyone else shut down for the night.

Five years ago, after his father retired, Drew was named the CEO of Hallman and Carter. Not granting him full ownership meant his father could have his hands in the business, critiquing and criticizing his son's every move until the day he died.

Nearly two decades before, when the economy hit a downward spiral, and the company did as well, his father bought out his partner, Glen Hallman. It was a move that made no sense to a young, 30-year-old Drew; he begged his father to reconsider, but his dad held firm. In hindsight, it couldn't have worked out better. Drew's doubt in his father's judgment during the buyout had kept his dad from handing H & C to him earlier. "Two," as Drew often referred to his dad, wasn't about to "let some snot-nosed kid, who didn't know his head from his ass, ruin a company he had worked so hard to grow." He'd heard it repeatedly over the years—both from his dad and from the reel that played inside his head from time to time. It didn't matter that he'd proven himself time and again or that he was a good ten years older than his father was when he had started the company. To Two, Drew was still a kid, and he knew that was how his dad would see him until the day the last shovel of dirt was thrown into his father's grave.

Before he retired, Two had created an ironclad document laying out the specific terms that governed Drew's role as CEO. Harrison II had hired a team of attorneys, still paid for by the company, to enforce that document to the letter. He had put safety nets in place. Drew had tried everything in his power to take ownership, but it was like trying to push a square peg through a round hole. No matter how hard he tried, it wasn't going to happen.

To make matters worse, for the past two years, his father, at the end of his battle with dementia and experiencing several small strokes each month, lived in a care facility for adults with memory loss. Two didn't recognize his only child much of the time. On good days, the best Drew hoped for was to hear his father speak his name. On bad days, Two screamed and threw everything in his reach. That kind of anger was something Drew had never seen growing up.

It was 6:30 p.m. when the call rang through from Living Waters. They begged him to come for a visit; his father was out of control. His tantrum had gone on for hours; nothing they tried had worked. He was their last resort before they medicated his father into a stupor that would leave him nearly comatose for days. Drew had seen him like this before: angrily reliving his life as if those things were happening in the moment. Other than a rare smile, there were few happy occasions anymore, nothing to make Drew want to visit, and yet, he felt obligated. After all, his father had been his only parent since the day his mother packed her bags and left without an explanation. She hadn't hugged him or told him she loved him; she simply walked out the door with a pair of expensive suitcases. Drew was eight. And, of course, there was the fact that his father was leaving him a multimillion-dollar company that he knew, with some help, he could build into something even better. Yes, *obligated* was the word that described how he felt.

Yet here he was driving his father's company into the ground. Since Two left, Drew had shifted money around more times than he cared to admit. He'd eliminated departments and cut the staff back to barebones. He hated to think about it, but the only thing that would keep him afloat was his father's personal funds, the investments beyond the company he would inherit. And that wouldn't happen until his old man drew his last breath.

He tucked a manilla folder into his brown leather satchel. It was the latest financial report; he needed to review it before his meeting the next morning. He threw the strap over his shoulder and checked his phone one last time. Then, after extending a good night to the cleaning crew, he headed to the heated parking garage. The parking attendant had signed out shortly after the day staff had left the building. His Mercedes was parked in his spot, closest to the door. A few other older cars remained in the ramp.

Living Waters Memory Care was nestled along the curve of the Long Prairie River, about seven miles from town. Arched outward in the front and inward in the back, the building mimicked the arc of the river. The grounds looked like a golf course: peaceful and pristine. Mums of every color swelled in full bloom alongside sedum and other fall flowers. Drew was not familiar with any of the flowers. The trees surrounding the home had begun their slide into fall. Flecks of red dappled the woods as the maples began their last hurrah.

Drew pulled into the lot and finished the call he had made on his way. Business never ended. He was fortunate enough not to have a wife and kids waiting for him at home.

He waved at Genevieve as he passed the front desk. "They'll be happy to see you," she called. "He's having a pretty rough day." A scream pierced the air; he recognized it from many of his other visits. He nodded toward the woman and hurried down the hall.

"Hey, Dad," he called as he entered Room 311. "How's it going?" Silence fell as his dad looked in his direction. Drew knew his father was trying to figure out who he was. Finally, a look of recognition fell over Two's face. He opened his mouth. Drew was positive a scream was about to follow, but instead, a weak smile turned up the corners of his mouth.

Drew moved closer to his father, tucking in the red plaid

fleece blanket that lay across his lap. "That's right, Dad; it's me, Drew."

"Drr-eww," his father slurred as he repeated the word. "Drew."

"That's right. How are you?"

The nurse behind him sighed loudly.

"It's okay," Drew said to her. "Go catch your breath. I'll be here for a while." She gave him the same watery smile his father had; tears of exhaustion trickled down her cheeks.

"Thank you," she said as she touched his shoulder.

Drew smiled at her. "Thank you," he whispered.

He found the folding chair tucked into a tall cabinet at the end of his father's bed and pulled it close to his wheelchair. "What's got you so upset, Dad?" He was used to their one-sided conversations, so he was shocked when his father responded.

"B-book," his dad said. "B-book," he said again.

"You want a book, Dad?" He got up and grabbed a picture book of Minnesota from the top of his dresser. "You want this book?"

Two shoved his hand away. The book fell to the floor. "B-book!" he said more insistently.

"A specific book?" Drew picked up a few other books, holding each one in the air for a yea or nay. Each one elicited a louder, more anguished cry from his father.

"B-BOOK!" he screamed.

Drew began searching the room: the top of the nightstand,

the closet, the dresser drawers. His dad continued to yell the same word over and over. Drew felt sweat run down the back of his neck as he searched. He wasn't used to dealing with his father's newfound anger. Other than for business purposes, the man had never raised his voice a day in his life—until two months ago.

In the last drawer of Two's dresser, Drew scooped his hands beneath the clothing. Touching something hard, he hoped he'd struck gold. He pulled it out and held it up for his dad to see. "How about this one, Dad?"

His father's shoulders sagged. "B-book," he whispered.

Drew looked at the cover. It was his father's college yearbook. Where had it come from? When he moved his father into the home, he hadn't remembered packing it. Had his father somehow snuck it in? Was it more important to his dad than he realized?

He handed it to Two and stood off to one side. "Your college yearbook, Dad. Are you in it?"

Two clumsily opened the book and pointed to a picture of himself. "Me," he said, smiling. "Me."

Drew grinned. "That is you, Dad...back in college."

Drew's father turned several pages until he came to a picture of the University hockey team. "You didn't play hockey in college. You played football, remember?"

Two repeatedly pointed his finger at one person in the hockey picture. "Your friend?" Drew asked. "Is that your friend?" He matched the names to the photos. "That's—that's Doug Sterling. Was Doug a friend of yours?" he asked. As far as he could remember, his dad had never so much as uttered Doug's name.

Harrison, the second, shook his head no. "Ahhh," he exclaimed, "so you *don't* like Doug Sterling." His father nodded. Drew was confused. Did yes mean he did or he didn't? In the grand scheme of things, it honestly didn't matter one way or the other.

Two scanned the page and pointed to a second face. Again, Drew matched the name with the photo. "It says that's Vern Hartung. Was he a friend of yours too?"

Two violently turned his head from side to side. "Who's Vern Hartung?" Drew asked, knowing he wouldn't receive a response.

His father continued to clumsily page through the book. Suddenly, he stopped and pointed to a woman. "Okay, it says Vivian Goldmeier. She's pretty, Dad," he teased as he elbowed his dad in the shoulder. "Did you like her?"

A wide smile grew across his father's face. "Ah, you did. You liked her, didn't you?" Drew couldn't be sure, but he thought his dad blushed.

Harrison, the second, flipped through a few more pages. He pointed to a picture that had a large black X drawn through it in a thick black marker. "Did you do that?" Drew asked. "Did you cross that couple out?" He looked at his dad and grinned. "Wait, is that the woman you like with someone else?"

He took the book from his father and tilted it toward the light. "Dad, that's a photo of Vivian Goldmeier and Doug Sterling." The minute he said their names out loud, he realized what his dad was telling him. "That's Viv Sterling, isn't it?" He set the book in his father's lap. "You and Doug both liked Viv, but he ended up with her." His father laid a hand to his heart. "Oh, you *loved* Viv."

Drew looked at the photo again. By the time he looked at his father, his eyebrows had furrowed and his face had gone blank. He caught the book as it slipped off Two's lap. His father had retreated back inside himself.

Drew's imagination spun in all directions. *What ifs...* raced through his brain while he stayed and helped the nurse get his father changed and into bed.

As he walked to his car, the biggest *what if* suddenly struck him. What if Viv Sterling was his mother?

CHAPTER 9

The previous night had gutted Drew. His time with his father and reading through the company's financial reports, hoping to squeeze another dime from anywhere, had left him completely exhausted. His morning meeting had gone about as he had expected. Pure and simple, it was a train wreck. The company was about a buck and a half shy of going under. He was imploding a company his father had built from the ground up.

If Drew didn't find something to save his ass soon, he was done, and so was Hallman and Carter. And, as if bleeding money wasn't enough, his father's attorneys were on his case about every little thing. His only saving grace was that Two wasn't aware enough to be disappointed in him.

By the time everyone else had left the office, he was about ready to throw in the towel. Spending the entire day putting out fires and kissing asses made him feel like a politician during an election year. He just didn't have the energy to deal with his father tonight, but he knew he had to at least check in.

Drew spun around in his desk chair and pressed his cell phone to his ear. He pushed the soles of his feet flat against the wall and locked his knees as he stared out the ceiling-to-floor third-story window. From there, Cedar Point was breathtaking.

From his office, he could see a body of water in nearly every direction.

"Living Waters Memory Care. How may I direct your call?" The person sounded breathless, as if they had run to reach the phone before the machine picked up.

"Hi. Drew Carter here," he said.

"Hello, Mr. Carter. This is Genevieve. I assume you're calling to check on your father."

"That I am," Drew told her. He truly wished it didn't feel like such a chore to check on his dad—or to visit him, for that matter. After all, Two had taken care of him for eighteen years—and then some. And when his mother left, his dad took on the role of both father and mother, and never once had Drew heard him complain.

"Are you okay if I put you on hold for a few minutes? I'm pretty sure I know the answer, but I don't want to give you the wrong information in case I missed something today."

"No problem." He heard the phone click and the hold music begin. It was a slow piece that almost lulled him to sleep while he waited. He jumped when Genevieve got back on the line.

"Mr. Carter, it was as I thought. Your father had quite a good day. According to the nursing notes, he spent a great deal of time looking through his old yearbook. He ate about a third of his dinner tonight and he slept for a few hours this afternoon."

Drew breathed a sigh of relief. "Thank you, Genevieve," he

told her. "I think I'll pass on visiting tonight. I have an early morning meeting I still need to prep for."

"Don't worry about your dad, Mr. Carter. He's in good hands. I'll let the nursing staff know you called. He'll be in bed for the night before long anyway. Is there anything else I can help with?"

"No, I think that's it," he told her. "Have a good night, Genevieve."

"You too, Mr. Carter."

He hung up, leaned his head back in his chair, and closed his eyes. He felt guilty for thinking he had earned a reprieve.

The cleaning crew had come and gone from his floor. The sensor lights had shut off one by one as they worked their way toward the elevator to the next floor. A narrow strip of light bled through the side window of his office and into the shared workspace.

The silence of the office created a sudden surge of loneliness. He missed his dad, not the way he was now, but the way he had been. He longed for the Sundays of watching football together and celebrating holidays—just the two of them. He craved one more father-son island hopping adventure. Even though they'd had disputes over the business, Two was still his best friend; he had been since the day his mom deserted them. Because of his dad, he'd never missed not getting married or having kids. And he'd never resented being an only child— until now. The hardest part of his dad dying was knowing he'd be alone afterward.

Drew needed a drink. His office was stocked with bottles of anything a current client, or a potential one might want. It was the first thing he'd learned from his father: hospitality. A welcoming atmosphere went a long way in keeping an old client or obtaining a new one.

The accent light in the cabinet came on as Drew opened the glass door and reached for one of the heavy tumblers. He poured himself two fingers of scotch and carried both the bottle and his glass to his desk.

After sucking down his first drink, he poured a second. The scotch dulled Drew's worries. He finally felt like he could draw full breaths. His anxiety kept him from turning ideas over in his mind, figuring new ways to solve his financial woes; the scotch held his fears at bay. There had to be something he hadn't thought of, something that would get him out of this mess without having to wait for his father's demise.

A lateral filing cabinet sat on the opposite side of his office. He had meant to have maintenance move it into storage, but the top of it served as a countertop for a series of three-ring binders that held information his father had deemed important. Was there something in those books he might have missed?

He flipped through the first notebook but found nothing remotely helpful. Even though the cabinets had been there for as long as Drew could remember, there wasn't a speck of dust to be found, including under the binder he had removed.

"Hmm," he muttered in surprise. If he had money, he'd give the cleaning crew a raise—but right now, it wasn't an option.

The top drawer was filled with old, framed photos, including one of his mother. Drew held the old, framed picture and studied his mother's face. He hadn't seen her actual face in over forty years; honestly, he wasn't even sure she was still alive. The drawer also contained a variety of coffee mugs and other gifts his dad had received over the years. It wasn't like his dad was a hoarder; he just didn't have a cruel bone in his body, so he kept every gift, unable to hurt anyone's feelings.

Drew leaned a hip against the top drawer and pushed it closed. He bent over and opened the bottom drawer. Files were tightly pressed together; one more sheet of paper would have collapsed the delicate organization, exploding it like the Booby-Trap game he loved as a child.

He paged through the tabs on the files. The first half was benign as far as anything that might help. It was all old contracts; some dated back twenty years or more.

His back ached from bending over the bottom drawer. Tylenol or more scotch were both possible medications to ease the pain; he chose the latter. With one foot, Drew dragged a chair over to the cabinet while he took a mouthful from his newly filled glass. He set his drink in front of the three-ring notebooks. He started perusing the second half of the files; the first folder he pulled was labeled *Jane Hart*. It made no sense for an employee file to be stuck in the middle of old contracts.

He tossed the file on the round conference table behind him. He planned to drop it on his secretary's desk on his way out the door; she could file it in the morning. On some of the files, the plastic tabs were so brittle, they cracked when Drew ran his finger over them. Just before the last file, his finger froze. One word was all that was written on the label: *Will*.

Of course, his dad had a will. Harrison Andrew Carter II was worth millions—personally and professionally—well, that was if Drew didn't destroy that before Two died. No one with that kind of money would leave his fortune to chance.

He wiggled it out from between the tightly compressed folders. He tucked it under his arm and grabbed his glass from the top of the cabinet. The motion-activated lights on the other side of the room turned on as he strolled toward his desk. He set the folder neatly in front of his chair and stood by the window, captivated by the lights of the city. A few boats, decorated with strings of battery-operated lights, dotted the lakes, but the most light came from the brightly lit statue of a Viking that stood on the water's edge. Drew raised his glass to the effigy. "Here's to you, big guy," he said. Then he drained it and plopped it down on the corner of his desk.

Drew was feeling little pain. However, he knew he would feel differently in the morning. The desk chair was old and still fitted to his dad's posterior, but over time, it was slowly becoming Drew's. He just couldn't make himself throw it away. He shifted his weight in the chair until he settled in. Slightly

OCD, he moved everything else off his desk and into a drawer, including his empty scotch glass. He creased the folder by rubbing the heel of his hand over the top before opening it.

The Last Will and Testament of Harrison Andrew Carter II were the only words written on the first page. Drew grimaced. In his mind, he saw his father's lifeless body lying in a casket. Tears formed in his eyes and threatened to fall. That, in itself, told him he was drunk. He was a sloppy drunk: emotional and sappy. It was the reason he never allowed himself more than one drink when he was with others.

He turned the page, hoping to learn something that would settle his frayed nerves, make him know the company was going to succeed before he ran it into the ground. He skimmed the first few lines—the "I, Harrison Andrew Carter II, being of sound mind and body, do declare..." With a finger, he tracked each line as they swam in front of him because of the scotch and tears.

Near the beginning of the second paragraph, a name popped off the page: *Jane Sterling Hart*. That was the second time tonight he'd been reminded of their ex-employee. Drew could easily believe his father would reward Jane, a faithful member of H & C for twenty-five years, with some money or some shares of stock in the company or both. His father was a compassionate man. Jane had made him tons of money over the years; of course, he would leave her something. To be honest, her absence was one of the reasons H & C was struggling now.

Clients had followed Jane out the door—attaching themselves to their rival companies in Moorhead or Minneapolis.

It was the next line of the document that pushed him over the edge. Drew saw red. He frantically scanned his desk for his scotch glass but remembered it was in his desk drawer. He jerked the drawer open and lifted the glass to his lips, but only a drop or two fell onto his tongue. Raising the glass over his head, he pitched it across the room. It shattered as it smashed into the far wall.

"Arghhhhhh!" he screamed. He picked up his desk chair and tossed it toward the middle of the room. He swiped his hands across his desk, sending the will and folder flying. "No! No! This is not happening!" he yelled. Everything in his office became a projectile. He threw it all—every notebook and photo, every decoration and award. He even threw the nearly empty bottle of scotch.

Drew couldn't sit down, and he couldn't stand still. Rage tore through him in waves, sucking him down again and again. He felt like he'd been punched in the gut; the deep breaths he took didn't help. His tie flew across the room as soon as he won the battle in getting it off; his suit coat followed—over his head, one sleeve inside out. He searched for something else to throw, but everything was already broken or downed. He kicked off one shoe and whipped it across the room; the second one sailed through the glass cabinet door and sent the shelving and tumblers through the gaping hole. The glasses broke as they hit the quartz countertop, shattering as they landed on the marble floor.

Exhaustion ripped through Drew, and he dropped onto the leather sofa, falling onto his stomach, lying half off the couch; one knee rested on the floor. His chest heaved as he gulped air. The room looked like a war zone; there was nothing he hadn't destroyed during his temper tantrum.

What the hell was he going to do? What was he going to tell the cleaning crew or his staff, for that matter? He pushed himself into a sitting position and stared at the mess. The white paper, his father's will, almost glowed in the mess that had once been Two's pride and joy—his office.

Angrily, he leaned forward and snagged it off the floor. A sliver of glass embedded itself into the tip of his finger. He pulled it out and watched the blood pool. Death would end this, he thought; he would never have to think about any of it again. But then he thought of his dad and all he had sacrificed for him over the years, and he knew he couldn't do it. He couldn't take his own life and leave his father to die alone.

The pages were wrinkled and damp and smelled like scotch. Blood dripped onto the paper, leaving smears of Drew's red fingerprints all over the stark white sheets. His eyes grew wide with rage as he reread the information.

He had just found out his father had been in love with Viv his entire life, but in his wildest dreams, he never imagined that Two was Jane's father also. And worst of all, his father had left half of everything to Drew's newly discovered half-sister.

He thought back to the day he hired Jane. It hadn't been his decision. On paper, there were at least a dozen better candidates. In the interviews, everyone fared far better than Jane. But no matter how much he argued, the old man wouldn't budge. Jane was the only one his father would agree to hire. Back then, it made him angry. His father had overruled him once again. Today, knowing Jane was his sister, it made him furious.

Drew white-knuckled the paper. He rolled it into a tight tube before sending it sailing across the room, unraveling as it flew.

"This is all on you, Dad," he hissed through clenched teeth.

There was only one way to save the company—Jane had to die before his father did. It was clearly stated in the will. *In the event of one of the heirs' untimely death before me, Harrison Andrew Carter II, the entire inheritance will be bequeathed on the single living heir.*

Instead of taking his own life, Drew had to take hers.

CHAPTER 10

Cole and Luke were no strangers to social media. Like every twenty-something, they had accounts on every platform: YouTube, Instagram, Facebook, SnapChat, and TikTok, as well as many others. While Cole was a prolific poster, sharing photos and stories about sporting events and parties, Luke was more of a follower. When Luke did post, it was almost always photos of Hoss, his two-year-old Newfoundland rescue dog. He was huge, but he was the friendliest dog that ever lived.

The brothers, 23 and 21, posted pictures of their mom on Facebook and Instagram, hoping someone would have seen her or had information about her. Daily, they skimmed through posts looking for something that might help locate her, but they always came up empty-handed and heartbroken.

The days were challenging for the boys, but the nights were even more brutal. When the lights went out, they would often lie awake, staring into the night sky, missing her more than they ever thought possible. At the insistence of friends, they had both gone back to work, trying to find a small piece of normalcy. Even the nightly video challenges with their friends began again, but they weren't the same.

The brothers lived together in a one-story house Sean and Jane had purchased when Cole graduated from high school.

Located on a dead-end street, on the east side of town, surrounded by cornfields, the house was in shambles; it begged for repairs, but they had gone undone. The property was in foreclosure and had just come up for auction. Jane, looking for a place to settle when she left Sean, had her realtor show it to her. She saw the possibilities in it and, instead of purchasing it for herself, begged Sean to go see it. He agreed to buy it *with* her, knowing *the boys*, as Jane and Sean always referred to them, planned to settle in Cedar Point after college. If nothing else, it was a good investment property they could flip.

The house was an enormous one-story built on a slab. Rumor had it, the building had once been used as storage by a local farmer. When his son-in-law was killed in a freak farm accident, he turned it into a home for his daughter and grandchildren. Everything that had once belonged to the original farmstead, had an unsettled feel. It was a perfectly eerie set for a horror movie. Only one other house was on the street. But because of its age and poor upkeep, it was also uninhabitable.

Almost every weekend while Cole was in college, the Hart family worked on the house. They ripped out walls, increased the insulation, tore out the concrete slab and installed radiant heat flooring, replaced the oversized fireplace, and redesigned the layout, placing the kitchen and a massive living room in the center of the house. A bedroom, bathroom, and work area were located on each end. Almost always alone, Jane spent evenings painting walls and woodwork. It was slow going, but it was gorgeous when it was completed.

Cole attended college in St. Cloud, about an hour away. As planned, he moved home after graduation. His business degree landed him a job at the Waterbury Corporation in Cedar Point as a market research analyst. When Cole was a junior in college, Luke moved to the Twin Cities to attend Hennepin Technical College, where he earned an Automotive Technician degree. He had a job lined up at Mike's Master Mechanics in Cedar Point before he graduated. They moved into their house within days of each other.

Cole, two years older and a good five inches shorter than his younger brother, was the caretaker of the pair. From the minute Luke was born, Cole declared him his best friend. There wasn't anything the brothers didn't do together—except date. They had very different tastes in women.

The house had one huge design flaw. When they drew up the plans, they'd forgotten a video room. So, on their own, the brothers erected a wall through the huge living room, creating a small sitting room on one side and a gaming room on the other. Impressed by their newly found ability, Sean bought them a double row of theater seating and a TV that spanned nearly the full length of one wall. With his signing bonus, Cole purchased video and audio equipment that would allow them to game with friends and acquaintances and livestream their gaming sessions.

Cole typically got a good hour of warm-up in before Luke got home. Dinner almost always came from a sack one of them picked up after work or it was delivered in a pizza box. Their mom stopped by a few times a month to fill their freezer with home-cooked meals packed in individual containers, but those were usually grabbed for lunches as a last-minute thought on their way out the door.

On Friday, a few days after their mother disappeared, their grandmother stopped for a visit and insisted on making them dinner. They wanted to say no but didn't have the heart. So, at 7:00 p.m., they ate a full roast beef dinner, complete with guilt and shame. The secret their father and grandparents had made them keep for years weighed on them with each bite. Their mother was missing, and having their grandmother there felt more than wrong.

***

The following Friday, Cole stumbled into the house around 6:00 p.m. He hadn't been drinking, but he wished he had been. It would have numbed the anxiety and fear he felt.

Gaming was the last thing on his mind; his encounter with the masked man was all that mattered. Driving out of work, a person in a white mask had appeared in his rearview mirror, hiding in the backseat. His Jeep Cherokee almost launched itself into the ditch across the road. Cole yelled as he fought to regain control of the wheel when he dropped onto the soft sand just beyond the shoulder. The gun pressed into the side of his neck told him it wasn't a joke. Too afraid to make one wrong move, he followed directions exactly.

Cole traveled the highway for just over a mile before turning down a narrow, rutted gravel road he had never driven before. Without hesitation, he stopped the Jeep when he was told to do so. The back door opened and closed at nearly the same time as the front door did. The person wearing an expensive suit coat and the mask crawled into the passenger's seat and made sure Cole knew exactly what was expected, including not calling the police. After several minutes of precise instructions, with Cole mostly listening or repeating back what he and Luke were to do, the person climbed out and disappeared into the brush. Cole wasted no time turning his SUV around and barreling out of the road toward home.

When he opened the front door, later than usual, he was met by a hundred-and-seventy-pound Hoss begging to be let out. After sending the dog into the fenced yard, Cole began pacing a loop through the house: around the kitchen island and along the edges of the living room and back. He'd pulled his tie off and removed his suit jacket, tossing them onto the couch on two separate trips. He had just passed the island for what must have been the fiftieth time when Luke walked in.

"What the hell? What's wrong with you?" Luke asked, watching his brother's unusual behavior. "The guys'll be here in like an hour and you haven't even changed. What's going on?"

Cole stopped. He looked up at his brother, opened his mouth to speak, but said nothing. He huffed a breath and continued pacing.

"Cole, you're scaring me. What? Did they find Mom?" Luke's shoulder fell. "Is she…is she dead?" he asked.

Cole shook his head. "No, but ah, something happened," he mumbled. He stopped walking. "We gotta talk, Luke. We seriously have to talk, but first, you have to call Buzzer and tell him and the guys not to come tonight."

"What? What am I going to tell him?" Luke asked.

"I don't give a crap what you tell him!" Cole shouted. "Just call him and tell him they can't come. Tell him I'm sick, or you're sick, or the dog's sick. I don't give a shit what you say. Just do it!"

Luke walked to the patio door and let Hoss back into the house while he called Buzzer. He told him Cole had a migraine and needed extreme quiet. Buzzer offered to host the evening's video night if Luke wanted to attend, but he declined.

Luke went to his bedroom to change. He threw his Carhartt shirt and pants into his laundry basket and tugged on a pair of gray shorts—old sweatpants he had hacked off with a dull pair of scissors he found in the garage during a pickup game of basketball one night. He pulled on a worn t-shirt with the phrase *Warning! I do dumb stuff!*, then dumped three cups of kibble into Hoss' bowl before making his way to the kitchen.

The fridge door handle felt sticky, so he wiped it with the

dishrag, then washed down all the counters. He was avoiding the conversation Cole was going to lead him into. He didn't know why; he just knew it would be something he didn't want to hear. Finally, unable to find anything else to distract himself from the inevitable, he grabbed two beers from the fridge and handed one to his brother, who seemed to be glued to the kitchen stool.

"Alright, what's going on, bro?" Luke asked, pointing toward the living room, indicating a change of scenery.

The two sat in opposite corners of the room. After watching Cole fall into the chair, Luke dropped heavily onto the oversized couch. Based on his brother's state, he knew it was bad, but he also knew it wasn't *Mom's dead* bad. Cole upended his beer and guzzled it to the last drop; he got up and grabbed another from the fridge. He shut the door, twisted off the top, and sucked down a third of that bottle before he could face his brother.

The story Cole told seemed so ridiculous Luke asked him to repeat it. "The guy wore an all-white mask and a suit? *And* he had a gun?" he asked, clarifying the story after the second retelling. "Are you sure that's what he wants us to do? I don't understand."

Cole shrugged. "All I know is what I was told. That, and if we call the police, Mom is as good as dead." He looked into his brother's eyes. "Honestly, Luke, I'm scared."

The boys sat in silence, each throwing back another beer

before the sun slid below the horizon. Cole flipped on the lights and disappeared into his bedroom before returning with his laptop. "We have to do it now. I'm just following directions. We can't let him hurt Mom."

CHAPTER 11

"Hey, this is Matt Entenza coming to you live from the studios of KDIG Radio in beautiful Alexandria. Tonight, we're talking about the missing Cedar Point woman, Jane Hart. My question for you: Did Jane Hart leave of her own volition or did something more nefarious happen to her? I want to hear your thoughts after this message."

It was 8:01 p.m. when Matt pressed the button to send the station to commercial. He nodded to his program manager through the glass window on the other side of the studio as he burst through the door—late as usual. He watched the phone lines light up as he waited for the commercial to end. It was apparent everyone had an opinion on Jane Hart's disappearance.

It was his job to play devil's advocate—to question, to plant seeds of doubt on every topic he covered. He felt bad about doing this to this poor missing woman and her family, but he'd been hired to sell entertainment, and he was good at it.

When the commercials ended, he pressed the first button. "This is *Chat with Matt*. You're on the air. Let's hear what you think about Jane Hart, the missing woman from Cedar Point."

"Hi, Matt. My name's Jen. I have to tell you, I'm scared. I used to think Cedar Point was a safe place to raise my kids, but if a middle-aged woman can disappear without a trace, it could happen to anyone."

"I hear your concerns, Jen, but how do you know she didn't just get fed up with her life and choose to leave? It's been done before." He gave control back to the listener.

"Matt, she left her kids. Moms don't do that—not even when they're grown. They're always your kids. Nothing good can come from her disappearance."

He moved his computer screen in front of him and enlarged the font. "Okay, so here's the thing. I was on Facebook a little while ago looking at the *Bring Jane Hart Home* page. Listen to what her sons are saying. This one's from her oldest son Cole. *Mom truly is not missing. We don't need your help. Something bad is not happening.*"

"His whole post is oddly worded. Maybe it's a cryptic message," Jen said.

"Well, everyone has an opinion. Thanks for yours." The radio host cut Jen off with a push of a button. "Okay, so, let's take another caller."

Matt pressed line 2. "This is *Chat with Matt*. Tell me where you're at regarding the disappearance of Mrs. Jane Hart."

"Hey, Matt. Dan here. A woman disappears in the middle of a small town like Cedar Point, and everyone automatically jumps to the worst conclusion—kidnapped or murdered. I mean, come on. Who's to say she didn't meet some guy through a dating app and she just ran off to hook up with him."

"Exactly!" Matt exclaimed. "Women leave their husbands all the time. Why would we automatically jump to the conclusion she's in danger. Thanks for the call, Dan."

Matt pressed another line. "Hey, caller, you're on the line with Matt. Let's hear your thoughts on the disappearance of Jane Hart."

"This is Theo. I've got the *Bring Jane Hart Home* Facebook page pulled up. I'm looking at that post from Jane's son, Cole, the one you read a few minutes ago. Pull it up, will you?"

"Still got it up," Matt said.

"Okay, I sort of agree with the caller who said the message may be cryptic."

"Another conspiracy theorist, huh? Well, go ahead. Make your point—just make it quick." Guilt coursed through Matt. He knew Jane—or knew of her. He didn't believe she would have run off, but his job depended on him to fan the flames. His listeners counted on him to be controversial and hardcore.

The caller continued. "Matt, if you read every other word of her son's message, this is what you hear. *Mom is missing. We need help. Something is happening.* It sounds like her son is pleading for help. Maybe he knows more but is afraid to say."

"Nutcase." Matt hid the word in the clearing of his throat. "Sorry about that, listeners. It's allergy season, folks. I can't control all of my bodily functions." He shut down Theo's line. "Come on, people; I thought you were smarter than that. There are a few crackpots in every crowd." He looked at the lights on the phone panel. "We still have one line open. Let me hear your thoughts on this caller's theory or any others you want to talk about regarding Jane Hart."

The last line lit up. Something made Matt press that button. "You're on the air with Matt. Go ahead, caller."

Luke pressed the speaker button on his phone as his brother moved closer. He lowered his voice at least an octave before speaking. "This is, ah, Sam."

Matt lowered his voice to match the caller's. "Okay, *ah, Sam*. What are your thoughts on the Jane Hart disappearance?"

Luke paused. Cole lightly poked him to get him started again.

"Well, ah, I think Mo..." Cole punched him harder. He almost referred to her as *Mom*.

"You think mo...what?" Matt asked.

"Well, I think mo... more people," Luke looked at his brother and slowly repeated each word Cole mouthed. "More. People. Should. Consider. All. The. Facts. Before. Jumping. To. Conclusions."

Matt laughed. "Come on, man. This is a talk show. It means you have to talk like a human, not a freakin' android."

"Ah, yeah. Sorry," Luke/Sam said. "I don't think people are considering all of the evidence found at the house."

Matt leaned closer to the mic. "What evidence? The police have been pretty hush-hush about the crime scene. Do *you* have inside information?"

Luke/Sam tried to make a save. "Ah, no, nothing specific, but, ah, Chief Enderly did say that, um, he couldn't talk about it. So, ah, they must have found some kind of evidence, something out of the ordinary." Luke angrily slammed his fist through the air, chastising himself for being so stupid.

"Hey, man, I don't know if you're being completely honest here. I think you know more than you're letting on, Sam?" He heard the click and knew the caller had hung up. "Well, it looks like Sam isn't interested in sharing his deepest darkest secrets with us. So, listeners, what do you think?"

The last light lit up again; Matt skipped the others, hoping it was Sam calling back. "*Chat with Matt.* Where are you on the subject of Jane Hart?"

It wasn't Sam's voice that buzzed across the radio. It was a computerized voice that had been programmed to provide a very specific message. "Stop sticking your nose where it doesn't belong," the non-emotional voice stated. "If you do not, someone is going to die." The line went dead.

Silence followed. The station was completely silent until Steve, the program manager, pressed a button to take them to commercial.

Steve yanked the studio door open. "We're trying to trace the call, but apparently, they used star-six-seven to block the number. We've got a call to the police too. But, Matt, you have to keep going. There may be more that comes out during the show."

Matt swallowed hard. He wasn't sure if *his* life had been threatened or if the message was about someone else. Either way, he wasn't sure he wanted to continue.

The commercial was coming to an end. From a few feet away, the program manager counted him back in.

"Hey, ah, this is Matt. Thanks for hanging around during the commercials." His voice cracked. The program manager circled his hand, prompting him to keep going. "It, ah…well, let's take another call." He pressed a line that had been lit up since the start of the show. "This is *Chat with Matt*. What's on your mind?"

"WOW! WOW!" The words blasted through the phone. Matt pulled his headphones away from his ears. "I *was* going to say I believed Mrs. Hart was a bit *heartless* and left her husband and sons to chase some hottie, but after hearing that last call, I've done a one-eighty."

Matt was still shaking. *Entertain your audience,* he told himself. "So," he said, finding his footing, "one call and you spin on a dime. Really?"

"That wasn't just any call, Matt, and you know it. Whoever recorded that message meant business. Did you trace the call?"

"We're not going there. I think we're done."

"Negligence…" was all the caller got in before Matt cut him off.

Matt pulled off the fleece jacket he usually wore in the cold studio. He wiped his forehead with it and pushed the next button.

"You're on the air. This is Matt. Who's calling?"

"My name's Jim. I just wanted to say that I worked with Mrs. Hart for many years. During that time, before she retired, she became kind of, well, I suppose, *restless* is the word I am thinking of." The phone line cut in and out as the caller spoke, sometimes dropping a word here or there.

"Jim, are you on speakerphone? You're hard to hear at times."

"Is that better?" he asked.

"It is. We can hear you now," Matt assured him.

"Sorry, I'm in the car. Anyway, I was saying I think she may have been having a mid-life crisis of sorts. I don't believe she's in danger; I would guess she may just be trying to find herself."

Matt leaned forward in his chair. "Tell me more about this mid-life crisis, Jim."

"Well, she, um, she seemed rather…distant before she retired. Yeah, and that's another thing, who retires at forty-seven? Wouldn't that be an indicator she was restless?"

"It could be…or maybe she was just tired of her job," Matt said.

"Exactly…a mid-life crisis," the caller agreed, misinterpreting the host's statement.

"That doesn't exactly make it a mid-life crisis. So maybe the woman wasn't running toward something new but was just tired of all the old crap she was dealing with."

"Are you dense?" The caller grew angry. "It's the same damn thing."

Matt smiled. Arguments made for great radio; he wanted to keep this guy talking. "Not really. Sometimes we look…" The line went quiet; Matt knew the caller had hung up. "Seems like Jim doesn't want to talk to us either. Looks like we have time for a couple more calls before the next commercial."

The host pushed a red button. "This is *Chat with Matt*. Tell me where you're at with the Jane Hart disappearance."

"This is Lucia. First, let me say this, that computerized call was frightening. I can't believe you're even still taking calls, but since you are, I want to stand by the caller who said women don't typically leave their families without some sort of explanation. Even if Mrs. Hart were having a midlife crisis, as the last gentleman claimed, her family would most likely have known about it. There are signs."

"So maybe leaving was her sign," Matt insisted.

"No, I mean long before. Restlessness, lack of interest, frustration, unhappiness, withdrawing from her family. I'm a therapist. It doesn't just happen all at once. They should have seen it coming."

"Okay, well, you can't argue with a therapist." Matt laughed. "Thanks for the call." Matt waved his index finger back and forth over the red buttons. "Let's see who's next." Finally, he dropped it on line 2. "You're on the air with Matt.

We're talking about the disappearance of Jane Hart from Cedar Point, Minnesota. Let us know where you stand."

There was a click before the computerized voice began. "I warned you before."

Seconds after the line went dead, the transom window in the studio shattered. A hanging lamp on the far side of the studio exploded. Matt dove under his desk as the KDIG station went silent.

CHAPTER 12

Black, puffy bags hung under Brian's eyes; he hadn't slept in over twenty-four hours. After receiving the call from the Alexandria police, he headed west, making the forty-five-minute trek in just shy of half an hour. The sound of the siren still buzzed in his brain, and if he closed his eyes for even a few seconds, he could see the flashing lights cutting through the darkness.

He'd done his due diligence at the radio station—talked to the program manager and Matt Entenza, the host of *Chat with Matt*. He had listened to the recording of the show so many times he could almost repeat it word for word. The Alexandria police took the lead, but they included him in every step. They were waiting for the ballistics report, but gleaning any useful information from that lone bullet was a long shot.

As the sun exploded over the horizon, he pulled out of the KDIG parking lot. He drove along the frontage road until he hit a Perkins. He knew he looked like crap and probably smelled even worse, but he climbed out of the squad car and lumbered inside.

The waitress poured him a cup of coffee and dropped a menu on the table. She was a tiny waif that looked like she would blow away in a storm. Her hair was pulled into a loose ponytail, and she wore no make-up, except to hide the black eye she was sporting. "Excuse me, ma'am," he said as she turned to walk away. "I'm ready to order."

She returned to his table, holding her notepad in one hand and a pen in the other. "Just bring me the biggest breakfast you've got and a full pot of coffee," he told her.

"Sausage, bacon, or ham?" she asked in a monotone voice.

"Surprise me," Brian said.

"Toast, English muffin, or pancakes?"

Brian smiled at her, but his grin elicited no reaction. "Definitely pancakes." His grin fell as he asked, "Are you okay?"

"Hmm." She shrugged and walked away.

He, of all people, knew the signs of domestic abuse, but unless she asked for help, there was little he could do.

An abandoned *Alexandria Times* newspaper sat on the table next to Brian's. He snatched it before one of the other patrons could. The headline read *I warned you before*, mimicking the caller's last line from last night's radio show. The paper was quick. Undoubtedly, some hotshot reporter was after a raise or a promotion or both.

The waitress set a tray on the table where the paper had been and began transferring food to Brian's table. "You know," he looked at her nametag, "Beth, I can help you," he said.

She gave him a sad smile. "That's okay," she mumbled. She tucked his check next to his plate before picking up the tray and returning to the kitchen.

Brian shoveled his food in—cutting his pancakes in four pieces, twisting each in a pool of syrup and plunging them into his mouth. After ten minutes and almost an entire pot of coffee, he grabbed his wallet from his back pocket. He spotted his waitress and intercepted her before she ducked back into the kitchen. He tucked two hundred-dollar bills in her hand. "You need to get out," he said, holding her eyes with his. "You're worth more than the way whoever gave you that black eye treats you."

Tears filled her eyes. She tucked the money into her apron pocket before looking back at him. "You're right," she whispered. She opened her mouth to say something else but closed it again. "You're right." Her resolve was much stronger. She touched his hand. "Thank you. Thank you for seeing me."

Brian's knees almost buckled. Those were the exact words Jane used to say to him when they were in high school. He took a step backward and nodded at her. "Take care of yourself," he mumbled awkwardly.

He stopped at the front counter to pay his bill but couldn't take his eyes off Beth. *I see you,* he thought. *I see you and Jane and every other woman who has been made to feel not enough.* After he tucked his change into his wallet, he searched the dining room for his waitress, but she had disappeared. "Have a good day," he said to the clerk as he headed out the door.

The squad smelled of stale onions. He lifted an arm and took a whiff. He instantly hit the buttons to lower the front windows and cranked the fan up high. He backed up and headed toward the exit. An older Chevy Malibu crept along the frontage road in front of him. The woman had dark, straight hair and pale skin. She had Jane's chin line and her tiny nose. His heart raced as he pulled onto the road behind her and followed her to the Target parking lot, maintaining a safe distance. She drove in and parked her car toward the back of the lot. Brian parked a couple of rows away, facing her. He readied the camera on his phone, setting the zoom as much as it would allow him. When she opened the door, Brian snapped her picture. But when he enlarged it, his heart sank. The woman wore a red shirt and tan pants, obviously a Target employee, but she was also a good ten to fifteen years younger than Jane.

"Where are you, Jane?" he said to no one. "Where have you gone?"

CHAPTER 13

After a quick shower, Brian shoved his arm through the sleeve of a freshly ironed uniform. He stared into the mirror as he buttoned his shirt from top to bottom, seeing himself, but really seeing nothing at all, except Jane. Jane Sterling. Jane Hart. *His Jane.* The one he had loved since they were kids. The one he still longed for multiple times a day. The one he avoided several times a week, always turning the other way if he thought there was even a minuscule chance he might have to talk to her. The reason he had never married. *That* Jane was the only thing on his mind lately. That was obvious when he trailed a woman who only slightly resembled her. The pain cut so deeply he could barely breathe. At times it came out of nowhere, nearly driving him to his knees.

Enderly jabbed his finger as he poked the pin of his badge through the fabric. "Sonofabitch!" he yelled before sticking the bloody tip in his mouth and rubbing it against his teeth. When it stopped bleeding, he ran his hands down the front of his shirt as he took one last look into the mirror.

Walking through the living room, Brian picked up an old photo he'd taken of Jane in high school; he went soft as he stared at it. Her eyes sparkled. She wasn't classically beautiful; she wasn't even pretty by most men's standards, but she was the most beautiful woman Brian had ever known. She had a heart of gold; it was her heart that made him love her. He pressed the picture to his chest and softly murmured, "I miss you, Jane. I miss you so much. But I love you even more." He set the photo on the side table, adjusting it so he could see it from his recliner—the one Brian fell into at the end of a long shift—if he even made it home. The chair hadn't been used since Jane disappeared.

"Siri, call Jeff Porter," he commanded into his iPhone.

"Calling Jeff Porter mobile," she sang back in her smooth voice.

His lead deputy picked up after two rings. "Hey, Chief. What's up?"

"I need your help this morning."

"Everything okay?" Jeff asked.

"Spent the night with the Alexandria police after last night's shooting at the radio station."

Jeff exhaled. "I read the article in the *Times* before I got your message this morning. They sure didn't waste any time, did they? The TV stations are all over it."

"Yeah. They know as much as I do. But, ah, I need you at the station this morning. I got another lead I need to check out. So it may take a while."

"Anything you want help with?" his deputy asked.

"Nah," Brian mumbled. "This one's a long shot. Just cover the station, okay?"

"Got it. I'll head over there now." His blinker echoed across the phone line. "Anything you want me to do while I'm there?"

"Yeah, but you have to promise me this stays between you and me. Got it? I don't even want Mauri to know."

"You know it," Deputy Porter assured him.

"I need you to spend some time digging into Drew Carter."

"Drew Carter? What am I looking for? Anything in particular?"

"Anything you can find on him. What I'm most interested in is any connection he has to Sean Hart or the Sterlings."

"Got it. See you when you get back. Be..."

Brian hung up before he heard Jeff's final message.

Enderly spent the better part of two hours driving up and down streets, through alleys, and into the industrial park before finding the man he was searching for. The squad slowed and Brian pulled up next to him and rolled down the passenger's side window. "Get in," he commanded. The old man didn't move. "I said, get in." Brian unbuckled his seatbelt, leaned over, and threw the passenger's door open, bumping the man with the door of the Ford Explorer. "Get in!"

The man stumbled as he climbed into the SUV. "Shut the door," Brian told him. The old guy stared at Brian like he didn't understand. "Shut the damn door." Before the door even completely closed, Brian was turning onto the highway.

He headed west out of town for nearly five miles before slowing and making a right-hand turn onto a grassy opening that gave the illusion of a long-ago road. The squad bounced up and down along the path until it came to a dilapidated building that appeared to have long since been abandoned. The roof had caved in on one side. The wood siding was twisted and cracked. Many pieces had fallen off and were leaning against the side of the house as if they had given up. The waist-high weeds had been flattened, creating a path toward an old trailer that was only in slightly better shape than the house.

Ironically, it was one of the most famous high school party locales in Cedar Point. The police and fire department had made numerous runs out here over the past fifteen years. Bonfires that fled their boundaries, music that drifted into town on still nights, and calls from parents looking for their errant teenagers had forced Brian down this road again and again, back to the one place he never wanted to go.

Brian walked around to the passenger's side and jerked the door open. "Get out," he told the man. Again, he was slow to respond. "Now!"

The old man slowly and painfully climbed out of the car. "Start walking," Enderly commanded, giving him a gentle push. "We're going to the trailer behind the house," he barked. The two walked single file toward the trailer. The elderly man shuffled along, driving a fat garter snake out of the weeds. He stopped so quickly, Brian almost knocked him over.

When they reached the trailer, Brian pushed the door open and pulled the man inside. The air smelled of a mixture of stale booze and mold. He opened a window above the table and another on the opposite side. The scent of decaying prairie grass joined the party, making it only slightly easier to breathe.

Brian walked down the hallway and peered into each room, his hand on the handle of his gun. The inside looked exactly as Brian had expected. Empty bottles, mostly broken or tipped over, were strewn across the floor and the counters. Trash was strewn about the trailer. Mouse droppings littered the floor and every flat surface.

He took the man by the shoulders and pushed him into a kitchen chair. Before Brian sat down, he grabbed the curtain from the broken rod and brushed it across the table, sending the dried mouse turds flying, making pinging sounds as they hit the cupboards and the floor. Finally, he sat in the chair adjacent to the elderly man. He leaned forward and crossed his arms. "Who the hell are you?"

The man was old, or so he wanted Brian to believe. His teeth were a mangled mess of yellow and brown; rotted cavities showed at the base. His clothes had seen better days.

"John Henry," the old man spoke slowly, slurring his words.

The man looked at Brian but said nothing more. Brian set his gun on the table. "Now, yours," he said. The old man stared at Brian's gun before finally reaching inside his jacket and removing his own. He laid it on the table next to Brian's.

"Okay, so, I'll ask again. Who are you?"

"Really," the old man mumbled. "My name's John Henry.

I'm just passin' through Cedar Point. Grew up in Duluth. Headin' somewhere warmer for the winter."

"That's bullshit," Enderly said. "Your name may be John Henry, and you may be from Duluth, but you sure as hell aren't the old geezer you want people to believe you are. I know that. And you know I know. So cut the crap."

The two sat in silence. Finally, John lifted one hand toward his mouth and removed the top row of fake dentures and placed them on the table before reaching in to extract the bottom ones. In their place was a set of nearly perfect teeth. They almost glowed in the dingy trailer light. John reached up and pulled his stocking cap from his head. The long, scraggly gray hair he had passed off as his own was attached to the shabby hat. It was obvious John's dirty blonde hair had been professionally cut.

"Now, who the hell are you?" Brian demanded.

John reached into one of the pockets of his cargo pants. Brian slowly moved his fingers toward his gun. John pulled a thin wallet from his pocket and handed it to Enderly. Inside was an ID and a badge stamped FBI. The name on the ID read John Henry Wallick; the photo matched. "FBI. Of course, you're FBI. I should have known," Brian said, handing the wallet back to the man.

John snapped the thin wallet closed and set it near the gray wig on the table. "Why are you here?" asked Enderly. "You've been hanging around Cedar Point since before Jane Hart disappeared. And since nothing happens in this podunk town

that I don't know about, what's your purpose for being here?"
He was met with silence. "Fine, we can work together, or I can
work against you. You choose."

John huffed through a sideways grin. "Well, it looks like
we'll be on the same team, then, doesn't it? But for your
information, I am FBI, and I can have you tossed out of here
until this case is closed. So, if you blow my cover, I'll do it. Do
you understand?" John asked.

Brian nodded. "I do."

"First," John said, "how did you find out about me?"

Brian smirked. "As I said, there isn't much that happens in
this town that I don't know about." His grin turned to a laugh.
"I was tipped off by an undercover state patrol who followed
you to the house you're staying at."

"Huh," John huffed. "These small towns are tight, aren't
they?"

"That they are," Brian agreed. "We look out for one
another."

John nodded. "Well, I was sent here three weeks ago to keep
an eye on Jane Hart," John explained.

"What?" Brian's jaw almost dropped to the floor. "Why?
Do *you* know where she is?"

John tilted his head to the side and shrugged. "I'm supposed
to. But she disappeared before we could get her into protective
custody."

"Protective custody? Are you kidding me? Are you effin'

kidding me?" The table bounced when Brian slammed his fist into it. "She could be anywhere! Hurt or scared—or...or worse."

"Yeah, I know," John said slowly. "I've got a few leads I'm working on." He took his gun from the table and tucked it back inside his jacket. He reached for his hat and the wig, but Brian pressed his hand on top of John's.

Enderly locked eyes with him. "Not yet. You need to tell me everything first."

CHAPTER 14

Jane Hart

The murky sky threatened to explode. Thunder rumbled in the distance as I searched the old garden for a few paltry strawberries that sometimes appeared during a warm fall. With the berries tucked in the front of my shirt, pulled up into a pouch, I combed through the tall grass, searching for the old water pump. My arm ached by the time the pump gave in. The water started as a slow trickle but eventually flowed in a steady stream. I rinsed the berries before catching a mouthful of ice-cold water. I had barely swallowed when I heard the engine of a car blend with the roar of the impending storm.

Sounds in the country are deceiving. They always appear closer than they are, so I took another long draw from the water pump. When the car bounced into the space that had once been the front yard of the old shack, I ran behind the trailer and flattened myself against the wall. The strawberries tumbled to the ground around me, but I was afraid to move, afraid to collect my breakfast. I became acutely aware of every noise: two car doors slamming, Brian's voice, and two sets of feet shuffling along the path.

Making it to the shed was too risky. The tall grass was sparse; it wouldn't cover me even if I got down on my hands and knees. I stood perfectly still, afraid to take more than slow, shallow breaths—even though my heart banged inside my chest and my lungs screamed for air.

As soon as the second person spoke, I recognized his voice.

The old drifter had been digging through garbage cans near the church a few days before I received that frightening call. I had no idea who he was or where he had come from. I saw him as someone down on his luck in need of help, so I fed him and offered him clothing. I often tried to give him money, but he accepted nothing but a pair of Sean's old tennis shoes and a sandwich. I also saw him in town: near the hospital when I volunteered and on Sundays near the church. Like everyone else, he seemed to be constantly searching.

***

The morning I received that life-changing call had started like every other morning. I had just set the mail and a cup of fresh coffee on a tray on the ottoman when my cell phone rang. After just a few words, everything shifted to slow motion; it all felt surreal. The light grew dim as colors blended together; I was unable to discern where one color ended and the next began. I was launched from living life to being a spectator, watching the instant replays over and over. As I listened to the man slowly speak to me, my legs gave out, and I dropped to the floor. I felt sucked down by an invisible weight I could not remove. Fear and disgust flowed through me, each vying for my attention. From my prison on the floor, I stared toward the lake, through the locked double doors, past the patio furniture, and beyond the hill that led to the water. The red maple leaves clung to the branches—earning another day's reprieve. It wouldn't be long before the fall winds threw them to the ground.

Suddenly, a shadow fell across the patio. It was a cloudless day, yet that dark spot moved in the afternoon sun. Nothing should have created that shape. Swiping a long-necked pottery vase from the side table, I crawled behind the couch. I tossed the arrangement onto the floor as I pressed my cheek into the thick carpet, watching through the narrow space beneath the sofa. I hadn't shut off the alarm, but had Sean intentionally not rearmed it when he left? That call had me doubting everyone—including my husband.

After some time, I saw the image of a person in the obscure silhouette cast across the patio; at least, that was what my imagination led me to believe. All I knew was I wasn't going down without a fight. My fingers squeezed tighter around the neck of the vase.

I was keenly aware of the passing of time. I heard every second as it ticked away on the oversized living room clock. Shockingly, a man stepped in front of the window. I clapped a hand over my mouth to stifle a scream. He perched his hands above his eyes and peered through the glass. I sucked in a deep breath; my pulse drummed in every part of my body. Was I going to die at the hands of the town drifter?

My cell phone double-buzzed before lighting up. The

number matched the earlier call. The text was short. *Mrs. Hart, this is John Henry, FBI. I'm on your patio.*

FBI? Was this a ruse? Was I supposed to believe that an old man who could move no faster than a shuffle was an FBI agent? Or was that part of his cover? I no longer knew what to believe—*who* to believe. The caller hadn't sounded anything like the old man I had befriended. From my hiding place, I could plainly see his dirt-smudged face. Again, he typed something into his phone and held it up for me to see before pressing a button. Another text lit up my cell. *I'm here to protect you.*

Picking up the heavy vase almost made me laugh. It appeared I was bringing a vase to a gunfight. Even I knew it made no sense, but then again, none of this did. Drawing in a deep breath, I got onto my hands and knees, resigning myself to the fact I had to trust someone and, based on the earlier call, I didn't have time to weigh who that was going to be. I just knew that at *that* moment, it wasn't going to be Sean or anyone else. The only one I could trust—was me.

I crawled out from behind the couch and moved along the edge of the room. The alarm beeped as I disarmed it and pulled the wooden rod from the door before cautiously sliding it open. I scanned the backyard but saw only the drifter. John Henry grabbed the top of his stocking cap and pulled, lifting off the thin gray hair with it. He smiled at me—not with his yellow, crooked teeth, but with a set of perfectly spaced white ones. It startled me to see someone else wear the clothing I associated with the old drifter.

"Mrs. Hart." It was the voice from the earlier call. "Jane. May I call you Jane?" I nodded. "Jane, let's go inside. It's not safe for you out here," he said as he scanned the woods on both sides of the house.

Immediately, I stepped backward. John Henry followed me in. He shoved the door to the side and pulled the curtains closed before he turned toward me.

"How do I know you're who you say you are?" I asked.

He reached into a pocket of his cargo pants. I lifted the vase ever so slowly, ready to strike if needed, but instead of a gun, he held a small leather case containing his ID. He flipped it open and held it toward me to see. Tears blurred my vision; I blinked several times to try to bring his name into focus.

"May I sit down?" he asked.

I pointed to the couch. He sat on one end while I took the chair on the opposite side of the room. I struggled to reconcile his appearance with the man I had come to know over the last few weeks. "J-john Henry?" I said.

"Yes. John Henry *Wallick*." His lips fell into a crooked, closed-lipped smile, the one I had seen so many times since he arrived in town. My fears eased slightly. "As I told you on the phone, you're in grave danger." I swallowed hard. This was the stuff of books and movies, not real life, and certainly not *my* life. "Someone wants you...gone," John said. "We're pretty sure we know who that person is, but for your safety, I won't tell you until you're in protective custody. That's the reason I'm in Cedar Point."

All I could do was nod; I was unsure what to say. What's the appropriate way to react when you find out someone plans to kill you? "Please, just tell me who it is," I begged, unsure if I even wanted to hear the answer.

John indicated his unwillingness to tell me with both his face and his shoulders. "I'm sorry; I can't tell you yet. Once you're safely hidden away, we'll let you know everything we know. I need to get you safely into protective custody first."

"When?" I wanted to know. "I need to talk to my sons, tell them what..."

"Jane, I'm sorry, but that's not possible. No one can know. We have your house under surveillance." My mouth dropped open. "Come with me," John said as he stood up. "I'll show you."

I followed him to the front of the house, where he nodded toward a nondescript silver Ford Escape. "And the path in the woods..." he said, looking toward the opening, "we have an agent stationed there also." He pulled the blind and faced me. "If anyone so much as sneezes in your direction, we'll know about it."

I turned and walked toward the back of the house. "You never answered my question. When will this happen?"

"Tonight, after dark, sometime around 7:00. We know your husband will be gone until late, so you should be safe until then."

I walked to the sliding doors and peeked through the narrow opening between the curtains. "Wait," I said. "How do you know Sean will be late?"

John grimaced. "The less you know, the better. Pack what will fit in one suitcase. I'll be back at 7:00. Understand?"

"What will you tell my family?" I asked.

"Nothing, at least for now. They'll just think you left on your own. We'll decide who needs to know what and when they need to know it." John Henry walked around the island, dragging his hand over the smooth quartz. "Make sure to leave your phone here. It can be used to trace you. Don't bring your purse or your credit cards. We'll make sure you have everything you need. Leave them in the same place you typically would. Nothing can seem out of the ordinary." He stopped circling the island and held my stare. "Seven p.m. Got it?"

I nodded. John pressed his fake teeth back into his mouth and pulled on his wig and hat combo. He slid the door open and disappeared just as he had appeared—with only a shadow.

As soon as he was gone, I locked the door, pulled the curtains, and reset the alarm. I pressed my head to the wall. My knees felt weak; they trembled, and I was afraid to test them out. One thing I knew for certain, I trusted no one—not Sean and not even John Henry whatever-his-last-name-was. For all I knew, he could be part of the plot to kill me.

Dropping onto the couch, I struggled to slow my thoughts,

to focus on what I needed to do. Years earlier, I had prepared for this moment, should it ever come, when I would disappear without a trace. The volatile relationship Sean and I had led me to believe he was capable of killing me. So I had to be prepared. But that preparation always included taking my sons with me. This was entirely different.

Did Sean want me dead? Or was it someone else? Could John Henry be part of his plan?

After some time, I moved into the bedroom. The clock on my nightstand next to the bed read *2:15*. I had less than five hours to erase my existence, to escape from both the FBI and whoever wanted me gone. I had spent my entire life researching, organizing, and planning. I used to think those were skills that would lead me to be a highly effective director at H & C, but instead, they had led to this exact moment.

Kneeling in front of my nightstand, I pulled the top drawer open. I removed the Mother's Day cards from Cole and Luke and an assortment of small items: bookmarks, pins, jewelry, daily quotes, and my bible. Once the drawer was empty, I set it on the bed and lifted the false bottom. Inside the hidden compartment was a small black string bag I had packed years before—in case I needed to leave my marriage. I inserted the cord into the burner phone and plugged it in to charge. There was enough cash to last me for weeks, if not months if I was careful. A small wallet held my new ID—a new name, address, and a doctored photo. I had been prepped by a group whose sole mission was to help abused women like me escape.

With the false bottom snapped back into place, I replaced everything exactly as it had been. Then I went to Sean's barren nightstand and pulled the false bottom from his drawer. The secret hiding place was the reason I had selected these nightstands. Sean had always hated them: too tall, too bulky. He had no idea about their hidden compartment and their importance to me.

Cautiously, I lifted the pistol and the box of copper-colored bullets and tucked them into the bag. It had been years since I had been to the shooting range, had learned how to load and fire this gun, but the memory was etched in my brain forever.

I set the bag on the floor before picking up the heavy vase I had held when John Henry appeared on my patio. I slammed it against the countertop. The fragments scattered everywhere. I grabbed the piece with the longest point and methodically ground it into my stomach, clenching my teeth to keep from screaming. Blood oozed out along the jagged cut. I wiped it on the countertop, let it drip onto the floor, and flicked droplets toward the wall. Tiny drops fell onto the carpet and down the hallway as I passed through. Grabbing Sean's tennis shoes from the mudroom, I pressed them into the blood that still oozed from my stomach. Finally, I moved them along the floor, creating a few faded, almost non-existent bloody footprints that led into the garage and to the garbage can before returning to the bathroom to bandage the deep wound.

With a bottle of peroxide and an old towel at hand, I dropped my head into the kitchen sink and emptied the contents of the container over my dark brown hair. The chemicals made my eyes water; I repeatedly blinked as I worked the peroxide through the long strands, watching it lighten to a strawberry blonde as the clock moved toward 4:00 p.m. Finally, I rinsed it out and wrapped the ragged towel around it.

I laid the damp towel on the counter to catch the six inches of thick hair I lopped off. The curls I worked to straighten each morning lay in ringlets that barely skimmed my shoulders. Drying it wasn't an option, so I finger-combed the curls and let it air dry. I peeled away my false eyelashes and scrubbed off my make-up before wrapping the washcloth, lashes, scissors, and hair in the towel and stuffing it all into a large plastic bag. That bag, plus a few other items I thought I might need, went into a second backpack I had retrieved from Cole's closet. I snapped off the bathroom light and took a deep breath.

I removed a gallon of bleach and a pair of disposable rubber gloves from the back of the laundry room cabinet. Trying to make it appear that whoever kidnapped me had attempted to clean up their *crime scene*, I made a pathetic effort to wipe the dried blood from the floor, counter, and the walls, purposely leaving tiny dots in numerous locations. Once I was done, I poured bleach down every drain in the house before tossing all the rags, the empty bottle, and my bloody shirt into the trashcan in the garage. I knew the police would find the stash and, based on the small specks of blood they would find, they would luminol the entire room and find both new and old blood. I had no doubt about that. It was a setup. I had framed Sean. I had to know if he was the one determined to see me dead. If it wasn't him, he'd be able to prove his innocence. After all, he was a top-notch attorney. Just ask him.

A pair of jeans, tennis shoes, and an oversized thick sweatshirt also took up space in my bag. I slipped on a pair of knit shorts and a water-blue t-shirt. I remained barefoot. Counting on my fingers, I ticked off every item in my possession—making sure I had only what I absolutely needed—nothing Sean would notice as missing.

For three hours, I raced against the clock. Finally ready, I took a few moments to collect myself and just breathe. I walked through the house one last time, visiting each room, calling up memories of Cole and Luke when they were small. There was no way to know if I would ever return; memories may be all I would ever have. Finally, I went to the key cupboard and entered the code. I removed a single key from a ring of five. This key, a gold Schaffer, unlocked the one place I was sure I would be safe.

The agents guarding the house needed to know I hadn't slipped away. I pulled my hair into a ponytail, slipped on a Minnesota Twins baseball cap to hide my newly colored blonde locks, and tugged on a lime green t-shirt over the blue one.

Peering through the wooden slats, I noticed the Escape had

not moved. The driver wasn't visible through the tinted glass, but I knew he was there. Agents don't leave their posts. I glanced toward the walkway that cut into the woods. The branches were still, but I knew someone was there; the trail was an easy way to get to me. No agent would leave it unguarded. I took a deep breath and pulled the blinds wide open and stood in the window long enough to ensure they noticed me. After a couple of minutes, I lowered them and retreated to the back of the house.

Pulling off the green shirt and the Twins cap, I headed into the bedroom and placed them in my dresser drawer, exactly where they had been. I tugged on a light blue cap, one that nearly matched my shirt. The backpack hung over the top of the string bag, as I disarmed the alarm and opened the sliding door. I listened carefully but only heard the rattle of katydids and the chirp of the crickets. My heart raced as I stepped onto the patio. After sliding the door closed, I tiptoed toward the stairs that led down to the water. With each step, I expected to hear someone call my name, but there was only silence.

At the bottom of the hill, I turned left and ran along the deserted sandy shoreline of the state beach. I ran to the nearest picnic table before veering right and racing into the shockingly cool water. If they used dogs, the water would make it more difficult to track me. Again, I turned right and raced through the shallow water, past my house and along a stretch of cabins—every one of them shut down for the winter months.

Just before the shore began to level, I arrived at a boathouse attached to a cabin through an underground tunnel. The passageway between the two had been built by bootleggers back in the late 1920s. The most notorious, Clark Swain, owned a hundred acres of farmland and forest, including this boathouse and the residence above. While most Americans enjoyed the good life during that time, farmers like Clark lost their fortunes when corn prices tumbled. To survive, he and his farmhands built stills and turned the corn into alcohol, hiding it in the boathouse. With the moonlight as their guide, they loaded cases of booze into a convoy of rowboats and paddled out to the barge that sat in the shadows of the bay. Before sunrise, the alcohol was loaded onto a train heading into Minneapolis. Once there, it was secretly delivered to the underground nightclubs. The money was good, and it kept Clark afloat for the first few years after the stock market crashed. But then his wife and son died in a barn fire, and Prohibition was reversed, and everything fell apart. Seeing no way to survive, Clark lost his will to live. Following a night of drinking his profits, he rowed his boat to the middle of the lake, tied an anvil to his ankle, and jumped overboard. With no relatives, his land was escheated to the state. Eventually, after the war, the state parceled it off into small pieces and sold it—mainly to the wealthy for summer homes. Those were the cabins I passed as I ran.

The silence of the shoreline was deafening as I made my way to the boathouse. The key turned easily, and I stumbled when the door opened.

Bill and Sheila Hayden, like most of the cabin owners, were from out of state. They didn't want to be bothered with shutting down the cabin each winter, so they turned the heat low enough to be economical, but not so low the pipes would freeze in the cold Minnesota winters.

I was the keeper of the neighborhood keys since I was the only one around during the harsh winter months. Sean didn't have a clue that I had access to most of the cabins between our house and the Haydens. I hadn't put names on the keys, but I knew which one belonged to each summer retreat.

The Haydens had pulled the blinds when they left after Labor Day weekend. I flipped the deadbolt on the door and dove headlong onto the couch, moaning slightly when the edge of the cushion bumped the new sore on my stomach. The boathouse and house were my safe haven—until the following day when the helicopters began flying over and the dogs started barking. After three days of listening to the foreboding sounds, I no longer felt safe; the cabin was too close to home. There was only one other place I knew I could go without leaving town.

Hanging on a hook in the kitchen, were a set of car keys for the gray Toyota Prius Bill and Sheila kept in the attached garage. I waited until dusk and backed the car down the driveway and onto the gravel road. I hadn't been to Brian's childhood home since we were in high school, but I knew it well.

Disguised in dark glasses and a hat, my bravery outbid my fear. As I approached town, I decided to travel the main drag. Unsurprisingly, my picture was posted in yards and in merchant's windows. Not the way I looked now—not my bleached blonde, mass of curls—but the exact opposite.

I kept my head down as people passed in front of me. But no one looked my way. Whether it was bravery or stupidity, I turned down a side street and watched throngs of people fill the grassy area around the gazebo. Pulled by something internal, I climbed out of my car and fell in with a group heading toward the park. I kept my head down and my eyes focused on the feet in front of me. And before I even knew what was happening, I was standing in the middle of a search group—looking for me.

My pulse whooshed in my ears. I expected someone to notice me—to realized who I was, but it didn't happen. And when the group disbanded, and I listened to Sean's rant about his lodging, I walked away. I was not, nor have I ever been, his priority.

By the time I drove out of town, the streets were nearly empty. They were filled with vehicles, but the people had boarded school buses that would take them to their search area. I released a ragged sigh, removed my glasses, and drove through town, toward the old house.

The lights bounced as the small car traveled along the grassy road. I pulled into what had once been the old driveway, traveling through weeds that were nearly as tall as the car. I pulled up to the old wooden garage, leaving enough space to open the doors. The deteriorating building had two heavy paneled doors; one opened in each direction. I turned the wooden latch on the outside of the garage and struggled to pull the doors outward over the driveway that had shifted over the years. After a brutal struggle, I got them open wide enough to ease the Prius inside. I fought just as hard to close them.

As I walked through the grass where I had driven, I scooped at it with wide arms, lifting it up, attempting to leave no trace of my arrival. I headed for the trailer behind the house, but something told me not to go in. Instead, I went into the shed where Brian and I had talked about our life together nearly every day of high school. A bed covered with a sheet of plastic was still set up in the corner. I pulled off the mound of junk and flipped the dusty sheeting. As night fell, I lay on top of the plastic, wrapping myself with the one dusty quilt Brian and I used to lay under. In the dark, I reminisced about how different my life would have been had I made other choices.

Between the memories and my incredible fear of snakes and mice, I didn't fall asleep until dawn, when the early morning light streaked through the cracks in the siding. I woke up much later than usual. Famished, I plucked several strawberries from the weed-ridden patch before finding the old water pump. That was when I heard the car bounce along the non-existent road.

I was petrified. Pressed against the trailer for the better part of an hour, I listened to my story as it came together—first from

Brian and then from John Henry. John shared much more with Brian than he shared with me. Was he telling the truth, or was he a pawn in someone else's plan? Hiding behind the tin can of the trailer, I prayed to wake up from the nightmare my life had become.

When the men walked out of the cabin and headed back toward the car, I finally took my first deep breath. But just before they reached Brian's squad, a shot rang out so close it silenced my hearing for several seconds. I ran through the grass and yanked the shed door open, locking it from the inside with the latch. I cupped my hands over my mouth and breathed into them to silence my panic.

"What the hell was that?" I heard Brian yell. His voice created a doppler wave as he and John raced past the shed and into the field.

In the distance, I heard three voices and a ripple of laughter. Before long, Brian and John Henry passed by the shed, and the car drove away. I wasn't sure where the other man was, so I remained silent until I heard another shot off in the distance. I had entirely forgotten about the duck hunters when I came out here. Shaking with fear and the realization I was 47 years old and had screwed up my entire life, I curled up on the bed and wept for what could have been as the rain suddenly arrived in buckets.

CHAPTER 15

Brian grabbed the station door with one finger and pulled it open. Having been a victim of the storm that passed through, he was drenched. In one hand, he held a damp paper sack filled with burgers and enough fries to feed a small army. A drink carrier with three large sodas balanced precariously in his other hand. He awkwardly set the drinks on Mauri's desk. She caught the tray as it started to tip.

"Aww. Ain't nobody going to tell me there isn't some sweetness tucked inside that gruff demeanor of yours." Mauri grinned as she daubed at the brown liquid with a tissue.

Brian dug around in the bag. He smirked as he pointedly dropped a burger in front of her. "One plain cheeseburger. No ketchup. No mustard. No pickles. No onions. No taste," he teased as he pulled out a small fry and set them next to her burger.

Mauri pulled a large soda from the carrier and inserted a straw. "You know me so well. What do I owe you, Boss?"

"You know what I want? One afternoon where I don't have to put up with any of your crap—about anything," he said as he swiped a finger through the air. He picked up the carrier and the bag and headed toward his office.

"Dammit!" Mauri groaned as she took a sip. "It's Coke!"

Brian grinned to himself, "Sucks to not get the drink you want, doesn't it?"

"What happened to Mr. Nice Guy who always pours a can of Pepsi into my glass of ice?" Brian shrugged. "You know damn well I'm dumping this crap down the drain, don't you?"

"I do, but it was so worth it," Brian called over his shoulder as he disappeared into his office.

"Hey, Jeff. I brought lunch."

"Mmm-hmm," Jeff acknowledged. His back was to Brian as he continued to stare at the computer screen.

Brian set the food and drinks on the corner of his desk. "Discover anything interesting?'

Jeff tilted the screen nearly closed. "Well, actually, I did. But let's eat. I'm starving. We can talk while we eat."

The chief opened the bag and pulled two Big Macs from inside. His deputy set the four large orders of fries aside before flattening the paper bag and upending them, creating a mound of potatoes and grease.

"Dammit! I forgot the…"

"…ketchup?" Mauri appeared, holding a bottle of ketchup. "When have you ever remembered?" She set the bottle next to their shared fries before leaving.

"Hey," Brian called, "I said no crap for an entire afternoon."

"You know as well as I do that's not happening," she called from her office.

Brian bit off a large piece of his burger. "That woman is the most infuriating assistant I've ever had."

Jeff laughed. "And she's also amazing at what she does. That's why you keep her," he reminded the chief.

Brian snorted. He grabbed a handful of fries and dunked them into the pool of ketchup his deputy had created. "Yeah…and that's what's so frustrating. I'd fire her ass if I didn't need her so much."

"You would not," Mauri sang from her desk.

"Shut the damn door!" Brian yelled.

Mauri walked into the room and grabbed the doorknob. Both men laughed when she gave them the one-finger salute as she backed out of the room, slowly pulling the door closed.

Jeff scooped up the last couple of fries. "You ever googled yourself, Chief?" he asked.

"No. Why? Should I?"

"You'd be surprised by what you'd find."

Brian's head tipped to the side and one of his eyebrows rose. "Did you google me? Should I be concerned?"

"No, I didn't google *you*, but after I did some checking on Drew Carter, I decided to google Sean."

"Enlighten me." Brian lifted the garbage can and swept the McDonald's bag and wrappers into it. He sent the tiny salt granules and crumbs flying onto the carpet.

Jeff picked up the small yellow notepad he'd been writing on. "It seems Sean Hart has a history—just not as Sean *Hart*."

"What?" Brian looked confused. "You mean he has another identity?"

Jeff nodded. "Yeah. But let me start from the beginning. First, I googled *Sean Hart*. The usual came up: name, address, etc. And, of course, the law firm where he works showed up. So, I read his bio on their site. Did you know he graduated from Hamline?"

"I did," Brian moved to the recliner. "It's where he met Jane." He sighed.

"Anyway, I searched Sean Hart and Hamline together, but there was nothing that connected them."

Brian shrugged. "Well, that was a long time ago. I wouldn't expect to find anything about him from back then."

"Right," Jeff agreed. "So, I decided to give Hamline a call. I asked the registrar to verify that Sean Hart attended Hamline." He smirked at Brian.

"And…" Brian pushed him to respond.

"Well, they never had a Sean Hart go through the law school, but they did have a *Sean Hartung* who graduated the same year Sean claimed in his bio."

"Really? What are the chances?" Brian snarked. "So, our boy isn't who he says he is. Does that surprise you?"

"Yeah, some," Jeff claimed. He ran the tip of his pen halfway down the notepad. "Well, I did some digging into Sean Hartung and found all kinds of information. Turns out he has a post office box in Alexandria, just two blocks from the law firm where Sean *Hart* works." He looked back at his notebook. "Ah, Box C2097."

"Okay, so he's hiding something from Jane other than his name. But what? That's what we need to figure out."

Jeff pressed a finger to his lip, "I also uncovered an obituary from just three weeks ago—for a, ah..." Again, Jeff scanned his notes. "Vernon Hartung—Sean's father."

Brian stood up, stepped toward his desk, and grabbed his soda. "Jane told me Sean had no family. Said his parents were older, and they had both passed while he was in college before they met—" He stared into the distance. "—which plainly wasn't true," he mused. Brian began pacing back and forth in front of his desk. "So, clearly, Jane had no idea Sean's folks were still alive."

Jeff nodded. "Well, his dad, anyway. According to death records, his mom died when he was about five. And, as far as I can tell, his dad never remarried." He waited for Brian to stop moving. "But there's more."

"Well, of course there is." Brian rubbed his forehead with his thumb and index finger. "It's Sean we're talking about."

"While I was digging, I googled Vernon Hartung. Appears Vernon and Doug Sterling were pretty chummy back in college. They both attended the University of Minnesota, played hockey at the U, and graduated from the pharmaceutical program together." Jeff pulled a few sheets of paper from beneath his legal pad. "I found photos of them. Looks like they both loved the ladies and the booze."

Brian slowly paged through the pictures Jeff had printed. There was no mistaking Doug; except for aging, he looked almost the same. The other man, Vernon Hartung, looked nothing like Sean. But it wasn't unusual for a parent and child to not look alike. Thank God *he* looked nothing like his old man.

He handed the pages back to his deputy. "So, where does this put us?"

"You haven't let me finish."

"There's more?"

Jeff snorted. "So, four years ago when the Sterlings moved to Duluth..." Brian nodded. "...well, they bought their house from Vernon Hartung. And what's even more bizarre is that in this hot real estate market, they paid only about half of what it was worth."

"Why would a guy, supposedly smart enough to be a pharmacist, sell his house for pennies on the dollar?"

"Well, I called the Duluth PD and got ahold of an old friend of ours—Wesley Alder." Jeff waited for Brian's expression before rolling his eyes; he didn't want to miss it.

"Wesley Alder. I haven't thought of that idiot in years. I can't believe he even graduated. I mean, seriously, at the shooting range, I swear, he missed the target every single time."

Jeff laughed. "Yes, and so, when I got him on the phone, he was more than happy to help out an old classmate." He shook his head in disbelief. "Anyway, it appears Vernon had a pharmacy down on Canal Park. He must have hired well because he was quite the drunk. Wes said he had several DUIs, but more importantly, he would disappear from the pharmacy for weeks on end, only to reappear as if he hadn't been gone at all."

"Really? So maybe he was in rehab or…"

"Nope, it was more like he spent days locked in his house drinking until every bottle was empty. Then he'd sober up and return to work."

"Does he still own the pharmacy?" Brian asked.

"No, he lost it. He'd taken out second and third mortgages on it and eventually defaulted on the loans."

"Makes sense then that he'd sell his house too. So where was he living?"

Jeff looked at his notes. "The obituary said he was living at The Bluffs on London Road. Pretty swanky joint. My guess is Sean was footing the bill."

Brian looked down at the carpet. He followed the swirls with his eyes as he wrangled with his thoughts. "So, if the guy needed money, why would he sell his house to the Sterlings for next to nothing?"

Jeff shrugged. "Good question. And one we're not likely to get an answer to since he's dead, and I'm sure Sean's not going to share—especially since he didn't let on he even had a family."

"True." Brian plopped into the chair across from Jeff.

"Okay, so Sean lived in Cedar Point most of his adult life, and one of his father's best friends from college lived here too, and yet, Sean and Vernon never spent time together here, in Cedar Point?" Brian stared at his deputy. "Or did they?"

Jeff bit his lip. "I think maybe Sean was protecting the lie about his family."

Brian frowned. "He's hiding something." He strummed his fingers on his desk. "Let's bring him in for questioning in the morning."

"Want me to give him a heads up?" Jeff already knew the answer.

"No. I think the element of surprise might work in our favor." Brian picked up the printed photos of Doug and Vernon Hartung. He slowly studied each one. "Hey, hand me the magnifying glass from my top drawer." He moved toward the window as he looked through the curved glass, studying the grainy photo Jeff had enlarged. "I knew it. Come here," he told his deputy. "Look at this."

Jeff took the paper and the magnifying glass from Brian; he tipped the photo toward the window and studied the area where the chief was pointing. He turned toward Brian. "That's weird," he laughed.

"It's Viv, right?" Brian asked. Jeff nodded in agreement. "And look at the man next to her."

Jeff tipped the picture back toward the window. "Seriously? You've got to be kidding?"

"Harrison Carter the second—one of the founding members of Hallman and Carter—where Jane worked." He took the photo from Jeff and threw it toward his desk. It sailed farther than he anticipated, landing upside down on the floor. "Why did we never know that the Sterlings and Harrison Carter were connected? They sure kept that on the down-low."

"And speaking of the Carters, I found no connection between Drew and the Sterlings or the Harts—other than Jane's employment," Jeff said. "But now that we know the old man went to college with Doug and Viv Sterling, there might be more. I'll keep digging."

"Good work, Jeff. This is why you're my lead deputy," Brian said as he patted him on the back. "Now get the hell out of my chair and go see what the rest of Cedar Point is up to."

Jeff laughed. "Yes, sir." He picked up his hat and tucked it under his arm before walking out of Brian's office. Almost instantly, he stepped back in and closed the door again. "I forgot to ask. Did the lead you were following this morning pan out?"

Brian hated lying to Jeff, but he had no choice. "No. It was a bust, but I owed it to Jane to check it out anyway."

Jeff watched Brian's face cave into despair. "We'll find her, Chief. I have a good feeling." Jeff left the room before Brian responded.

"Not me," he whispered. "I don't have a good feeling at all."

CHAPTER 16

The clock glowed 10:15 p.m. Brian was still in his office. Mauri had gone home hours before insisting he do the same, all the while knowing he wouldn't. Jeff had stopped by with dinner around 7:00—hot and healthy, courtesy of his wife.

His deputy stayed for almost two hours, reviewing questions for their meeting with Sean the next day.

Brian popped the top of a third Coke and sucked down nearly half the can before setting it on his desk. He turned toward the window and stared into the trees on the far side of the small field.

Sean Vernon Hartung. What are you hiding?

He reached behind himself and grabbed the folder, paging through it again. He shifted a couple of pages, switching the order of the questions, then made a second and third pass through his notes. The order felt good, but his gut told him things were missing—things he wanted to know but couldn't ask yet. Jeff had pushed him to wait on some of the questions until he did some more digging. Brian had reluctantly agreed, but it left him beyond frustrated—especially sitting in the dark alone, knowing Jane was somewhere out there.

He dropped the folder on the corner of his desk and opened his computer. Slowly, he typed Jane's name into the search engine and waited for the screen to populate. Newspaper articles, links to TV newscasts, YouTube videos, and social media sites popped onto his screen. Hallman and Carter made the list, as did the church Jane attended.

Brian clicked through multiple links. He deleted Hart and typed Sterling, focusing on her maiden name. A couple of pages in, his jaw dropped open. Jane's name appeared along with two photos. One was a baby photo that, to be honest, looked like every baby Brian had ever seen. The second was a photo of a toddler about two years old, claiming to be Jane.

Confusion washed over him as he perused the page. What the hell was this? The headline read—*Family Reunited*. Brian enlarged the article and read through it several times. It couldn't be *his* Jane Sterling, but according to the report, that was exactly who it was.

He read it again.

A Cedar Point, Minnesota family has been reunited with the child they wondered if they would ever see again. Just under two years ago, Douglas and Vivian Sterlings' daughter, Jane, was kidnapped less than a month after her birth. Mrs. Sterling told police she had taken her out for a drive to try to calm her. Shortly after turning down a gravel road, a rusty blue pick-up began to follow her. According to the infant's mother, the thick dust kept her from identifying the truck further. Vivian Sterling claimed that the truck sped around her and blocked her from proceeding onto the highway. She reported two men jumped out of the truck, pulled her from her car, tossed her keys into the grassy field, and left with her daughter.

On Wednesday, the two-year-old was found wandering the streets of Alexandria, Minnesota. The officer assigned to the child's disappearance recognized her from an age progression photo he recently had made. Police will continue to follow leads as to the child's whereabouts for the past two years. As for now, the Sterlings are thrilled to have their daughter back.

How did he not know about any of this? Did Jane know? She had never mentioned it, and they had talked about everything.

Brian threw back the rest of his soda, stacked the can on top of the other two, and went to grab a fourth. The article buzzed through his brain as he began a new search: *kidnapped Jane Sterling.* Several articles popped up, but none stated anything more than the first one had. He continued to search for more information, but he knew he was headed down a rabbit hole. Sometime around 2:00 a.m., he finally closed his computer.

He made a few calls, leaving messages at each place. The last place he called was Crosby's Insurance. The office had been closed since 5:00 p.m., but he wanted Jay to get his request the minute he walked through the door.

Too tired to drive home, Brian asked Siri to set his alarm for 5:30 a.m., just in case he fell asleep harder than expected. He stretched out in the recliner in his office and closed his eyes. The four cans of Coke played all night long; they laughed at him for even thinking sleep was possible. He finally drifted off around 4:00 a.m.

CHAPTER 17

"Hey, Boss!" Mauri greeted Bryan when he walked into the office. "Glad to see you slept in." He cringed. He'd left his office long before his 5:30 alarm. A quick shower and a decent pot of coffee were the only things he had been able to focus on. Three rubbery breakfast sandwiches had made their way into his stomach, along with a rock-hard cinnamon roll from nearly a week before. He'd spent most of the time on the phone with his deputy, sharing what he'd learned about Jane. The plans they'd laid out so carefully the night before had been thrown out the window and new ones were fixed in their place.

Mauri got up and followed him into his office. "Everything's a go. The fridge is loaded with water and soda. And, ah, here are your messages." She handed him two yellow squares of paper before spinning around and returning to her desk. "Let me know if you need anything else," she called.

Brian watched her leave. There hadn't been one nasty remark, not one flippant comment. He was perturbed, not with Mauri, but with himself. Mauri deserved a better boss than he'd been lately.

Refocusing, Enderly swiped the folder from the top of his desk. After paging through it, he rearranged the items yet again. He pulled a package of yellow sticky notes from his top drawer

143

and scribbled thoughts that had badgered him in the middle of the night when sleep hadn't played fair. He stuck them on several pages as reminders.

"Hey, Mauri," he summoned her. She was standing in his office before he even finished saying her name.

"Yeah, Boss?" she asked.

A tired smile passed across his face. "Thanks," was all he could muster.

"You got it, Boss," she said, swinging her arm through the air in front of her.

Jeff stuck his head in Brian's office. "Just checked the equipment, and…"

"Already did that," Mauri yelled from her desk.

The two men laughed. "Damn! She's good!" Jeff admitted.

"Don't tell her that," Brian whispered.

Mauri yelled again, "I already know."

A single eyebrow raised on Brian's face as he shook his head.

Jeff glanced at his watch. "You ready, Chief?" he asked. "Want to talk through the changes one more time?"

An audible sigh was Brian's only response before commotion broke out in the main office.

"Enderly, you better have a damn good reason for making me drag my ass down to this hellhole. You know full well we could have talked in my office or on the phone or at my house, but nooo, you make me come to you," Sean bellowed. "This is ridiculous! You know I'm a lawyer, right? I'll see your ass in court if…"

Brian stepped out of his office with the folder tucked under one arm. "Hart, shut the hell up. Any decent lawyer knows the more you protest the more you look guilty."

Sean leaped toward the chief. Brian steeled himself for the blow, but Sean thought better of it and veered sideways at the last second, landing his thigh against the corner of Mauri's desk. His face crumpled as he kneaded his leg; he turned away to keep from showing his pain.

"We can do this the easy way, or we can do it the hard way, Hart. You choose," Brian told him. Sean nodded toward the conference room. "I kind of thought so," Brian said as he pulled the thick folder from under his arm. "Do you want your lawyer present?"

"I am a lawyer, you idiot," Sean seethed as he limped toward the room.

Brian followed him. "Okay by me," he said with a smirk.

Deputy Porter pointed to a chair. "That's not my usual chair," Sean complained.

"Well, today, you're not playing the role of lawyer, are you?" Jeff had almost lost his patience. "Sit your ass in the chair I tell you to."

Enderly coughed to stifle his laugh. It was so out of character for Jeff to let anything or anybody get his ire up, but Sean Hart wasn't just anybody. He was a smart-assed attorney who believed he was above the law.

Brian dropped the folder on the table close enough for Sean to see his name printed in block letters across the front. Sean's eyes grew wide when he saw the dense folder. The chief had lots of experience with *Sean the lawyer*; he knew the thicker the folder, the more agitated Sean became, so he had padded it with blank sheets of paper before leaving his office.

Sean leaned back in his chair and crossed his arms. He pointed to the folder with his chin. "You're bluffing with that thing. You've got nothing on me. I'm innocent."

Brian loudly cleared his throat and shrugged. "Well, then, you've got nothing to worry about, do you?"

Jeff turned on the camera and the recorder. "For the record, state your full name."

"What?" Sean seemed confused.

"You know how this works, Sean," Porter told him. Then he repeated the request slower, enunciating each word as he stared directly at Sean. "For. The. Record. State. Your. Full. Name."

"Oh for..." He sighed loudly. "Sean Vernon Hart." He looked directly at the camera and added, "Attorney at Law."

"Good for you, Sean. Good for you." Brian clapped three times. Then he looked at the camera and said, "Looks like we might have another hostile witness."

"Also, for the record," Porter began, "would you like to have your attorney present?"

Sean looked like he was going to blow a gasket.

"Wait!" Brian said. He turned toward Sean. "I believe Sean's answer to that question was, 'I am a lawyer, you idiot.' Is that correct?"

Sean leaned back in his chair. His face went blank, but he knew Brian was right. Hostility made a person look guilty. If his client had acted as he had, he would have removed them from the room and read them the riot act before bringing them back in. He focused on his breathing for a few seconds before deciding to play nice.

"I don't need a lawyer present. I'll be serving as my own counsel." He leaned toward Brian. "I just want you to find my wife. I haven't been able to work or sleep since she disappeared. My brain won't shut down at night." Sean gazed at his hands as he folded and unfolded them over and over again, playing the devoted and worried husband.

Brian almost clapped again. If he'd learned anything in his twenty-five years in law enforcement, it was that lawyers made the best actors. But he wasn't buying any of what Sean Hart was selling.

"So, sleep eludes you...but golf doesn't?" Enderly shrugged. He knew he'd struck a nerve. "I heard you spent yesterday afternoon at the Links over in Fergus. Hard to believe a guy who can't sleep or work because his wife's missing can focus on golf." He bit his lip. "You know, I don't golf, but, ah, doesn't it require an intense sense of focus?" he teased.

"Besides, didn't I tell you to stay at the Moonlight?"

"I wasn't..." Sean slammed his fist on the table. Then he chastised himself for letting Brian get to him.

"Can it, Sean." The chief opened the file and pulled out three photos. "They have these amazing new things called cameras." Brian closed his eyes and took a deep breath. "They don't lie." He laid one photo on top of the other. "Here you are teeing off. And here you are inside the clubhouse. And here's another one of you flirting with the beverage cart girl." Brian pointed one hand toward the pictures. "Pretty hard to deny."

Enderly waited for a response, but Sean's lips pressed into a tight line—silenced by rage. He may as well have pretended to turn the key and throw it over his shoulder like kids do when they refuse to speak. All three men knew the hole-digging had begun. The more he said, or the more he tried to deny, the worse it would be.

Brian sat upright in his chair. "Okay, so, let's move on." He again opened the folder and pulled out a multi-page report and another stack of photos. He tossed the pictures in front of Sean.

Sean choked as he inhaled. "What the hell? This isn't possible," he yelled. "I didn't kill Jane." The photos were dark. Large and small blotches of blue, created by the luminol, peppered the kitchen, hallway, living room, and bathroom. Bluish footprints tracked from the mudroom into the garage.

Brian snorted. "No one said you did, but based on the photos, something went down in your house." He and Jeff watched Sean's face. "That's a lot of blood."

Sean's hands shook as he concentrated on each photo. "I-I, I don't know anything about this."

"Well, that's just weird." Brian twisted his mouth up in one corner. "The footprints match your shoes exactly."

"Not possible," Sean whispered. "I didn't…"

"Okay…" Both officers kept their eyes fixed on Sean. "So then…do you know anything about the bleach that was used to clean up the blood? Or how about the bloody and bleached-soaked rags in the garbage can in the garage?"

"N-no." Sean's face melted into confusion. Brian almost felt sorry for him.

Enderly opened the folder again and pulled a story he'd printed from an online newspaper. "Okay, let's leave that for a moment. Did Jane ever tell you she was kidnapped as a child?"

Sean froze. His eyes told the chief everything he needed to know. "Did Jane tell you about it, Sean?" Still, he said nothing. "Did Jane know? How did you find out?" He could see Sean's blood begin to boil. "Tell me. When did you know?"

"Where's Jane now, Sean? Was she kidnapped again?" Jeff asked calmly, adding to Enderly's barrage of questions. "Where is she? Where are you keeping her?"

In a fit of rage, Sean sent Brian's folder flying across the room. A raspy yell filled the conference room as Sean pressed his fists against the sides of his face. He shoved his chair backward and stormed toward the door. "Screw you, Enderly."

The chief leaned back and folded his hands behind his head. "You know we're not done, Sean."

"Oh, yes we are!" he screamed as he stormed out of the station.

Before Sean even left the station, Mauri poked her head through the doorway. "Well, it looks like that went just peachy!"

Jeff laughed. "It did. It went exactly as we hoped."

CHAPTER 18

Sean side-armed his keys toward the kitchen countertop when he walked into the house. They skidded across the length of the island and off the far side, slamming into the front of the lower cabinets. He was beyond angry. Enderly had no proof he'd done anything to Jane. None whatsoever! Because he hadn't!

He kicked off his Ferragamo loafers and dropped onto the couch. With one hand, he loosened his tie. It wasn't even noon and he felt like he'd been chewed up and spit out multiple times. Enderly and his deputy had hit a nerve. As an attorney, he would never have allowed his clients to answer their damn questions, but as a possible suspect, he was in a different seat. He was pissed—royally pissed. He had a good mind to press charges against the Cedar Point police for badgering and anything else he could throw at them.

That morning, Jeff Porter had met him in the parking lot of his office building. He'd told him he was taking him in for questioning. Sean had fought it; he said that wasn't the way it worked. They could ask him to come or they could arrest him, but they couldn't just haul him in. Jeff's calm demeanor had angered him. The deputy told him if he wanted to find his wife, he'd come with him, and if he didn't get in the car, it would look like he had something to hide. It was the oldest line in the book, but Sean couldn't let Porter think he knew anything about where his wife was.

He had a deposition at 9:00 a.m., but his assistant could handle it. Other than that, he had just planned to use the day to catch up on other cases. Finally, he agreed to meet Porter at the station.

Jeff studied Sean's face. "You'd better be there or I'll hunt you down."

Sean had rolled his eyes. "Calm down, Barney Fife. I'll be there by 10:00." He stood in the parking lot and watched the deputy drive away. Everything was falling apart.

The entire interrogation had been a shitshow from the moment he arrived at the station. His hands hadn't stopped shaking. Sean got up and poured himself a shot of whiskey, thought better of it, and made it a double before returning to the couch, where he rehashed the morning. He planted his feet on the leather ottoman, crossing them before shifting into a comfortable position.

Brian assured him they were just talking, but within ten minutes, he knew it was a full-out interrogation. Enderly thought he was guilty and, evidence or not, he was going to pin it on him. It would only be a matter of time before the police would show up and arrest him.

Memories flooded through him: of the morning at the station, of Jane, of his childhood. He dropped his feet to the floor and set his drink on the wooden tray on the oversized ottoman. He leaned sideways and extracted his wallet from his back pocket. With a flick of his wrist, the bifold wallet opened. He removed the photo insert and stuck his finger into the compartment that held it. Inside was a worn and faded photo of two small children. Across the back, in his mother's distinct handwriting was scrawled—*Sean, 4 1/2 and Emily, 1 1/2*. Time and love had faded the photo.

Both children held an ice cream cone; their free hands were linked together. Chocolate was dripped down the front of their shirts. Their smiles were awkward: eyes narrowed, and teeth pressed tightly together as they lifted their cheeks upward. Sean remembered his mom laughing as she snapped the photo. It was one of her good days—one that was as clear as if it had happened yesterday.

Sean loved this picture. He loved Emily. After all, she was his sister. But it was more than that; Emily was the only person who could ever make his mother smile. His mom had been sick for so long that when she smiled, his heart felt happy. There was a glimmer of hope. Before Emily, his mother had spent days in bed, not moving and not talking, just staring at the closed blinds as if she could see through them. After Emily, everything changed—at least in the beginning.

There were still days when his mother stayed in bed all day, days he fed himself and his sister. On those days, Sean was the adult, and his mother was the child. Sean learned how to change

Emily's diapers when she would get fussy and cry. He played with her every day. And, when the first number on the digital clock was a straight up and down line, they would take a nap together.

When she was younger, he learned to make her bottles using a can of powder his parents kept in the cupboard. He fed her from jars his father opened before he left for work or ones he found in the refrigerator. And when his mom was awake, he and Emily would sneak into her bedroom and he would lift his sister onto the bed, hoping to make his mother smile. Sometimes, she would scoop them both into her arms and hug them until they couldn't stand it for one second longer. Other times, she didn't even notice them.

When his sister was hurt or sick, she didn't call for their parents; she yelled his name. When she would wake up in the middle of the night, he'd pull his teddy bear and blanket from his bed and climb up the side of her crib to sleep with her. No one loved his sister more than he did. Not his mom, and definitely not his dad.

On the days when his mother got up in the morning, she'd cook the most amazing breakfasts and lunches and dinners; there was more food than anyone could eat. She'd sing and dance and spin them around in circles. Their mother would tell them how much she loved them. She read books and played games with them. Sean never wanted those days to end.

On her good days, their mother showered, fixed her hair in

long pretty curls, put on a flowery dress, and sprayed her best perfume—not just on herself, but on him and his sister too. When his father walked through the door, she'd meet him with a drink, lifting one leg as the two of them kissed for a long time. He and Emily would stand in the hallway watching them. He'd cover Emily's eyes and giggle. His sister would copy him— with a long, loud fake laugh that echoed down the hallway. On those nights, he fell asleep as soon as his head hit his pillow, happy and safe, dreaming about the perfect day. But when he opened his eyes in the morning, his world didn't feel so innocent anymore. He wouldn't know what to expect until he went to check on his sister. If Emily were out of her crib, he would take a deep breath and blow it out through a smile. If she was still inside, he knew it was the start of a bad stretch of days.

For some reason, his father always knew when to come home and when to stay away. On his mother's bad days, he never came home until long after they were all in bed. On those nights, if Sean got up to use the bathroom, the house smelled disgusting, like the stuff his mom rubbed on Emily's gums when her teeth were coming in.

With Emily, Sean never felt lonely. No one ever stopped in for a visit anymore and they never went anywhere, but he didn't care; he didn't even notice. Sean didn't go to school. He didn't know he was supposed to; school was a foreign concept. And even if he had known, he would rather have stayed home with his sister. She was his best friend.

Once Emily came to live with them, he wasn't allowed to go outside anymore or open the curtains. "Your mama needs the dark when she's sick," his father always told him. But even on her happy days, the rules didn't change. Sean didn't care; he was so busy playing with his mom and sister that it didn't matter.

The older Emily got, though, the sicker their mom became. That was what his father called it—her sickness. He brought golden-brown bottles home from his work—bottles of pills. *Medicine,* he told Sean. His father told him to keep his sister away from the bottles because what was inside could kill her. Sean wondered how medicine that was supposed to help his mom could hurt his sister, but he did as he was told. He needed Emily.

Shortly before Sean turned seven, his father and mother got into a huge yelling match. It had been a good day until his father came home late for dinner. Instead of kissing him when he came through the door, she threw his drink at him and slapped his face. The noise scared Emily and made her cry. Sean bent down and wrapped his arms around her tummy; he locked his fingers together behind her back and awkwardly carried her to her bedroom. The entire time, his sister's feet kicked him in the knees. He bolted the door before hoisting her into her crib. He threw books and toys over the top of the railing before crawling in with her. For a long time, he read to her, not actual words, but words he'd memorized from hearing them before. He sang her songs and played peekaboo and pattycake until they both fell asleep.

The room was dark when his father angrily banged on the bedroom door. "Dammit, Sean! Unlock this door. Open it, now!" he yelled, violently jerking the handle up and down. His dad's words were garbled and hard to understand, but even as disoriented as Sean was, he knew he needed to move fast. When his father was this furious, there was no telling what he might do.

Sean jumped over the top of the crib and landed on his hands and knees on the floor. He raced to the door, slid the bolt sideways, and yanked it open. His father, barely able to stand, supported himself by leaning one hand against the door jamb. His breath smelled dreadful, but Sean didn't dare turn away. "Get your sister and get in the damn car!" he hollered.

Sean froze. He hadn't been out of the house for as long as he could remember. Tears filled his eyes. He wanted to ask his mom if it was okay, but his father shoved him toward the crib before stumbling down the hallway toward the front door.

Emily rubbed her eyes and whimpered when he woke her. He stood in her crib and lowered her over the side, the way he had done hundreds of times before. He poked her pudgy hands through the sleeves of her sweater and tucked her feet into a pair of shiny black shoes that were too small. She whimpered when she tried to walk, but Sean hugged her and told her it would just be for a little bit.

He sat on the floor and tried to force his sneakers on, but no matter how much he curled his toes, he couldn't make them fit. His feet had grown too much. Neither he nor Emily ever wore shoes in the house, and because they never went outdoors, his mother hadn't bought him new ones; she hadn't even noticed they'd outgrown the ones they had.

His father appeared in the doorway again and angrily grabbed him by the arm. "Get your ass in that car, boy!" he yelled as he swatted his behind with his free hand. Sean shoved one arm through the sleeve of his jacket before grabbing Emily's hand. In his other hand, he carried his shoes. The two of them ran into the driveway, where he lifted his sister into the car.

His father took off before the back door was shut and Sean almost fell out as his dad raced backward into the street. There were no car seats. It had been so long since he'd ridden in a car, he didn't know about seatbelts.

Sean pressed his face to his window; he was mesmerized by the lights and the houses and trees. Rushing to get Emily into the car, he hadn't noticed how the night air felt on his skin or how the stars in the sky glowed but hoped he would have the chance wherever they were going.

Emily had instantly fallen sleep. The car zigzagged back and forth on the road—sometimes slow and easy and other times sudden and jerky. Within minutes, Sean's stomach began to flip-flop. He tightened his jaw and clutched his stomach.

Finally, leaning his head over the edge of the seat, everything he had eaten for dinner spewed onto the floor.

"What the hell, boy? Are you stupid?" his father screamed. He called him other things that made Sean want to cry, but he refused. He was a big boy now; his mother had told him that a million times.

The car finally slowed and came to a stop between a bunch of old buildings. Sean looked out the window; the narrow space was dark and dirty. There were overflowing garbage cans next to every building. He had no word for this place; he had never seen anything like it before.

His father barked at him, "Stay in the car and watch your sister and don't let anyone see you. Understand? And for god's sake, clean up that puke before I get back." Then he was gone. Sean watched him disappear through a metal, windowless door not far from the car.

He hid on the floor of the opposite side of the car and watched Emily sleep. Before long, the acidic smell of his vomit made his eyes water; he could barely breathe. He grabbed the handle of the window and tried to roll it down, but it was stuck. Careful not to disturb his sister, he moved to the seat above where he had thrown up and rolled that window down just enough to let in some fresh air. He leaned his head against the glass and breathed in the cool night air.

Sean almost nodded off to sleep when he remembered he was supposed to clean up his mess before his father got back.

But when would that be? He peeked out the window to see if anyone was around before quietly opening his door. The ceiling light came on, but he found the button near it and shut it off. While he went out to search for something to wipe the floor with, he left the door open. A few minutes later, Sean returned with an old rag he found lying next to a garbage can, but Emily was gone. A feeling he had never experienced before rushed through his little body.

Where had she gone? "Emily," he called quietly. "Emily, where are you?"

His father had left specific directions to not let anyone see them. Moving along the narrow alleyway between the buildings, toward the bright lights and the cars that sped past, Sean panicked about being noticed. Terrified someone would see him, he hid in the shadows. He peeked in both directions, but his sister was nowhere. "Emily!" he whisper-yelled. Sean's heart thudded in his small chest. This was the worst trouble he had ever been in. Finally, he returned to the car, praying his sister would find him before his father did. After scrubbing the floor, he tossed the rag into a nearby garbage can, curled up on the seat, and cried himself to sleep.

When he woke, it was still dark. The car was moving again, but he didn't dare open his eyes. When the car stopped, his father yelled, "Get your sister out of the car and into bed." Then he slammed the door and left Sean alone. *His sister,* he thought. *Had she returned?* He looked in the front and the back seat but couldn't find Emily anywhere. Defeated, he climbed out of the car and went into the house and to his bedroom. The digital clock had the straight number that went up and down, but it was the nighttime number because it was dark outside. Sean lay in his bed; he didn't sleep, but he wasn't awake either.

Daylight streamed through the window when he heard his mother scream. She was up; it was supposed to be a good day. His mom raced into his room. "Sean, where's Emily? Where's your sister?" He threw his arms around her neck without saying a word, but she untangled them and dropped him back into his bed. "Emily's missing! Where is she?" she shrieked as she raced from the room.

"I don't know," Sean whispered. He was afraid of telling lies. Had he just told his mother a lie? Was he going to that place called *hell* that she often told him about—the one for bad boys who didn't help their mamas or take care of their sisters? He honestly didn't know where Emily was; he just knew she hadn't been in the car on the way home. "I don't know, Mama," he cried again.

From behind the couch, he watched his mother race around the house screaming the words "Oh my god!" over and over. From the doorway of his bedroom, he listened as she told someone on the phone that his sister was missing. Minutes later, his father burst through the front door. He immediately came to his room. "Sean, where the hell is your sister? Where's Emily?" he screamed, cupping his big hands around Sean's arms and lifting him off the ground by his shoulders, shaking him back and forth.

"I don't know," Sean cried. "You're hurting me." He tried to wiggle free, but his father was too strong.

His father threw him to the floor when the telephone rang. Sean scampered beneath the bed and pressed himself against the wall on the far side. He heard his father's soft voice as he spoke to his mother, a sharp contrast to the sound of her gut-wrenching wails just moments later.

Sean saw his father's feet slowly cross his room. "Emily's gone, boy, and it's all your fault. I told you to watch her. You couldn't even do that, could you?" his father screamed as he stamped his foot hard on the floor. Sean covered his ears as his father yelled about him being worthless and no son of his. His father sat on his bed and sobbed. Then, after what felt like an eternity, his dad walked out of the room and out of the house, leaving Sean alone to listen to his mother sobbing.

By the time the straight up and down line on the clock appeared again, his mother had stopped screaming. Her sickness was back. She was in her bed, staring at the closed curtains. He crawled up on the bed and kissed her cheek and wrapped his arms around her neck. Because she looked at him, he thought it was going to be okay, but instead, she angrily pushed him away and said, "You're not as big of a boy as I thought you were." Then she rolled over so she couldn't see him.

Tears rolled down his cheeks and a sob escaped. "I *am* a big boy, Mama. I am."

A week later, when Sean woke up early one morning, he couldn't find his mother anywhere. She wasn't making breakfast and she wasn't in her bed. Quietly, he opened the door between the garage and the house and gasped. His mom was hanging from the boards at the top of the garage. A chair was tipped over, lying beneath her. He raced to stand the chair back up; he tried to grab her feet and put them on the chair. "Mama, stand on the chair. I'll help you," he told her. He grabbed onto her feet and tried to press them onto the chair. "Hold still, Mama," he begged. But she swayed back and forth. Finally, he gave up and wrapped his arms around her legs and kissed her ankle.

He curled into a ball on the garage floor and stared at his mother until he fell asleep. His father found the two of them in the garage when he returned around midnight.

What kind of a big boy was he? His mother was right. He'd lost Emily, and he had lost his mother. He hadn't protected either one of them.

***

Sean tucked the photo back into his wallet. Then, throwing his head back, he downed the rest of his whiskey. A second drink, much larger than the first, went down quickly. *I loved you, Emily,* he thought. *But you had to be punished for leaving me—back then and now.*

CHAPTER 19

A *For Sale* sign was posted in their Alexandria home's front yard the day after Sean's mother died. There was no funeral, no opportunity for him to say goodbye. He watched as his father made a deal with the funeral director to *take care of her*, to bury her somewhere nice. When his dad handed a check to the man, Sean saw the director's eyes grow wide; a smile spread across his face before he enthusiastically responded, "Yes, sir." His dad spun around and walked out of the building. Sean followed, afraid to let his father out of his sight. After losing his sister and his mom so suddenly, he didn't want to lose his dad too. His last memory of Emily was of her asleep in the car. The last one he had of his mom was of her hanging in the garage.

Before the house even sold, his father loaded everything they could fit into the car and drove away. Sean kneeled on the front seat and stuck his head out the window, watching their house until it became nothing but a speck. He didn't know why he cared. The outside of it was as foreign as any of the other homes they passed. The only time he had seen it was when he lost Emily—the night he became an only child.

Boxes were piled on the front seat between him and his father and on the floor beneath his feet. The radio played music Sean had never heard before; it wasn't like the simple songs his mom sang to him and his sister on her good days. He stole a glance at his father, but his dad's eyes were glued to the road. Afraid to ignite his father's wrath, Sean dozed off and on for much of the next four hours.

"Sean, wake up." His dad tapped him, rousing him from a happy dream of his onetime family. "Look!" He pointed toward a vast body of water. "Look! That's Lake Superior."

He rubbed his eyes and leaned closer to the window. "What's that?" he asked, pointing through the dark sky toward a huge lighted mass on the water.

"That's a ship, son." His dad laughed. "It's a huge boat. It hauls iron ore out of Duluth."

Sean cautiously eyed his father. Something had changed since they had left their home. He seemed happier, more relaxed than he had just four hours before. "Where are we going, Dad?" he finally asked.

"We're moving to a new house—one with lots of room and lots of windows and a great big backyard."

Sean stared at the ship. "You mean I can play *outside*?"

"Of course you can, son." His father laughed. "That's what boys do."

Sean was confused. "But. But," he said again. "I couldn't go outside before?"

His father continued to watch the road as he maneuvered the car through the steady traffic. "Well, your mom was sick then."

His dad put a hand on Sean's knee and wiggled it back and forth. "You know what? Let's not worry about that anymore. Let's just look forward to our new adventure."

"I wonder what Emily would think about this place," Sean excitedly pondered out loud.

"Sean!" His dad's voice angrily boomed. "You know damn well Emily wasn't real. She was just part of your imagination, boy." His father continued to drive. "We're not ever going to talk about her again. Do you understand?"

He didn't know how to answer. Emily had been real; he knew it. He had hugged her and taken care of her. He loved her.

"Do you understand?" his father asked again, squeezing Sean's leg so tightly he yelped.

Sean wanted to cry. Emily hadn't existed only in his imagination, but he could no longer be sure. "Yes, sir," he whispered, his voice shaky with uncertainty.

His father let go of his thigh and roughly tousled the hair on the top of Sean's head. His smile had returned. "That's my boy. Emily and your mother are gone. It's just the Hartung men now."

***

Sean loved their new adventure; he experienced something fun and exciting every single day. His dad stopped smelling like the bottles he used to hide under Sean's bed in their old house. In the evening, after Sean returned from school, his dad would make dinner. Then, they'd go outside and play catch or walk along the shore and throw rocks into the huge lake that seemed to go on forever. In the wintertime, they would go skiing, sledding, and skating. When the weather was too cold to be outside, they would watch movies and order pizza. His dad even read to him before bed. But best of all, he kissed him on the forehead before he turned off his light each night. Even after his dad bought the pharmacy down on Canal Park, he still found time for Sean.

Life was perfect—for about eight years, then things slowly began to fall apart again.

By the time Sean was in high school, he spent most of his nights at hockey practice or locked away in his bedroom studying. His father had begun arriving home later and later each night, and the familiar smells from his past resurfaced. He watched his dad sink deeper and deeper into the drunken stupor of the past. At times, his father stayed locked in his den for days on end, drinking himself into oblivion. But it no longer mattered to Sean; he couldn't be bothered with his drunken father. He had his eye on the prize, a goal he set for himself way back in junior high. Sean wanted to become an attorney to help people. He knew it was ironic to want to help others when he let his father suffer alone every day.

Emily and his mother had long been forgotten. But on lonely nights, when stressed about a test or some big assignment, the image of his mother hanging from the rafters infiltrated his thoughts—day and night. For weeks afterward, he'd see her everywhere—in his mirror when he got ready for school, on the crowded Duluth streets, and outside his bedroom window before falling asleep at night. He often wondered if his mother had had someone to turn to, would she have left his father for a better life? Or would she still have killed herself?

On the day Sean graduated from Central High School, he was ecstatic. He had an acceptance letter to Hamline University for the pre-law program sitting on his desk at home and the keys to a new black Ford Mustang burning a hole in his pants pocket. Even though he was drunk much of the time, his father had somehow scrounged together enough money to buy it for him.

Standing in the entryway of the school, Sean waited for his dad to arrive. He held a white rose tipped in crimson boutonniere for his father. He stabbed the long pin through the stem again and again as he watched people pour through the door, but none of them belonged to his father. One of his buddies caught the wide sleeve of his graduation robe and pulled him down the hall. Sean angrily tossed the flower into the trashcan as he passed and joined his class.

Positioned on the side of the stage, behind the curtain, waiting to be called to give his speech, as all Central High School Valedictorians had done before him, Sean scanned the crowd for his dad. He could not locate him in the sea of faces; Sean was still searching when they called his name. His counselor tapped him on the shoulder and pointed toward the podium.

Sean adjusted the microphone and delivered a speech to his classmates and their families, one that was not only powerful but inspiring. Just before he finished, he glanced down to check the wording of his final thought. "And so, go forth and change the world—not just for yourself…" Suddenly, he heard a lone person clapping. He looked up from his notes and saw his father standing directly in front of the stage: tie unknotted, shirt untucked, barely able to stand.

"Whoo-hoo! T-that's my son," he slurred. "Good j-job, boy!"

Sean glared at him. He pressed an index finger to his lips before pointing to the door. His father stopped clapping, somehow confused. A few of Sean's teachers moved forward and escorted his dad out of the auditorium. When his father walked through those back doors, Sean took a deep breath and started his last line again. "And so, go forth and change the world—not for yourself," he paused and then tilted his outstretched hand toward the door, "but for the people who cannot do it for themselves."

Thunderous cheering broke out. The audience was on their feet—whistling, hooting, and shouting. Despite his seething anger, Sean smiled. He walked back to his chair and sat on his hands to keep them from shaking. It wasn't until he walked across the stage to pick up his diploma that he finally felt like he could breathe.

He didn't go home that night. Instead, he partied with his

buddies and spent the night with a college girl he didn't know and would likely never see again. By the next day, his father couldn't even remember what had happened. Sean chose to keep it that way.

***

In college, Sean pushed himself even harder than he had in high school. Remaining at the top of his class was his biggest priority. Professors adored him; he was their star pupil. He was awarded special privileges others did not receive. Sean wore those entitlements like Joseph's coat of many colors.

But two years later, everything changed.

It was the first week of his junior year. He had enrolled in a class called *Case Studies LR301*. Dr. Martin Dixon, Sean's favorite professor, had been assigned to the course. The intent of the class was to look at old cases—both from the perspective of a researcher and an attorney. For some cases, the students were required to defend the accused. The others had yet to be solved. They were challenged to bring an end to the mystery. Their first case was the latter.

Dr. Dixon assigned groups and appointed a lead researcher. The group Sean was assigned to was comprised of two females and three other males. He wasn't overly thrilled with any of the men. Arrogance ran deep in all three, but the women were organized and rational thinkers. He had worked with them before and had developed a strong bond.

There was a momentary commotion as students moved to

their groups and awaited their case study. The professor delivered instructions and a timeline. Dr. Dixon dropped a large, sealed envelope in front of each lead researcher and a packet of reading information for each group member.

After some discussion, Sean's team packed up after agreeing to regroup in the Student Union around 7:00 p.m. With no afternoon classes, Sean walked the half-mile to his on-campus apartment.

The apartment had four large bedrooms, each with a private bath. The suites branched off a shared living room, kitchen, and laundry. Being a junior finally afforded him the luxury of having his own room.

Except for the soft hum of music coming from the bedroom next to his, the apartment was quiet when Sean walked in. By luck, two of the people he shared the apartment with had attended Central High School. This person, however, was from the opposite end of the state. Other than a brief introduction, he had yet to get to know him.

Sean slapped together two peanut butter and jelly sandwiches and dropped them on a napkin before grabbing a soda from the fridge and heading to his bedroom. He plopped into an oversized chair and planted his feet on the edge of his bed, eating as he read. The article was about a child who had been kidnapped as an infant and later found, as a two-year-old, wandering the streets of Alexandria in the middle of the night. The case was titled: *Where was Jane Sterling?*

His yellow highlighter and pencil worked overtime; he spun the mechanical pencil between his fingers as he read. It wasn't until he neared the end that he felt a hammering in his gut. The girl was found in Alexandria, Minnesota—the place he had lived as a small child. He was too young to remember ever hearing the story, yet there was a thread of familiarity.

Sean finished reading. Everything inside of him felt jittery; his stomach burned with adrenaline. He picked up the envelope and held it in his hand. He was the only one in his group to have access to the additional information, and he had agreed not to open the envelope until they met later that night. His pulse raced and he started to sweat, yet he wasn't sure why.

Unable to prolong the inevitable for any longer, he moved to his desk and tore the envelope open, removing the thick stack of papers. Inside were several smaller envelopes with labels affixed to the front of each. Still standing, Sean shifted through them until he came to the one labeled *Photos*. He pushed everything else into a drawer and opened the white envelope.

The first picture was of an infant. Based on the color of the blanket, she was a girl. He set it to the left side of his desk. Written on the back of the second photo was the phrase *Jane Sterling, Age 2*. When he turned the picture over, his legs gave out and he dropped into his desk chair. He tugged off his t-shirt and used it to mop off his sweaty face and chest. Memories bombarded him—each one hitting him harder than the last. The little girl was Emily, the person he called his sister, the same person his father told him had only lived in his imagination. She was the girl he had forgotten about at the same time he'd let his mother's memory drift away. Emily had existed; his father had lied to him. But Emily wasn't really *Emily*; she was Jane Sterling.

Sean dove from his chair to his bed without ever standing up. He lay on the edge of the wide bed, staring at the picture of Emily. Disbelief and grief slammed down on him from every direction. He had never mourned his sister because he had been told she only lived in his imagination—she hadn't been real. His father had lied to him. Overcome with emotion, Sean sobbed hard, at times gasping for air. The tears fell, not just for his sister but for everything he had lost.

A sharp rap on his door drew him from his cocoon of grief. He wiped his eyes with the t-shirt. "Sean, you okay, man?" his roommate called.

Sean cleared his throat. "Yeah, ah, just working out."

"Okay. 'Cuz it kinda sounded like you were crying."

"Seriously? Nah, I'm good." He heard his roommate walk away. He turned his fan on high and let the breeze hit him like the memories had—at full force.

Two hours later, Sean finally looked at the last picture in the stack. It was a high school photo of Jane Sterling from her hometown paper. From the article, he surmised she lived in Cedar Point, Minnesota, less than half an hour from Alexandria. The other thing he knew was that she was 17 years old and a senior in high school. But more than anything else, he knew he had to find her. He wanted Emily, or Jane, back in his life, but he didn't know how to make that happen without implicating his father in the kidnapping.

Sean again picked up the photo of two-year-old Emily; his hand shook as he stared at it. His disbelief had turned to anger. There was no doubt about it, she had to be punished.

CHAPTER 20

Brian sifted through the thin stack of messages Mauri handed to him as he walked past her desk. He plucked out the one he had been waiting for and tossed the others on his desk. Jay from Crosby Insurance was in a meeting until 2:00 p.m. but had told him to call after that. He glanced at the bottom corner of his computer screen: *1:27 p.m.* Enderly had a meeting at 2:15, so it had to be quick. The call was pivotal. If his hunch was correct, it would launch his meeting in a whole new direction.

"Mauri," he summoned.

"Yeah, Boss?"

Brian jumped at her immediate appearance. He pressed his hand to his chest and yelled, "How in the hell do you do that?"

She leaned against the doorframe of his office; her arms were tucked behind her back. "It's just one of the many services I provide," she joked. "You should probably know I can read minds too." She raised her eyebrows. "Does that freak you out a little? 'Cuz it should."

The chief pointed at her and raised his eyebrows. "Yeah. You're a bit of a—freak."

Mauri laughed as she walked into his office and set a cold can of Coke on his desk.

"What the hell?" he said, in utter shock. "How did…"

"Oh, for crying out loud, Boss." She cut him off. "It's 1:30. You have a Coke *every* day at this time. I could set the station clock by your need for caffeine." She grinned at him and walked out of his office. "Hey Boss," she called when she returned to her desk. "Just an FYI, that's the last can. By the time I leave this afternoon, all empty fridge space *will* be filled with Pepsi."

Brian laughed. "Like hell it will," he hollered back.

He checked his watch and walked out of his office and past her desk, knocking on the corner of it so she would notice his departure. Then he walked out of the station door. Less than ten minutes later, he returned with a shopping cart stacked with so many cases of Coke that Mauri was positive the welds would split. Tommy, one of the college checkout boys, followed him, struggling to push a second cart that was equally overflowing. They moved the squeaky carts past her desk and into the breakroom, where the two of them unloaded every case, stacking them directly in front of the fridge door. Brian knew Mauri would be the one to move them—if not today, then tomorrow. Silently, she stood in the doorway and watched.

Brian handed the young man a ten-dollar bill and sent him on his way with the two empty carts. Mauri stepped into the room to allow Tommy to pass just as Brian stacked the last case well above the top of the fridge. He picked up a cold can of Pepsi he'd bought at the checkout counter and handed it to her. "Enjoy it because until you move all those cases, it's probably the last one you'll get for a while."

Mauri took the can and popped the top. She took a long draw and wiped her mouth on her sleeve, playing rugged like her boss. "Okay by me. I only drink two cans a day anyway." She held the can in the air. "Number two," she said, swinging the bottom of the can.

"Tomorrow, then," Brian told her, laughing as he walked past her.

Brian settled into his office and opened his computer. A few minutes later, Mauri walked in and sat in the chair in front of him. "Hey, Boss. Don't know if you remember, but you gave me the rest of the week off for my sister's wedding. So, looks like you're going to have to move all that Coke." She burst into hysterical laughter. Her arms were clutched tightly against her stomach as she bent over, unable to control herself.

"Oh, crap!" Brian slammed his fist on his desk and sighed before joining in the laughter.

***

It was a few minutes after 2:00 when he dialed Jay's cell. The two of them had played football together back in high school. They'd had a lousy team—two years with only one win, but they had enjoyed it. They were easily the biggest linebackers in the conference.

"Hey, Brian," Jay said when he picked up his cellphone. "Hold on one second. I want to close my door." Brian heard the door shut before Jay got back on the line. "Okay, I have the information you asked for—which, by the way, I really shouldn't give you because technically..." Jay let the sentence hang. "Anyway, since Jane's missing, I think there's a little wiggle room here."

"Thanks. I owe you," Brian told him as he pulled out his list of questions.

"Anyway, yes, there is a life insurance policy on Jane. It was taken out by the Sterlings. The policy was purchased a couple of days after Jane was born. In terms of a life insurance policy, it wasn't a ton of money: $150,000."

"Term or Whole Life?" Brian asked.

"Term. I'm sure it was because of the cost. Originally, they purchased a childhood policy. But when Jane turned 18, that policy expired. They purchased another thirty-year plan ending when Jane turns 48."

"Wait! If Jane was 18 and it was a different policy, wouldn't she have had to sign it?" Brian was spinning.

"She did sign it. At that time, the policy was upped to half a mill. I have an electronic copy. I can send you the signature if that's what you're questioning. Just remember, people's handwriting changes over time, so it may not look the same."

"I'd know Jane's writing," Brian said.

"Okay. I'll text it to you on your personal cell. I don't want this to get out."

"Don't worry. If I need to, I'll get the paperwork for you to release the information officially."

Brian's phone buzzed. He enlarged the signature. It wasn't Jane's; it didn't match any of the notes she'd sent him back in high school, the ones he had read repeatedly the past thirty years. "It's not her signature."

"Are you sure?"

"Positive. Jane and I were inseparable back then; you know that."

"Interesting," Jay mused.

"Who's the beneficiary?"

"Vivian Sterling," Jay told him. "The one and only."

"Not Doug?"

"No. Just Viv."

Brian rubbed one cheek. He could feel the heat building. "Seriously? Okay, was there ever a break in the payments or a stop and start of payment?"

"Hang on a sec." Brian waited while Jay clicked through several screens. "Weird. There was a break in the policy for almost two years. But you must know that since you asked."

"When was it?"

"Umm, not long after the policy was taken out. I don't understand why it was never canceled during that time."

Brian could hear Jay's computer keys clicking away. "There's a note here that says *extenuating circumstances*. Does that mean anything to you?"

Brian sucked in a deep breath. "Yeah. I know exactly what that means. I'll get back to you about it once we find Jane."

His office door jostled from the pressure of the station door opening and closing. He knew his 2:15 appointment had arrived. "Jay, one more question. I hate putting you in this situation, but I won't throw you under the bus. I promise."

"Okay," Jay responded hesitantly.

"Does Jane have a life insurance policy that lists her husband as the beneficiary?"

"I knew you'd want to know that. She does. She has a policy for five million. But now I'm questioning everything. Jane would have had to sign that policy too. I'll send you that signature also."

"Thanks," Brian told him. "You know I appreciate this." His phone buzzed again. He shook his head as he glanced at the signature.

"Brian, wait! There's something else you need to know."

His ears perked up and he leaned forward just as someone knocked on his door. Brian covered the phone. "I need two minutes," he yelled.

"There's another policy on her also."

"Really? Taken out by Jane?" Brian asked.

"No, it was taken out by Drew Carter." Brian's mouth dropped open.

"What? How's that possible?"

"Well, some companies consider certain employees to be a valuable resource, so they take out something called Key Employee Coverage. Hallman and Carter must have believed she was too important to lose. Here's what's peculiar; once an employee leaves a company, the contract is supposed to end. For some reason, H & C has continued paying on the contract since Jane retired. But what's really odd—the payout was increased about a month ago."

"How can that be? Who's the beneficiary? Is it H & C?"

"No. It's not. The beneficiary's Drew Carter."

"Drew?" Brian shook his head in disbelief. "Are you sure?"

Jay took a few seconds to respond. "Yes. Shortly after it was taken out was when, well, you know."

"Sonofabitch," Brian whispered as a second, more intense knock jarred the door. "Two minutes!" he yelled angrily.

"Brian, just so you're aware, all of this was done before I took over last month. I haven't made it through all the files—honestly, any of them since I started. Alan Crosby must have had his hands pretty deep into somebody's back pocket."

"Yeah, too bad the poor bastard's dead. I'd like to ask him a few questions—including whether the fall that killed him really was an accident." Brian nearly pushed the end button but thought better of it. "Jay, one more thing."

"Yeah?"

"It might not be a bad idea to leave town for a while," Brian said just before he ended the call.

***

Brian walked out of his office and directly into the conference room. Mauri and Jeff had everything set and ready to go. Doug Sterling looked grayer than he had the last time they had talked. This time, the conversation needed to be more private. He needed to speak to Doug without Viv.

"Doug." Brian nodded toward him in greeting. "Jeff, is the machine on?"

"Ready." Deputy Porter turned to Doug. "For the record, state your full name."

Doug sighed. "Douglas Joseph Sterling," he stated. His voice sounded like he'd already given up.

"Before we start, do you wish to have your lawyer present for questioning?"

"You know I can't afford one," Doug told him.

"I do." Brian nodded. "We could have the court appoint a public defender if you would like."

"Do I need one?" Doug looked from Brian to Jeff. "Am I going to be arrested?"

"No, but some people want to have an attorney present regardless."

Doug's head barely moved, indicating no. "No. I don't need one."

"Okay then, I just have a few questions for you," the chief told him. "Did you or Viv take out a life insurance policy on Jane when she was an infant?"

Doug nodded.

"Please respond out loud," Jeff reminded him.

"Sorry. Yeah. Yes," he corrected.

"So, you admit to taking out a life insurance policy on Jane. Did you have policies on your other children as well?" Brian asked.

Doug shook his head no but remembered he had to respond out loud. "No." He stared down at the table. "I don't know if you ever knew this, but a few years before Jane was born, we had a son named Jordan."

Brian shot a questioning look toward his deputy. They both wore the same bewildered expression, indicating this was new information to them.

"When Jordan was four years old, he was killed in an accident." His words were ribbon-thin and frail. "We didn't even have the money to pay for his funeral." Jeff handed Doug a bottle of water. His hands shook as he took a drink. "Thanks," he said, nodding toward the deputy. "My father died not long before JJ did, and he hadn't left a penny. We used our savings to pay for his funeral and to help my mom. So..." Grief deeply etched Doug's face. "Well, you get it." He shrugged.

Brian gave him a few moments to pull himself back together. "So, then, you took out the policy on Jane because of your son's death. Is that correct?"

Doug nodded. "Yes."

"Why not on the older girls?" Jeff asked.

Doug tipped his head to the side and shrugged. "Well, we couldn't afford three policies. We could barely scrape together enough to make the one payment." He glanced from Jeff to

Brian and back. "And with twins...well, how do you decide which one's worth money?"

This time, Brian nodded. He could tell JJ's death still weighed heavily on Doug, even after almost fifty years. "Did you extend the policy once Jane turned 18?"

Doug stared at Brian. His voice grew stronger. "No. Why would we? When Jane left for college, I handed her a check and wished her well." He wrinkled his forehead and sighed. "I know it sounds terrible, but Viv never bonded with Jane. And I hate to admit it, but she dragged me down to her level of disgust, and after a while, I treated Jane the same way she did." His eyes welled. "Honestly," he stared at Brian as a lone tear trickled down his cheek, "when she drove away that day, I figured she'd be so much better off without us."

Brian folded his arms across his chest and waited a few moments while he lassoed his anger. "The last time you and Viv were here, you told us about your calls to Jane."

"Those calls were initiated by Viv. I wanted to leave Jane out of the mess we'd gotten ourselves into."

"Okay, but from what Viv said, *you* made some of the calls. Is that correct?"

Doug shook his head. "No, I didn't make any of the calls, but I was forced to talk to Jane. You, of all people, know Viv is a force to be reckoned with when she wants something." Brian nodded. He knew all too well.

"You did talk to Jane, right? And the purpose of the calls

was to ask her for money. Are you sticking with that story?" Brian folded his hands and rested his elbows on the edge of the table.

Doug clenched his jaw. "It's not a story. It's the truth. We *are* broke. We've gone through our savings and our investments. The money my dad left me is long gone. I used all of it to try to make Viv happy, but..." he shook his head. "And as bad as it sounds, Viv saw Jane as an easy way out of our financial troubles."

Jeff leaned forward also. "What about your other daughters, Lily and Laurel?"

"Huh," Doug scoffed. "They live like the rich and the famous, but they're worse off than we are."

"The apple doesn't fall far from the tree," Brian whispered under his breath.

"I'm sorry. What?" Doug asked, adjusting his hearing aids.

"Nothing." Brian looked at Jeff. "So, for the sake of conversation, let's just say that, ah, someone took an insurance policy out on Jane when she turned 18. Do you have any speculation on why that might have happened?"

The veins in Doug's neck bulged. "I'm not speculating on anything," he nearly shouted. "You wanted facts. I came here to give them to you. You've got them. Can I go now?"

Brian raised the palm of one hand toward Doug. "One more question. Who's in charge of your finances, you or Viv?"

"I don't see what that has to do with anything," Doug

barked. "But if you must know, it's Viv. Other than the money my dad left me, she controlled our money from the day we got married."

Brian cast a sideways glance toward Jeff before he stood up and reached across the table to shake the older man's hand. "I appreciate your time, Doug." Then he walked him to the station door and gently clapped him on the back. "If you think of anything else, will you please call me?" Doug nodded as he slipped out the door into the warm September afternoon.

When he returned, Jeff stared at him with eyes wide. "It's Viv," they said at the exact same moment.

CHAPTER 21

Jane Hart

The last week of each month, Sean was in Duluth on business. According to him, the firm had several clients at the Superior Correctional Institution there; Sean and his team worked from a conference room at the prison. They had at least two cases coming up on appeal. But where he went didn't matter to me. What did matter was that the house would be empty and the alarm would be off. Sean never set the alarm—day or night. He couldn't be bothered. I knew I could count on that.

After the close call at Mack Enderly's shack, I returned to the Haydens' cabin. It was impossible to know where to hide, but their lake home was the safest place once the helicopters stopped circling. I settled back in and lay low for over a week. I watched the local news reports during the day when the flashing lights of the television screen wouldn't draw attention like they would in the dark of night.

Sheila's iPad, the one she housed recipes on, lay on the kitchen desk. When I couldn't stand not knowing, I used it to search for information regarding my story. Fortunately for me, according to the media, the police believed I was no longer in Cedar Point. For the first time since my narrow miss with Brian and John, I had something to be grateful about.

In Bill and Sheila's Prius, under the cover of darkness, I had driven by my house several times. No cars were ever parked outside. Neither the police nor the FBI appeared to be keeping vigil over the house any longer. I wasn't sure if someone was stationed on the trail, but even if they were watching from there, I knew it was safe to enter through the service door into the garage.

With the summer neighbors gone for the season, and the local families back into the swing of school, the lake was empty. Because of the shallow waters, this end of the lake was used mainly for swimming. Fishermen preferred the deep bay on the other end. I hadn't seen a boat on the water in nearly a week.

Bill had left an oversized black hooded sweatshirt hanging on a hook in the mudroom; I grabbed it and threw it near the boathouse door. It would blend into the night. Although dotted with millions of stars, the sky had been relatively dark. Night after night, the moon slowly grew smaller until it was just a tiny sliver. I waited until just after dusk to make the mile trek back toward the place I had called home for twenty-six years. The narrow crescent of the moon provided almost no light as a guide, but it allowed me to hide in the shadows of the trees. I was familiar enough with the shore to find my way in the dark.

When I reached the house, I silently made my way up the wooden stairs, gauging the placement of my feet, missing the one creaky board I had repeatedly asked Sean to replace. As I had expected, the house was completely dark. I knew Sean would stick to his usual schedule. Even with me missing, he wouldn't miss an appointment or drinking himself stupid at the bar. For him, family rarely came first—or rather, *I* rarely came first. It was never about what I needed or wanted. It never had been.

I took a slight turn to the left, off the stone path, and made my way to the service door of the garage. I stepped onto the cement pad, kneeled, and moved my hand along the ground until I found the large rock that covered the extra key. It took me several moments to find it. For a split second, I wondered if Sean had moved it, but that was giving him too much credit.

Quietly, I unlocked the door, tucked the key into my pocket, and slowly pushed it open. Except for the shadow of my car, I could see nothing else. The windowless garage created a blackness that swallowed up nearly everything inside. I silently pressed the door shut and ran my hand along the wall until I felt the switch. The bright light made me jump when it flashed on.

Sean's BMW wasn't in the garage; I knew it wasn't parked in the driveway either. You couldn't pay him to leave his car outside. He was sure someone he had put in prison planned to seek revenge on *his car*—not Cole and Luke or the house or me. It was his car he was worried about.

With the toes of one foot, I unlocked the wheels of the large metal tool chest before pressing both hands against it and rolling it several feet to the right. Inside the top drawer, I found a long-handled Phillips screwdriver and inserted the cross tip into one of the four black screws that held a sixteen-inch square of sheetrock in place. Sean had purposely hidden the opening behind the oversized tool chest, knowing no one would roll the massive chest out of the way. After removing the last screw, I stuck a putty knife into the crack along one side of the sheetrock and pried it out. Hidden behind the false wall was Sean's safe. I hadn't known about it until three years ago. I had come home sick, surprising Sean. Between the moment I hit the opener and the time I crawled out of the car, Sean tried to cover the opening, but he had failed. I pretended not to notice as I rushed into the house. He never questioned me, and I never brought it up. But the next day, I checked it out just to make sure I hadn't been mistaken.

The combination to the safe was elusive as I tried to open it, hoping to find something that would tell me if Sean was the person who wanted me dead. I tried every possible series of numbers I could think of. Birthdays, our anniversary, holidays, but nothing worked. Then a number popped into my mind; it was a number Sean had used on his bike lock over the years, a number that meant something only to him. I entered 398 and the door of the safe popped open. Of course, Sean's college GPA. From the day he graduated, he had been incredibly proud of that number; arrogant, boorish even. He threw the 3.98 in my face often; compared to my GPA of 3.6, he claimed himself to be a freaking genius.

A half-foot stack of neatly arranged nine-by-twelve-inch envelopes and manilla folders tightly filled the small safe. I wiggled my hand up one side and pulled the thick pile toward me. A few loose items floated to the garage floor. As I picked them up, I wondered why they weren't in a folder. Sean was the most organized person I knew; he bordered on OCD. He was obsessive about everything. Even his boxers were arranged in his dresser drawer by color. His ties and shirts were arranged in a rainbow pattern, and his nearly three dozen pairs of shoes were placed on the shelf by style and color. The toe of each pair was exactly one inch from the front of the slanted shelf. At first, I thought it was cute, but soon it became just another of his annoying habits.

For a split second, I considered weeding through the folders right there in the garage, but an uneasy feeling washed over me as I set them on the floor, righting them when they started to tip. I pulled a plastic shopping bag from the recycling bin and tucked everything inside, taking care to keep them in order.

By the time the section of sheetrock and the heavy tool chest were back in place, my pulse had begun to slow. I took a deep breath; my shoulders fell, and I knew I was safe—until I heard a car barreling down the gravel road. This was the time of year when we were virtually isolated from traffic. It was rare to see even one car a day. Everything in me screamed to hide.

I flipped the ceiling light off and planted myself in front of my Armada as the garage door opened, gears groaning. I tucked the plastic bag inside Bill's enormous sweatshirt and pushed the hem into the waistband of my jeans. As Sean eased his car into the garage, I moved to the far side of my SUV, crouched behind the tire, low to the ground. I didn't dare move for fear the bag would give me away.

"Sonofabitch," Sean said as he opened his car door. "Who the hell do you think you are?"

My heart thudded inside my chest. I was sure he had seen me. But instead, he slammed his car door, pressed the button to close the garage door, and stormed into the house. Sean had been talking to himself, something that commonly occurred when he was angry. Luck had been on my side. Still, I remained frozen. Sean couldn't be trusted; he loved to play games. He could be lying in wait on the other side of the door. I held my breath and listened.

After hearing only silence, in the weak light of the opener, I snuck out the back door, twisting the lock on the handle before pulling it shut. I didn't bother to return the key; I couldn't take the chance. The lights were on in the house, sending ribbons of yellow onto the yard. Lights continued to snap on upstairs and down. Sean hated the dark. He hated having the curtains drawn or the lights dimmed; he always had.

Instead of racing down our stairs, I ran through the trees toward the cabin next door. Their stairs were concealed by a clump of newly planted pine trees. I returned to the Haydens' at a much faster pace. Sprinting along the shore, I tightly wrapped my arms around my stomach to hold the plastic bag in place. Twice I stumbled in a pocket of soft sand. The edge of the waves reflected the sliver of moonlight and kept me on the path. My imagination exploded; I was positive Sean was on my heels.

I raced into the unlocked boathouse, twisted the deadbolt, ran through the tunnel and up the stairs to the central part of the house. It was dark, but my eyes had grown accustomed to the murkiness on my return. My heart felt like it was going to jump out of my chest. It didn't slow until I was hidden behind the closed door of a windowless walk-in closet on the main level of the house. I tore off the black hoodie. The plastic bag plunged to the floor; its contents tipped out but remained in order.

The small room spun as I clung to a low clothes rod. I dropped to my knees before falling face-first onto the plush carpet. By the time the adrenaline had stopped surging, I was too exhausted to move. I fell asleep with my arm over the bag. At some point during the night, I covered myself with the sweatshirt and slept to nearly dawn.

CHAPTER 22

Sean poured himself a stiff drink and stood at the sliding glass door staring toward the lake. The glare of the living room lights allowed him to see nothing but his reflection. Even with all the lights blazing and the curtains thrown open, Sean was still panicked by the darkness inside.

His plans were falling apart thanks to Jane. Where in the hell was she anyway? He had to find her. He threw back the rest of his drink and wandered to the kitchen for another.

Returning today hadn't been his plan, but with his father gone, there was no need to stay in Duluth any longer. His team had spent the morning meeting with clients, going over an upcoming trial and looking into the potential of a second. Afterward, they bid Sean goodbye, climbed into one car, and headed back to Cedar Point. Sean had always driven separately; they were used to it. They often ribbed him about having an aversion to riding with others, but he defended his choice, claiming to listen to law podcasts and reviewing work in his head. Truthfully, even if it wasn't for his father, he would have driven alone. Small talk grated on his nerves. He didn't give a rat's ass who was dating whom.

When his team would head south, he would head up the shore to the small apartment he had moved his father into or to the assisted living facility where his dad had lived near the end. On Saturdays, from his father's apartment, he would work from a room indicated as a den on the plans, but one that more closely resembled a closet. At night, the two visited the diners of their past or drove up the shore, reminiscing about the good years—from the time Sean turned five until he turned twelve. But since his father's death, only the negative memories flooded through him.

That morning, after Sean watched his team drive away, he crawled into his car and laid his head against the steering wheel. For the first time since becoming an adult, he was lost.

Unsure of his next move, he released a deep breath, started his sporty black BMW, and raced toward the gate of the prison parking lot. "Mr. Hart," the security guard greeted him as he handed him a clipboard with documentation to sign. Sean pulled a pen from his front suit pocket, spun it in his fingers, and handed the paperwork back to the guard unsigned.

"Dammit!" he said. "I think I forgot something inside. I need to run back in."

"No problem, but can I ask you to back up rather than pass through the gate and turn around?" He pointed to an open space just behind them. "If you leave, we'll have to go through the sign-in process all over again," he explained. "Policy," he shrugged. "You know how it is." He glanced at the paper and leaned close to Sean's window. "Spot 15," he reminded him.

"Got it," Sean acknowledged. He backed into the spot and

headed back toward the prison.

He rolled down his window and sat in the car for the better part of thirty minutes, scribbling notes on a legal pad in his mostly illegible handwriting. When he finished, he dragged his finger down the page, reviewing what amounted to a confession in the wrong hands. A smile spread across his face as he tucked the pad into his satchel, threw the strap over his shoulder, and walked back to the building.

"Hello, Mr. Hart." The woman at the front counter seemed confused. "I thought you had left."

"I did, but I forgot something. I need to speak with someone, and since I'm his counsel, I'll need a private room. Can you make that happen?" Sean wore his game face. His voice exuded confidence.

"Who is it you want to talk to?"

Suddenly, a snowfall of doubt swirled inside of him. The glibness he felt seconds earlier collapsed. He glanced down at the floor before his eyes returned to the woman. "It's, ah, Mack Enderly," he said.

"I'm sorry. Who did you say?"

"Mack Enderly," he said slightly louder.

The keys on the woman's keyboard took a beating as she typed the information. Her fingers moved at the speed of light, yet it was still too slow for Sean; all he wanted was to get out of this room.

A look of confusion crossed the receptionist's face. "It says

Corey VanDressen is Mr. Enderly's legal counsel." Her eyes held Sean's. "Has there been a change? Do you have paperwork that shows you are now representing Mr. Enderly?"

Sweat beaded on Sean's forehead. He rested his elbow on the counter and leaned into his hand to hide his uneasiness. The placard told him her name. "Well, Joyce, let me think," he said, covering for his lie. The woman knew he was lying, and he knew she knew. "It's all been signed, but I, ah, don't have it with me. One of my junior assistants must have picked it up by mistake. My team has already left for home." He flashed her his brilliant smile. "Is there, um, any way you could get me a private room to speak with Mr. Enderly—just this once?"

The woman sighed. "I'll tell you what. I can call Mr. VanDressen's office and…"

"No, it's fine," Sean held his hand up. "I can meet with him wherever."

"Well, you aren't on Mr. Enderly's visitation list, but then again, other than Mr. VanDressen, there is no list." She glanced at the clock across the room. "Since it is visiting hours, and you're already cleared for visits, I can see if he'd be willing to meet with you." She banged out a message on the keyboard. "Just so you know, it won't be a private room," she reminded him again.

"I'm aware," Sean grumbled.

She nodded toward the small waiting room. "Have a seat, Mr. Hart."

Sean sat, but he didn't want to. Everything inside of him wanted to run, to escape before he did something he couldn't take back. Even the receptionist had his number. He crossed his legs, uncrossed them, and recrossed them. He picked up a magazine and paged through the entire thing in less than a minute. Finally, he got up and wandered to the water cooler; he downed one cup and had just started a second when Joyce called his name. Water ran down the front of his suit coat.

He pitched the half-full cone-shaped cup into the trash and swiped at his jacket, sending the droplets flying.

Joyce pointed to the door adjacent to her and buzzed him in. He handed his driver's license to the guard and emptied his pockets before pulling off his belt and his watch and dumping them all into a plastic bin. He walked through the metal detector and was subjected to frisking on the other side. "Can you hand me my briefcase?" Sean asked.

"Sorry, Mr. Hart." The guard lifted the basket and Sean's briefcase and put them into a cubbyhole behind him. "Since you're not representing Mr. Enderly, you aren't allowed to take any of these items in with you. They'll be here when you leave."

It burned Sean beyond belief to be treated like an ordinary visitor. He was an attorney, not some putz visiting a family member who had been stupid enough to get caught.

He clenched his jaw and, after being buzzed in, walked through a second door where he was met by another guard. The man steered him to a round table in a large room where several other inmates hosted visitors. He pointed to the exact chair Sean was to sit in.

"You may not touch the prisoner. If you do, you will immediately be asked to leave. Do you understand?" The guard must have made this statement at least a hundred times a week. It sounded robotic, like a digital recording.

"Yes," Sean snarled. "I've got it." He rolled his eyes at the guard and sat down and waited for Mack.

The guard crossed his arms and glared at Sean. "Do you? Do you understand that I can end this visit right here, right now?"

Sean grimaced. "Yes."

"Yes, what?" the guard asked. Sean knew he wasn't kidding.

"Yes, I understand I may not touch the prisoner."

"Okay, then. I'll let Mr. Enderly in."

A second guard escorted Mack to the table and sat him on the opposite side, facing Sean. "Well, well. If it isn't Sean Hart—the man who got me tossed into this hell hole," Mack said, unimpressed by his unexpected visitor. He adjusted his chair, pulling it closer to the table. "So, what do you want, Sean?" His glare was intimidating, and Sean hoped he never had to meet him outside of the prison walls.

"I'm pretty sure it was *you* who got yourself tossed in prison, Mack." Sean pretended to be braver than he felt. He held up his fist and, with his fingers, counted off each of Mack's crimes. "Stealing a car; no, make that two cars, multiple DUIs, and oh yeah, taking a life—not just once, but twice, as I recall."

"Screw you, Hart!" Enderly hissed. "I'm still waiting for you to tell me why you're here."

Sean grew nervous again. The words he had written earlier had faded into a jumbled mess and he struggled to recall them. "I, ah, guess I just want to know."

"Know what?" Mack growled, losing his patience.

Sean looked up at Mack; he leaned his head closer to the prisoner. "What's it like to kill someone? How does it feel?"

Mack's face burned red. Because of this hellhole, he had been sober for years; he'd forgiven himself. "F-you, Sean. You think you're such a big man because you have a wife and kids and a highfalutin job. You think you can look down your nose at the rest of us and judge us just because you've been handed everything on a silver platter. Money does that to a person. It makes you think you're superior to everyone else," Mack's voice grew louder. "Well, I got news for you. You still shit the same way as everybody in here. You're not so different."

Rage engulfed Sean. "Listen, asshole!" he said through clenched teeth. "You know nothing about me and my life."

The guard suddenly appeared next to the table. "Is there a problem?"

"No, just catching up," Sean was quick to answer.

The corrections officer turned to Mack. "It's all good. This guy's an asshole from my past. He's just tryin' to bust my balls." Mack nodded at the guard. "It's fine." The sentinel studied both men for a few moments before leaving.

"Why are you really here?" Mack asked as he folded his arms across his chest.

Sean looked around the room, searching for the guard and gauging the closeness of the other tables. Finally, he leaned forward and whispered, "I, ah, figured that someone like you, someone in here might, ah, have connections."

Mack seemed confused. "For what?"

Again, Sean looked around. "You must, well, know...guys."

"I know a lot of guys. What the hell are you asking?" Mack's booming voice caused the people at the table closest to them to look their way.

Sean put his palms out and lowered them. "Calm down." The guard was looking directly at him. Sean turned toward Mack and changed his approach. "I, ah, think you misunderstood. I'm doing research. I'm wondering if there are guys who get out of here who are still... well, you know... lifelong criminals. Guys who don't hang their name on the outside of a legitimate business."

Mack nodded. "Hmm, so, you're looking for a hitman."

Sean shook his head violently. "No." For the second time in the past hour, he was sweating profusely. "It's for, ah, research. I'm looking to talk to some guys who haven't, say, shut down business."

Mack winked at Sean. "Sure. I get it. *Research*." He emphasized the last word. He bit his lip, bobbed his head, and shrugged. "Yeah, I know some guys like that. I s'pose you're looking for names."

Sean nodded. "For research," he said again.

Mack looked toward the guard, but he was focused on another table. He turned back toward Sean. "There's a guy who's getting out of here in a week or so. His name's, ah, Wren Brigham. Hasn't changed a lot since he got here. He'll do what you want. I'll give him the message to contact you when he gets out." Mack glanced toward the guard before he leaned farther across the table, careful not to touch Sean." I need to know what you're offering, though. If it's not enough, he ain't gonna do it." Mack looked hard at Sean. "And then somebody out there knows more than they should. Understand?"

Sean jerked away from Enderly. "It's research. I told you. I just want to talk." He was sweating profusely; the fabric under his armpits was damp and he was certain it would only be a matter of time before it soaked through his jacket.

Mack's head bounced up and down in the tiniest movements. "Whatever you say, Sean. Whatever you say. But you gotta be paying enough or he ain't calling. So how much? Otherwise, it ain't worth me even talking to him."

Sean repeated the name *Wren Brigham* several times to himself. He needed to remember it so he could write it down when he got back to his car. "Ah, ten thousand?" Mack shook his head and pointed to the ceiling with his thumb. "Twenty?" Sean asked.

Mack shrugged. "Yeah, I'm pretty sure he'll do it for that." He looked toward the guard again. "I'll get him the message before he's out. I'd expect a call toward the end of next week."

Sean could barely breathe. Even though he'd told Mack Enderly otherwise, he'd just asked a criminal for the name of someone who could get rid of his wife. His hands shook and he tucked them between his knees. "This is private, right? Between you and me?" he said, waving his index finger back and forth. Sean knew Mack hadn't talked to Brian since he had been incarcerated. Their relationship had been severed the day he killed his mother. Even if Mack ever walked free, he was sure Brian would have nothing to do with him. "Remember," he told Mack, "It's for research."

Mack grinned. "Yep, research." Then he winked at Sean a third time.

Sean stood up and pushed his chair into the table. "I'll put some money in your account before I leave."

"It's the least you can do." Mack nodded at him. "Hey, how's that wife of yours?"

"Missing," Sean said over his shoulder as he walked toward the guarded exit.

***

Sean waited to be buzzed out. He collected his belongings and, true to his word, deposited $100 into Mack's commissary account. He whispered the name *Wren Brigham* as he walked to his car. Once inside, he wrote it on the yellow pad with the rest of his notes. Then he drove toward the exit.

"Mr. Hart." the gate guard greeted him again. "Must not have been able to find what you forgot, huh? Took you a while."

"I needed to speak with one of my clients again."

"Well, have a good day," the guard said as he pressed the button that opened the iron gate.

Sean drove through the opening, but rather than turning toward home, he turned right and headed up the shore toward Doug and Viv's house, the place he'd lived with his dad before he left for college. He drove back and forth in front of the house several times, pacing himself with the steady stream of cars that passed along the scenic route.

The Sterlings owed him. He just had to figure out all the details.

Sean turned back onto London Road. He headed south, back to Cedar Point, talking to himself the entire way, reliving every negative thing that had ever happened to him. As he drove into his garage, he was still talking to himself.

CHAPTER 23

Jane Hart

It was dawn when I woke. Every inch of my body ached from falling asleep on the closet floor. I slowly pushed the door open, not turning on any lights. After showering, I pulled on a clean pair of Sheila's jeans and a white t-shirt. I slid everything back into the plastic bag and carried it with me into the kitchen.

Yesterday's coffee was still in the coffee maker. I dumped it out and made a fresh pot, then dug around in the pantry for something to eat. I settled on peanut butter and crackers. Still hungry, I opened a small can of cling peaches and ate them directly from the metal container. When the fruit was gone, I tilted my head back and poured the syrupy juice into my mouth. I missed real food.

As the morning light began filtering in through the curtains, I settled on the couch. I pulled the stack of envelopes and folders from the bag and set them on the low table in the same order Sean had placed them in the safe. I drew a deep breath before I removed the first item from the stack. Clearly, there were secrets hidden inside this mass of files or Sean wouldn't have locked them away.

The first envelope I grabbed was filled with old tax records for someone with a name remarkably similar to Sean's—*Sean*

Vernon Hartung. It couldn't be. Was it possible my husband had hidden his true identity from me our entire married life? Was Sean actually *Sean Hartung*? I paged through the documents. The W-2's were from Sean's law firm. What was the likelihood two people were working for the same small company with nearly identical names? Interestingly, the forms displayed an Alexandria P.O. box, not our Cedar Point address. I shook my head and let out a small sigh. While it should have surprised me, this didn't. I had always suspected he'd been hiding something. His insistence we keep our finances private and file our tax returns separately always made me wonder. But a different name? Had Sean been living a double life? Did he have another family tucked neatly away somewhere close by?

I slid the pages back into the envelope and flipped it upside down on the floor. Sean was meticulous about everything, anal even. He would know I had been snooping if things weren't placed in the same order. The following two items were manilla folders—one for each of our sons. They contained photos, fingerprint cards from when they were young, their social security numbers, and their current passports. Why would Sean have their passports? Why would he have any of this information? Cole and Luke were adults; this was their business now, not his.

The folders went into the stack, flipped upside down. The next envelope contained only a couple of items. I dumped the contents onto the coffee table. As I slid a photo from beneath a sheet of paper, my stomach lurched. Staring back at me was an old picture of my parents. Drawn across their faces was a dark black X with the word *destroy* written along one line. The writing was Sean's; there was no doubt about that. But Sean didn't even know my parents; he hadn't had anything to do with them the entire time we lived in Cedar Point. He never asked about my family. I had always assumed he just didn't care. Maybe he cared too much. Why did he want to ruin Doug and Viv? Had they done something to him? Or did he see destroying them as a way to get back at me?

I picked up a copy of an article about my parents buying their house in Duluth, on Lake Superior. It was from the *Duluth Tribune.* The write-up was benign except for one passage: "The mansion was purchased from Vernon Hartung for a song and a dance." First, why was this news? Also, who was Vernon Hartung? Was he related to Sean, or at least to the Sean Hartung I had just learned about? And why would anyone sell a house for so little? Did the four of them have some illegal business deal going on? Well, that was obvious. But what? I carefully replaced the photo and the paper and tucked them back into the envelope before adding them to the stack.

I grabbed the next envelope. It was torn; old and new photos fluttered to the floor. *Dammit!* I thought. There was no way of knowing what order they had been in. I picked them up and started flipping through them. Most were black and white. They appeared to have been developed in a makeshift darkroom. The backs were rougher, and the pictures were grainier and more faded than those processed professionally.

For the first time ever, I saw pictures of Sean as a child, or who I assumed was Sean. I was still wrestling with the name discrepancy. He was the spitting image of our son, Cole: the same dark hair and crooked smile. The same four people and names appeared repeatedly: Vernon, Sarah, Sean, and Emily. Because the man and woman were often referred to as *Mom and Dad*, I assumed the photos were all of Sean's family.

The woman and the girl disappeared around the time Sean would have been about five or so. At that time, the backdrops also changed. The early photos had been taken only indoors, in what appeared to be a house. Later, there were a variety of differing locales. The pictures of Sean and his dad seemed to end around the time Sean would have entered Junior High but began again shortly after we were married. There were some as recent as July. I knew because, in one photo, Sean was wearing a shirt I had given him for his birthday at the end of June.

In those photos, Vernon, obviously the name of Sean's dad, looked fragile. His coloring had taken on a sickly gray shade. As I picked up a newspaper clipping, I realized just how sick he had been. Vernon Samuel Hartung had died on the 18th of August. Sean had spent a couple weeks in Duluth around that time. Had he been planning his father's funeral? But when he returned, he had acted no differently than usual: silent and uncaring. That was the Sean I'd grown to know over the past twenty-four years. I would have never guessed someone close to him had just died. I didn't even know his father had still been alive. The story he told me was that his parents had passed before he started college. Sean was full of secrets. I was beginning to realize I didn't even know the man.

I placed the photos back in an order that made sense to me before tucking them into the torn sleeve and carefully setting it on top of the others.

The paper of the next envelope was softer and appeared worn as if it had seen its share of traffic. I turned it upside down and let the pages slide out. On top was a stapled packet of crinkled pages, dotted with what appeared to be coffee stains. When I saw the title of the article, my jaw dropped open and my stomach churned. The pages slipped through my fingers. Shockwaves rippled through me as I grabbed the papers and blinked several times, trying to bring the headline into focus: *Where was Jane Sterling?* The article, obviously old, was about me—or at least someone who shared my name. Had I been missing before? I dropped the packet on the table and began pacing across the living room, not thinking and not taking my eyes off it for fear it would disappear. Falling forward, I sucked in a jagged breath.

I grabbed a second cup of coffee and returned to the living room before picking up the packet again. As I paged through it, I realized several articles had been photocopied and stapled together. Yellow highlighter along with Sean's scribbles marked nearly every page. There was no date anywhere on the paper. I pushed the contents of the folder around on the coffee table. After finding this, keeping things in the correct order no longer concerned me.

A goldenrod-colored syllabus was in the mix. It seemed to be from one of Sean's law classes. There I found a date—*Junior year of his undergrad program.* That meant Sean had known about this, about me, since long before we met. But what exactly did he know? And why didn't he ever tell me?

Three times, I read the five stapled pages, as well as Sean's handwritten notes, before any of it began to sink in. I had no idea I had been kidnapped as an infant or that I had been found wandering the streets of Alexandria in the middle of the night when I was two. I was 47 years old, and this was the first I had heard of it. My sisters hadn't spoken about it, my parents hadn't mentioned it—even Grandma Betty had kept it a secret. Were they worried it would make my life worse? That it would somehow ruin me? I don't think my parents could have hurt me more than they already had.

I grabbed Sheila's iPad and typed in *Jane Sterling, missing child, Minnesota.* A slew of links popped up. Many old newspaper articles about the abduction appeared; there was nearly an equal number about my return. According to multiple sources, an arrest had never been made. Nothing made sense. I had a million questions but no one to ask. I dug through the remainder of the smaller envelopes on the table. Each was labeled with a yellowed sticker and contained more information about me, but there was nothing I hadn't already seen online.

My coffee was cold, so I got up and dumped it out. I didn't need or want more; I was jittery enough already. What I needed was time to process what I had just read. How could this even have happened? And how could I not have known? Was it possible my kidnapping was the reason my parents treated me so poorly? Had they missed out on the chance to bond with me when I was an infant? Did they see me as someone else's child when I returned home? That would all make sense. It would explain why they treated me like I wasn't part of the family. Maybe in their eyes, I wasn't.

Was there more information about me in Sean's mystery pile? I pulled a large, yellowed envelope from the stack and opened it slowly. It contained three photocopied pictures, stacked one on top of the other. My name was written across the bottom of the first photo. I honestly had never seen a picture of myself as an infant; I didn't even know one existed. In my mind, I always believed Doug and Viv hadn't cared enough to take pictures. Not living with them for those first two years would explain why there were no photos. It finally made sense to me. The second picture was one I had seen in my Google search just minutes before. It was me at two years old. Something about the photo looked familiar, but I shrugged it off. Of course, it looked familiar. It was me. But still... The last image was of me in high school, my junior year.

If I thought Sean's lie about his name was big, or learning his father hadn't died until recently, or even that Sean had known about me since I was in high school, they were nothing compared to the bombshell of finding out I had been kidnapped as an infant.

Except for a thick tan envelope on the bottom of the pile, the rest of the items were loose, devoid of envelopes or folders. There was undoubtedly a reason they were in the order they were. But only Sean would know why.

The first few were newspaper articles about awards Sean had won. The next few were pictures of my parents' house in Duluth—the one that had once belonged to Sean and his father. The fact he was connected to my parents drove me crazy. Why? How? But more importantly, how had I not known? Did the boys know any of this?

At the bottom of that pile was a second obituary for Sean's father from a second newspaper. Someone had chosen to use an older photo of him. The resemblance between Cole and his father and grandfather was uncanny. The longer I stared at the picture, the more I had this overwhelming feeling something was wrong. Suddenly, a wave of familiarity washed over me; I was positive I had met Vernon before. But when? Sean would never have introduced him to me. From the day we met, Sean told me he had no family. And I'd never even been to Duluth.

The clock on the wall ticked loudly. I'd already spent over three hours entranced in information that frightened me. Time to think was what I needed; there was so much to take in, so much to figure out, so many questions that needed answering. But it was like trying to assemble a thousand-piece puzzle without looking at the cover. I had no idea what it would even look like when I was done. The pieces were all there, but some were broken or lying on the floor or still in the box.

Again, I started to pace. I walked through the house, from one end to the other. I made that trek at least a dozen times or more. Each trip, as I neared the coffee table, I slowed to a crawl, hoping for the missing piece to jump into my hand, but I was always disappointed.

My brain hummed with emotion, frustration, and anger. It felt like a freeway with cars moving too fast, getting on and off, changing lanes, and slamming on their brakes without warning. Then, suddenly, on one of my many treks, as I neared the boathouse door, everything in my head went silent. I stood perfectly still while the thought slowly became clearer, like a photo from an old Polaroid camera. I raced through the tunnel, up the stairs, and into the living room. Learning the truth scared me, but not knowing was even more frightening.

I flipped over the pile I had looked at, fanning out the envelopes and folders until I found the one I was searching for. I shoved everything to the side and dumped out the photos of Sean's family, the ones I had taken such great care to sequence. Caring had long since disappeared. Frantically, I shuffled them around until I came to the photo I was searching for. It was the picture of Vernon, Sarah, Sean, and Emily. I laid it on the coffee table and grabbed the three others of me from the envelope that had been upended in my desperate quest.

My stomach dropped. Sean's sister, Emily, and the photo of me at two years old were identical: the hair, the face shape, everything, right down to the doll we were each holding. My eyes darted around the room yet focused on nothing but my heart thudding in my ears. It was me. Sean never had a real sister; Emily didn't exist. I was his sister. It was Sean's family who had kidnapped me when I was an infant. They had destroyed my family.

I flopped over on the couch, curled into a fetal position, and sobbed. Sean's family had taken away my parents' ability to bond with me. Doug and Viv didn't hate me; they just hadn't had the chance to grow close to me. The Harts, or the Hartungs, or whoever the hell they were, had taken everything from me. I sat up and slammed my fists on top of the low table. "You bastards!" I screamed. "How dare you ruin my life?"

My blood boiled. I was no longer hurt; I was furious. In a fit of rage, I swiped my arm across the table, sending everything flying, including a glass bowl that housed the remote controls for the television, the DVR, and the gaming systems. It shattered into a million pieces. The table runner flew into the air and fell to the floor.

Amidst the mess, I noticed the one envelope I hadn't looked at. It had been sealed with box tape. I grabbed it and ripped it open from the side. I didn't care what Sean might think or do. Honestly, I wished he was dead like the rest of his family. My life had been one big lie for forty-seven years. Everyone had lied to me. "You can all rot in hell, every last one of you," I seethed as tears continued to run down my face and neck.

The contents of the final envelope splayed out across the low table as I angrily dumped them. I shoved things around, not looking for anything in particular, not even sure what I would even find. There were more photos of Sean and me as kids. We were always smiling and laughing. But these pictures didn't make me feel warm and fuzzy the way pictures of kids often do. Instead, they made me angry; I wanted to shred them into tiny pieces.

An old immunization record from a clinic in Des Moines, Iowa, drifted to the floor. Of course, a closer clinic might have been aware of my kidnapping. A small pink envelope held a lock of my hair, or rather, it held a lock from *Emily's* first haircut. A tiny pink newborn hat was among the mix, as well as a flat white and yellow rattle.

I shoved more photos to the side. Nausea swam through my stomach to even think about being part of Sean's family as a child. Near the bottom of the pile, the corner of a heathered blue and white sheet of paper protruded. I pulled it out and almost choked. It was my birth certificate—or again, *Emily's* birth certificate. Iowa Methodist Medical Center was embossed across the top. Vernon and Sarah Hartung were listed as the father and mother of Emily Jane Hartung. The date of birth was four days after mine. The birth certificate looked authentic. Undoubtedly, Sean's parents had connections and money.

I continued to push items around, unsure of what I was even looking for. A passport surfaced. When I opened it, my picture stared back at me. I was sure I had lost it, but that hadn't been the case. For some reason, Sean had hidden it from me.

Something stiff jabbed my hand as I slid things around on the table. I pulled it from the pile. The pink envelope housed a congratulations card. There was no return address, but Vernon Hartung's address had been typed on a typewriter with an old ribbon. I lifted the flap and removed the card. Inside was a yellowed letter written on sheets of rice paper like my mother used to practice calligraphy. The card was signed *Doug and Viv*. It was had been postmarked six weeks after I was born. Based on the articles, I calculated that to be about two to three weeks after I was taken. The Hartungs had evidently been friends of my parents. Doug and Viv must have believed the two families were giving birth around the same time. But Sarah must have faked her pregnancy.

I pushed the card back into the envelope and picked up the letter. It was multiple pages, written in my mother's neat handwriting. The farther I read, the more I realized the error in my thinking. My heart raced and I began sweating profusely. I believed the Hartungs had kidnapped me from my parents. The truth was, my parents had been part of the plan; they had initiated the entire thing. They had purposely given me away. The story of my kidnapping was no different than the ones in the books my mother buried herself in. No one had cut my mother off and grabbed me from the backseat. No one had thrown my mother's keys into a field so she couldn't follow; *she* had done that. There had been no blue truck. It had all been part of some fabricated story.

Tears streamed down my cheeks as I sobbed harder than I had in my entire life, and I let them fall. I was in shock. Nothing made any sense to me. It was as if I was watching a movie, and all I could hope for was a happy ending—but I already knew the outcome, and it was far from happy.

After several minutes, I read the next part of the letter. It explained that the new birth certificate for Emily had been obtained through a "friend." It also requested the monthly payments be sent in cash, in various types of envelopes, and with no return address. My mother stated it would be less obvious that way.

Sobs racked my entire body as I cursed and screamed. I had been wrong again. My parents hadn't just given me away; they'd *sold* me—to the Hartung's. For my entire life, I had believed they didn't want me, didn't love me. But five minutes earlier, when I thought Sean's family had kidnapped me, I forgave them. I believed they were the way they were because of our inability to bond when I was an infant, but that wasn't it. My parents had *never* wanted me. After the rollercoaster of the last few minutes, I realized I had been right all along. So why did it hurt so much to know the truth now?

I wiped my face on the bottom of Sheila's t-shirt. My hands were shaking, and I could feel the same vibration ripple through my entire body. Not wanting to do so but, unable to stop, I finished the letter. Several lines threatened what would happen if the Hartungs didn't keep quiet or if anyone found out about their fraudulent arrangement. There was no signature at the end, just one simple sentence. "So glad you've taken over our misery."

Emotionally, I was drained. I didn't have the energy to learn one more thing, but I had to know everything, so I continued to dig, sifting through stacks of photos and information. How had I ended up wandering the streets of Alexandria in the middle of the night?

I pulled a second card from the heap of junk. The postmark was just over two years after I was born, just days after I had been found. The same typewriter had been used. I threw the unsigned card to the side and unfolded the single sheet of paper I had pulled from within. Again, it was in my mother's handwriting. The message was short, but the words that had been chosen were direct and pointed.

We had a deal. You screwed it up. Until the day she turns 18, I will expect payments to continue. You know if this comes out, it will destroy your family. If the police get involved, we're all going down. You are as complicit in this as I am. But no one will ever believe a drunk like you. So, make sure it doesn't come out or there will be hell to pay.

A torn clipping from an old newspaper was also tucked inside the envelope. It was an obituary for Sarah Hartung. According to the article, her date of death was August 5th, just three days after the letter was postmarked. Was it suicide? Or had someone killed her to keep their dirty secret quiet? Had Sean's dad sent her to her grave?

I pushed the photos in one direction and the things I had already looked at in the other. Two small envelopes remained. One was gray; the other was white; Sean's law firm's address was on the outside of the latter. The gray envelope was worn and torn in multiple locations. It housed two sheets of graph paper with writing on both sides. It listed monthly dates and the amounts of each payment made to my parents right up until my eighteenth birthday. The total was staggering. I couldn't believe anyone could have paid that much money, especially back then. It explained how my father had been able to buy the pharmacy and the house we lived in on the double lot. I also clarified the trips my parents took my sisters on.

I set the pages aside and opened the second envelope. Inside were pictures of checks written to Sean Hart from my mother. The checks were significantly bigger than the ones Vernon had been sending to my parents. The dates were sporadic, not monthly like the ones they had received. The first check had been written shortly after my parents moved away from Cedar

Point.

If my parents had blackmailed Vernon all those years, who was to say that Sean wasn't blackmailing Doug and Viv? I didn't know what to believe anymore, but it was clear I couldn't believe any of them.

I stumbled into the kitchen and opened the refrigerator. It wasn't food I wanted; it was a distraction. Other than a few condiments, there was nothing in the fridge anyway. I had been eating food from the pantry and the freezer for nearly three weeks.

I shoved the refrigerator door shut and pulled the pantry door open. As I examined the shelves, the doorbell rang. "Police!" was all I heard before I dove inside and quietly closed the door.

CHAPTER 24

Deputies Carlos Serrano and Lance Finley entered the station. They walked by Mauri's empty desk and knocked on the doorframe of Brian's office.

"Hey, Chief," Lance called.

Without a word, Brian waved them in and pointed to the chairs opposite his desk. A thought-provoking email had popped in not long before his men arrived. Once he finished, he closed his laptop and turned his attention to his officers.

"Anything?" he asked.

Carlos shook his head. "We checked every cabin, garage, boathouse, and building along that entire five-mile stretch. There was no sign of anyone. It looks no different than it did a few weeks back. Nothing was unlocked and it didn't appear that any of the buildings had been broken into."

Brian nodded. "Have you talked to Diane or Jim to see what they found?"

"Same. There's nothing out of the ordinary."

Lance tipped his head and shrugged. "Well…." He dragged the word out as he looked at Brian. "We did find one thing that seemed kind of odd." He looked at his partner. "Sean Hart was home, sitting on his front porch in the middle of the day."

"Really? That's odd. The man's a workaholic and typically

not home until late. Did you stop and talk to him?"

"We did," Carlos nodded. "We told him we were checking out the cabins, making sure everything was on the up and up." Carlos grinned. "But, um, not sure he even cared. He was feeling no pain."

"Ah, day drinking, huh? Wonder what that was about."

The deputies looked at each other and laughed. "He claimed he'd just won some big case and was tying one on to celebrate, but I'm not sure I believe him."

"Oh, really?" Brian's eyebrows raised. "His wife's been gone for less than a month and he told you he was *celebrating*. Interesting." He lifted the lid of his laptop as he spoke. "Well, it was good you checked it out. I need you two to run down that road every couple of days or so when you have a chance. Switch up the times you drive by. Maybe send Fryer and Johnson down there a couple of times a week too." Brian was back to staring at his computer screen, his actions dismissing the men. "Hey," he called as they reached the door. "I want you to keep an eye on Sean. If he so much as farts sideways, I want to know about it."

"Got it." Carlos nodded. "Do you..." Brian's office phone rang; he waved them out the door.

"Chief Enderly here," he answered as he leaned back in his chair.

"Chief, Bob Harmon, warden up at Superior Correctional Institution."

"Yeah, Bob. How can I help you?" Brian asked as he tucked one hand behind his head and leaned back in his chair.

"I've got some information on a case you've been working on. Thought I'd give you a call."

Brian leaned toward his desk and grabbed a pencil from the cup. "What case is that?"

"I'd prefer we talk in person, Chief. I know it's a long drive up here but is there any chance we could meet tomorrow?" the warden asked.

"Is it really necessary to do it in person?" It was closing in on the end of the month and he had reports due. But more importantly, he was committed to finding Jane.

"It is," the warden told him.

Brian glanced at the calendar on his computer screen. "Ah, geez," he said, more to himself than to Bob. "I'd have to switch some things around, but I suppose I could be there by four. Otherwise, it'll be Monday if I come. I could send my lead deputy up tomorrow morning if that would work better for you."

The warden wasted no time responding, "No. I think it's best if I talk this over with you. This isn't something I want to drop into the hands of your deputy—no matter how good he is."

"Can you at least give me a hint?" Brian's curiosity stirred.

Bob ignored the question. "Sounds like we'll see you tomorrow at 4:00. Looking forward to talking then." The line went quiet, and Brian dropped his phone into the cradle.

Immediately, he lifted the receiver back to his ear and dialed Porter.

"Hey, Chief," Jeff answered. "Baxter, stop barking!" he yelled before he turned back to the phone. "What's up?"

"Damnedest thing. I just got a call from the Superior Correctional Institution up in Duluth. Their warden claims he's got info on a case we're working on. I'm wondering if it has anything to do with your conversation with that dimwit Alder the other day."

"Maybe?" Jeff questioned. "But it seems kind of far away to have information about a case here, doesn't it?"

"Yeah, but the Sterlings live up there, so maybe it's something to do with them," he speculated. "God, I hope so. Anyway, I'm headed up there tomorrow. Need to be there by 4:00."

"Want company?"

"I do, but I'd rather have you here. Mauri's out tomorrow too." Brian told him.

"Got it. Guessing you'll want to be on the road by what? Eleven thirty or so?"

"That's what I figured. Gives me time to grab lunch. Thanks for covering the station."

"No problem. Hey, before you go, I heard about the Coke incident with Mauri." Jeff snorted.

Brian laughed too. "Yeah. I'm sure you did. It's probably the talk of Cedar Point by now."

"Oh, it's gone *way* beyond Cedar Point." Jeff laughed harder.

Brian grinned. "Alright, smartass, just be here tomorrow by 11:30."

"Will do, Chief."

***

With his seat pushed back as far as it would go, Brian pulled out of the station and onto the main drag at exactly 11:30 a.m. He was grateful to have the Explorer; upgrading the squads had been the best thing they had done. Enderly had made the trip to Duluth numerous times in the old Crown Victoria he used to drive, but it wasn't comfortable for anyone, let alone someone his size.

Around 12:30, Brian pulled off the freeway and into a McDonald's. It had only been an hour, but he needed to stretch his legs.

Technology was not his thing. Enderly knew he would screw up his order if he tried the touchscreen menu near the door. So, after a quick trip to the bathroom, Brian ordered at the counter. He carried his tray to a booth and squeezed between the bench and the table. Once settled, he downed his Big Mac and fries while some toddler screeched at him from the next booth.

"Badge!" the kid screamed. "Gimme!" he said with both of his hands turned up and his chubby fingers wiggling in and out. "Gimme! Gimme! Gimme!"

Brian continued to eat, ignoring the kid the same way his parents did. He fished his cell phone from his front shirt pocket and scrolled through his messages as he shoved the last of his fries into his mouth. Nothing urgent.

Still chewing the last of his burger, he squeezed out of the booth and headed toward the trash. With a quick in and out of the tray, the remnants of his lunch dropped into the can. When he set the tray on top of the bin, he noticed the missing persons flyer of Jane hanging in the entry. His heart dropped into his stomach, and he grabbed the frame of the windowed wall to keep from collapsing.

Where are you? It was as if she had fallen off the face of the earth. It had been almost a month since she disappeared, and yet there were virtually no leads. He reached up and touched her face with his hand as he walked out the second door. It was a silent promise.

Finally on Highway 23, just past St. Cloud, Brian settled in. He called the station just to kill time. He and Jeff had barely begun their conversation when all hell broke loose on Jeff's end.

"Gotta call you back, Chief. Chet and his wife just walked in for their...ah, *counseling session.*"

"Of course, they did. It's almost the end of the month! Better you than me, buddy. Better you than me," he said again. But before Brian even finished, he knew Jeff had hung up, desperate to get them settled and out the door as quickly as possible.

He laughed out loud. The Murphys were frequent visitors at the station. Chet loudly complained about Suzette and her mafia thug brothers, but Suzette stood her ground, informing him in no uncertain terms that if he paid the damn money he borrowed from them, they wouldn't threaten to tan his hide once a month. Honestly, if this were a sporting event, Brian would root for the Pennucci brothers; Suzette's family didn't take crap from anyone. If just once, they would follow through on their threats, Chet would see the error of his ways and the revolving door of the station could finally be retired.

The Murphys needed a referee, not a counselor; they needed a divorce lawyer, not a cop. There was no question, for a couple of sixty-somethings, they were about as feisty and nasty as they came. They could spar like a couple of wild roosters and then leave the station with locked arms. Brian was thrilled Jeff was the counselor of the month.

The gas gauge indicated a need for fuel, and Brian needed his afternoon Coke. In the next small town, he pulled into a Holiday Station and took care of both; a full tank of gas and a thirty-two-ounce drink: more soda than ice. After another twenty miles of narrow two-lane highway, he settled back on the freeway for the last ninety minutes or so.

Once through the prison gates, Brian pulled into the Law Enforcement Parking area. Visiting hours were over, but the security guard at the gate had called in his arrival. The warden met him at the door.

"Warden Harmon?" Brian nodded as he walked up the sidewalk. The man was smaller than he had imagined. His balding head and his small stature didn't seem fitting for someone running a prison. *Walk softly and carry a big stick,* Brian thought. *This guy must carry a massive stick.*

"Call me Bob," Harmon said as he stuck out his hand.

"Brian," he told the warden as he reciprocated.

"You're early," the warden told him.

"Traffic was lighter than usual for a Friday afternoon." He followed Bob into the prison, waiting for him to unlock the double set of doors. "You must be fairly new here?" Brian questioned.

"Took over about a year ago," he said as they walked down the echoey hallway. "Love Duluth, but coming from the south, last winter was so cold, I thought I was going to freeze my ass off every morning just getting to work." Brian laughed. "Hell, I think my seat heaters even went on strike. If we would have had one more day below zero, my wife said she'd leave me, hightail it back to Atlanta. Truthfully, I'm pretty sure I would have been right behind her. Lord, it has to be a better winter this year or I'm going to be one lonely man."

"I hear you." Brian laughed. "Last winter was exceptionally cold all over the state. I grew up here, but that was a tough one, even for me." He laughed again. "Just be glad you're in Duluth and not over in Embarrass. They set weather records there every year."

The warden stopped walking. "I heard that name on the news all winter long last year. I thought it was a joke, like the news reporters making fun of the weather. Why in hell would anyone name a town Embarrass?"

"Well, you can blame the French trappers for that one." Brian grinned as they continued walking.

At the end of the hallway, they came to a door with a wooden placard: *Warden*. Bob slipped a key into the lock and opened the door. "Need anything? Water? Coffee? Soda?" he asked as he walked around his desk.

"Nah, I'm good," Brian told him. "Curious about your call, though."

The men took seats on opposite sides of Warden Harmon's desk. "I figured you would be." He pulled out a notepad similar to the one Brian used. *Kindred spirits. Screw technology,* Brian thought.

"So, listen, this is kind of—unusual, but we, um, well, had a guy in here the other day asking around for someone who wasn't really, let's just say—*reformed.* Someone who might be looking to make some money on the outside." He watched Brian's face. "Are you following me?"

Enderly nodded. "Loud and clear. Who was this guy? Someone I should know?"

Bob's elbows were pressed into the padded arms of his chair and his hands were locked together in front of his chest. He watched Brian over the top of his frameless glasses. "Name's Sean Hart."

Brian looked up at the ceiling and balled his hands into tight fists. "Dammit! I knew that no good sonofabitch was up to something."

"He's an attorney, huh?" the warden asked. Brian nodded. "Anyway, he was here with a team from his firm meeting with some prisoners who are clients of theirs. They all left, but when he got to the gate, he informed the guard he forgot something. At the front desk, he claimed he was someone else's counsel and needed to speak with him...in a private room." Bob guffawed. "We only hire the best, and Joyce was on her toes. Because he was a lawyer and had previously been cleared, she let him in, but she made him follow the same rules as any other visitor. And, on top of that, she made sure the guards knew she didn't trust the guy."

"Impressive," Brian said. Joyce was the warden's Mauri.

Bob leaned back in his chair, crossed his legs, and planted his arms in his lap. "What's even more impressive? As soon as Mr. Hart left, the prisoner went to one of the guards and filled him in on their conversation. I've spoken to him also. He said Sean told him he was looking for someone just to talk to. *Research,* he said, but the inmate didn't believe him."

"Why's that? Did Sean do or say something to make this guy question his story?"

"Well, the prisoner he was talking to knew Mr. Hart. Brian,

the prisoner was—your dad."

Brian felt the blood rush up his neck and into his cheeks. He touched a cool hand to his face. "Wow!" Brian's eyes flitted back and forth. "I, ah, haven't talked to my, um, dad in years." His throat was dry; he pressed the side of his fist to his lips and cleared his throat.

Bob pulled a bottle of water from the fridge under his desk and handed it to Brian.

"Thanks," he said between gulps.

Enderly stared at the carpet as he tried to get his emotions in check. Pain, anger, frustration, and sadness rumbled inside of him, each vying for his attention. "I don't know what you know about my dad, but he, well, he wasn't the father any kid wanted or deserved." He took a deep breath. "Let's just say he didn't live up to my expectations."

Bob grabbed another small bottle of water from the mini-fridge and handed it to Brian. "I sort of figured. Having a parent in prison is often one of the driving forces to becoming a cop." He watched Brian for a few seconds as he upended the second bottle, emptying it and setting it next to the first. "Based on what you said, I would assume that's why you chose to wear the uniform." Brian slowly nodded. "I read through his file after I met with him. It's a tough read. I'm sure it was even harder living it."

"This, ah, wasn't at all what I expected when I got your call yesterday. Somehow I've made myself forget my dad is even here." Brian's throat was dry again. "Can I get another water?"

"Of course. Would you rather have a soda or something else?"

"No, water's good." Harmon handed him a third bottle and waited for Enderly to settle down.

Brian shook his head. "I honestly thought I'd never have to see that bastard again. I figured if he got out, we'd go our separate ways and that would be it." He looked out the window. "Shit. I can't even tell you what I'm feeling right now. I don't even think I know."

"I understand. That's why I didn't want to tell you over the phone." He gave Brian a few moments to process.

"Okay, so did my dad hook Sean up with somebody? Did he give him a name? Because that would be something he would do, especially if there was something in it for him."

Bob pressed his lips tightly together and tilted his hands outward. "That's the thing. He gave him a name and told him this guy was getting out next week."

Brian's eyes blazed with anger. "Surprise! Surprise! He'll never change."

"No, Brian, listen. Your dad pulled a name out of thin air. It wasn't a real person. Then when Sean left, Mack came straight to us to tell us what happened."

"Seriously? You're telling me he lied to Sean? He set him up?"

"Yeah, that's exactly what I'm telling you." The warden

nodded.

Brian stared out the window, watching the trees dance in the cool north breeze. "My dad's never been a quick thinker. I'm curious; what name did he use?"

Bob opened a folder and scanned his notes. "Wren Brigham."

Brian grabbed the top of his legs and squeezed as hard as he could. His eyes stung and he bit his lip.

Harmon quickly stood up and moved behind Brian. He rested a hand on his back and looked him in the eyes. "Are you okay? The name Wren Brigham must mean something to you."

Brian drew in a deep breath and slowly blew it out. "It was…it's the, ah, the name my mom had, ah, picked for the baby she was carrying when she was killed. Wren Brigham Enderly would have been my brother or sister." He stood up and walked to the far side of the room, his hands locked behind his head as he relived that day. "She'd just found out that morning that she was expecting. She wrote the name on a piece of paper and asked me what I thought of it. My mom grew up in Wrentham, Massachusetts. Brigham was her maiden name."

"Can I get you something?" Bob asked. "A soda? Tylenol? A paper bag to breathe into?" He smiled gently.

Brian dropped his hands to his sides. "No. I'm okay. I just can't believe my dad even knew about that name. My mom hadn't even told him she was pregnant. I was the only one who knew." He turned to Bob. "I think I need to talk to…the, um,

Mack. Yeah, I need to talk to him."

"I agree, but can you? Right now, you need to be a police officer and not a son."

"Wow!" Brian locked his fingers across the top of his head. "I have to. I need to hear it from him." He looked at the warden. "I just need a few minutes to pull myself together."

"Brian, you have some pretty big unresolved issues with your dad. If the first part of this meeting goes well, maybe you could spend some time just talking," Bob suggested.

"It'll be a cold day in hell before that happens."

CHAPTER 25

Brian followed the warden down the hall through several sets of locked doors. The familiar hum of the fluorescent lights fought with everything he was thinking. When Bob stopped, Brian sucked in a deep breath.

"You doin' okay?" Bob asked.

Brian set his briefcase on the terrazzo floor and shook his hands at his sides. "I never thought I'd be standing here."

Bob pushed the heavy steel door open and held it for Brian to walk through. Hesitantly, he stepped into the room in front of the warden. In the last half-hour, he had mentally prepared himself to see his father, but when their eyes met, he froze. This wasn't the man of his past. Even though his dad was older, he looked healthy, younger than he had when he was first incarcerated. Regular meals and years of being sober had changed him. His cheeks weren't hollow, and his eyes no longer sunk into their sockets. They had life. Had Brian not known he was meeting his father, he wasn't even sure he would have recognized the man who sat before him.

"Son," Mack said as he checked him out, "it's good to see you."

Brian said nothing. He was here to get the story and get out. He had to think of his father as he would any other witness. To

Brian, that's all he was. "Heard you had a visitor," he said as he dropped into a chair opposite his dad.

Mack leaned back. "This is how it's going to be? This is just business to you?"

The two men stared at each other for the better part of a minute. "That's why I'm here," Brian finally told him. "Right now, I need to know what you know."

"Mack," the warden pointed toward Brian, "tell Brian exactly what happened during your visit with Sean. Tell him what you told us."

Mack's shoulders sagged. "Sure."

For the next half hour, Mack relayed the story of Sean's visit, answering questions asked of him by the two men.

Brian jotted notes on a yellow pad he had pulled from his briefcase when he first sat down. "Did Sean threaten you or offer to pay you for a name?" he asked.

"No. But it was Sean. Money's money. I'd like to say he hasn't changed at all, but he seemed...well, almost scared. I didn't see that arrogance he used to have when he first moved to Cedar Point."

"Of course not." Brian flipped the page of the notepad before he looked at his father. "He was looking for a hitman. That should scare the crap out of anybody."

"Mack, did Sean use the word *hitman*?" the warden asked.

"Not exactly. He said he was doing *research*. But Sean was clearly lying."

"I've watched the video multiple times. I can't make out any of the conversation. It's just the security video of the room. Brian'll get a chance to look at it when we finish here. But was there anything Sean did that made you think he was looking for someone for more than just research?" Harmon asked.

Mack bit his lip and tilted his head backward. He concentrated on the ceiling as if the answer was written there. Brian could tell he was fast-forwarding his memory of his time with Sean. Finally, he nodded. "Yeah. He was very concerned about where the guards were when he was talking. He didn't speak unless he knew they were on the other side of the room."

"I did see that on the video." Bob looked toward Brian. "He looked around a lot and leaned in when he talked. You'll have to see if you agree when you watch it later."

Brian entered the information onto his notepad. "Anything else?"

"Yes. Every time he said the word *research*, he emphasized it. I'm guessing he wanted anyone listening to know he was doing *research*." Mack closed his eyes. "Oh, one more thing. He was sweating like a pig the entire time."

Brian made the last couple of notes and flipped the pad of paper closed. "Okay, I got everything I need," he said as he glanced at Bob.

The warden looked at his phone. "I've got something important I need to deal with." His eyes met Brian's. "I'll be back in a few minutes."

"I'll go..." Brian tried to tell him, but Bob was already outside, locking the door from the hallway.

Brian was furious. He didn't want to spend one more second with his father, but Bob hadn't given him a choice. He tucked his notepad back into his briefcase and snapped the locks shut. Then he leaned back in his chair and folded his arms across his chest.

The father and son never broke eye contact until Mack finally spoke; when he did, he looked down toward the floor. "Brian, I want you to know how sorry I am about...well, everything." His voice quivered and his eyes grew glassy. "I'm the reason you grew up without a mom." He waited for a response but was met with only a harsh glare. "I, ah, well, I ruined my life and everyone's around me—especially yours. You know better than anyone that I deserve to be locked in here. I deserve to die in here for what I did to you and your mom...and to that other poor woman."

Brian uncrossed his arms and leaned forward. "Well, that's an easy thing to say now, isn't it? Too bad you didn't figure that out before two people died. Not to mention all the crap you did to me." He stood up and walked to the opposite corner. "Hindsight's twenty-twenty, Pops. Here you don't have a chance to be anything but sober." He turned and pointed out the window. "But what about out there? If they let you out, would you choose booze over everyone else? Because that's what you did, Dad. You chose alcohol over your only son. I needed you,

Dad, but you didn't give a rat's ass. You locked me in that cellar and beat me every chance you got."

Mack folded his hands and rested his elbows on the table. He leaned his chin against them. "I know, son. And Lord knows I've made enough mistakes to last a million lifetimes. I just hope that, at some point, you'll be able to forgive me for all the bad decisions I made."

"Huh!" Brian snorted. "Forgiveness is a really tough thing to give, especially because you've had multiple chances to redeem yourself before you ever got locked away for good." He turned toward his dad. "Do you understand that after Mom was killed..." he pointed angrily at his father, "a crime you only got away with due to a technicality of a faulty tire, you had the chance to turn your life around." Brian held three fingers into the air. "For three weeks—three, Dad, you were sober. But on the day I came home from the hospital, you drank every drop of booze you could find." Brian placed both of his hands on the table and leaned toward his father. "I needed you. I needed you to be there for me." He stabbed one finger into his chest and watched his father's face. When he saw nothing, he swiped his hand across the table, sending his briefcase flying off the far end. "But you couldn't do it, *Dad*." The last word he hissed through gritted teeth. He stood next to the two-way mirror and wondered if Bob was out there watching. He knew he was. This was a setup. "Do you know that every night after I came home from the hospital, I cried myself to sleep? Do you have any idea how hard I prayed you would come into my room and wrap your arms around me and tell me everything was going to be okay? I needed to hear that." Brian hoped his words wounded his father as much as they did him. "But you never did. Because of you, I spent my entire childhood wishing I had died in that accident along with Mom." He turned toward his dad again. "Because if I had, I wouldn't have had to grow up without a mother *and* a father."

Mack sucked in an audible breath. "Wow," he whispered. "I guess I deserve that."

"Damn right you do. You were a poor excuse for a father even before Mom died." Brian stepped toward the table. "Do you have any idea how much Mom loved you? I begged her to leave you, but she never would. By the time I was five years old, I wanted to be as far away from you as I could get." Brian stepped backward, fearing if he got too close to his father, he would sucker-punch him. "But for some damn reason, she believed you were salvageable. She used to tell me stories about when you first met, how kind you were, and how much you loved her." He balled his hands into fists. "Do you know I used to dream about *that* man? That was the family I prayed for every night before Mom died."

"I loved you and your mother so much, Brian." Mack's chin dropped toward the floor.

Brian held up one hand. "Don't! Don't even tell me that crap. You loved your booze way more than you loved either one of us. We were just collateral damage."

"I was sick, boy. I didn't know how to stop." He shook his head. "It was a small town. I didn't know how or where to get help."

Brian's face burned. "Screw you, old man. If you wanted help, you would have found a way." He walked around the table and faced the barred window. The tall prairie grass leaned toward the south in the strong autumn winds. "Did you know Mom was pregnant when she died? Did you know she was carrying my brother or sister?" He spun around to face his dad. "Did you?"

Mack grimaced as he nodded. "I did. She told me just before we walked into the party. She thought it might make me drink less knowing I had another child on the way. But that was why I was drinking." His voice grew shaky. "Brian, I couldn't be a father to you. How was I supposed to take care of another child? I was scared. I sucked at being a dad."

"Well, that's the one thing we can agree on. You know, people are afraid of a lot of things, Dad, but they figure it out. You just weren't willing to figure out anything other than where to get your next drink." Brian turned back toward the window. He took several deep breaths. "Where'd you come up with the name Wren Brigham?" His back was toward his father. He couldn't even look at him. "That was the name you gave Sean, right? The name of the supposed hitman?"

His father clicked his tongue. "When your mother told me

she was expecting, she told me the name she'd picked out. That name has stayed with me all these years," he said, folding his hands in his lap. "Every night before I go to sleep, I pray for you *and* Wren."

Tears escaped, rolling down Brian's cheeks and spilling onto his shirt. "So, you finally found God, huh, Dad?"

Mack's words were barely audible. "Brian, I've always known God—but somewhere back then, I lost Him."

Brian silently stood at the window for several minutes before finally sitting in the chair opposite his father. "I'm having a hard time finding God myself right now," he admitted.

"I heard about Jane." Mack reached across the table and placed his hand on his son's. Brian moved his hand slightly but didn't pull away. "I know you've always loved her, Brian. I could see that from the time you were just kids." A sad smile drifted across his face, then disappeared almost as suddenly as it appeared. "I've been praying for you to find her every night since I found out she was missing."

Brian looked up at his dad. "Thanks," he muttered. He was drained, physically and emotionally exhausted.

He heard the key in the door. Bob walked in and stood at the end of the table. "I trust you two had a good talk," he said.

Brian exhaled a laugh. "You should know. I'm sure you saw the whole thing."

Harmon looked from Brian to Mack. "Sometimes, we just need a little push in the right direction," he said as he sat down and crossed his legs. "Sometimes," he said again.

CHAPTER 26

During the four-hour drive back to Cedar Point, Brian relived the time with his dad, not the time discussing Sean, but the fifteen minutes afterward, when Bob took it upon himself to change the direction he and his dad had headed. It wasn't what he had expected or wanted, but it was what he had needed. He had no idea how much until it was over.

When a guard came to pick up his father, Brian stood up and walked to the door. He couldn't hug him; he wasn't even sure he wanted to touch him. But just before his father left the room, Brian held out his hand. It wasn't a peace offering; it was just something he felt compelled to do. He wasn't sure he would ever see his dad again. No, that wasn't true. He knew he wouldn't, but their unexpected time together had brought closure to his anger and pain. Letting go was as exhausting as holding it all inside; it just didn't last as long.

With Mack's hands cuffed behind his back and the guard's hand hooked through one of his father's arms, the two men walked down the hall. Brian watched him walk away. His dad turned once to look at him. Brian was confident it would be the last time their eyes would ever meet. He could forgive him, but he couldn't forget.

When Bob closed the door again, Brian felt something he

hadn't felt in years—lonely. He wasn't sure why; he wasn't even sure that was what he truly felt. He just knew it was different than the way he expected to feel.

Before heading home, he and the warden watched and re-watched the video of Sean's visit with Brian's dad; they worked out the details of the call that would be made to Sean from the fictitious Wren Brigham. For that, Brian didn't need Bob's help, but he wasn't ready to leave the last place he had spent time with his dad.

For nearly two hours, the men strung together the trap that would take Sean down, working out every detail.

Around 7:00 p.m., Bob's wife showed up with a takeout order from Little Angie's Cantina down on Canal Park. The three of them chatted for almost an hour and a half. The warden's wife had a wicked sense of humor. With one weight lifted, Brian laughed more than he had in the past month. Bob hadn't been kidding when he said his wife would leave him if they had another frigid winter like the last. She was very clear about what she would do to her husband before she moved back to Atlanta, and it sounded painful—painfully funny.

Their close relationship made Brian miss Jane even more—if that was possible.

When Shannon Harmon left, the men spent another hour finalizing the call to Sean. Finally, when they were satisfied with the plan, the two men walked out of the prison together.

It was nearly 2:00 a.m. when Brian turned the key in his

lock at home. Twenty minutes later, he had showered and was in bed. As exhausted as he was, sleep eluded him. His brain hummed, not with memories of the day but with thoughts of Jane. He rolled over, threw off the covers, pulled them back up, and finally gave in to the idea that sleep wasn't going to happen.

With only the rangehood light turned on, he made a pot of coffee. Brian stood in front of the counter in just his boxers and an old t-shirt as the machine sputtered. It slowly brewed as the rich aroma filled the air. Brian knew he needed a new coffee maker, but like everything else in his life, it had taken a backseat to finding Jane. Finally, he lifted the glass decanter in one hand and threw a mug under the trickle of coffee. He held it there while he added more hot liquid from the pot.

In the dim light of the kitchen, he sat on a leather stool, drinking the caffeine he knew he'd need later. He pushed a stack of random junk aside. He'd never let his place get this messy, but cleaning was the last thing he could focus on. Leaning an elbow on the granite countertop, he rested his head in his hand. Getting up hadn't stopped the spinning in his brain. If anything, it had intensified.

Finally, Brian pulled a notebook from the stack and stretched his arm to the far end of the island to retrieve a wayward pen that had rolled away when he shoved the pile. He opened the notebook to a random page and began making notes. One thought led to the next, and before long, the page was filled with ideas and questions. Circles with connecting lines ran across the paper in every direction.

When he finished, Brian ran his finger over the page, tracing the lines, occasionally stopping as a new thought took shape. Once done, he picked up his pen and drew dark, repeated lines under three names: Sean Hart, Viv Sterling, and Drew Carter.

Finally, Brian stood up and stretched, yawning as he emptied the last of the coffee into his mug. The new ideas that had popped up during his brainstorming session, things he hadn't considered before, excited him. His eyes never left the page between sips of coffee. All three had motive and means. They all had something to gain by getting rid of Jane. For the first time in four hours, Enderly shivered, unsure if it was from the cold or fear for the woman he had always loved. As he headed to his bedroom to get dressed, he was positive it was the latter.

Daylight slipped in when Brian opened the bathroom blinds. Brushing his teeth, he saw his father staring back at him in his reflection. After talking with him yesterday, he realized how much they looked alike. His entire life, he had believed he looked like his mother, but now he wasn't so sure. He and his father definitely shared the same sad eyes.

Brian snapped off the light and wandered through the living room. He touched the photo of Jane that sat next to his recliner, letting his fingers linger on her lips. In the kitchen, he tore the sheet of paper from the notebook, folded it, and tucked it into the front pocket of his jeans. Then he headed down to Fat Pat's for breakfast.

Before settling into a booth, he waved to the waitress and stopped to speak with a few of the locals. By the time he made it to his table, a pot of coffee had appeared.

"The usual?" the waitress asked.

"Sure. Why not?" Brian smiled at her.

Once she walked away, he pulled the paper from his pocket and smoothed out the creases.

"Interesting reading," Sean whispered in Brian's ear.

Enderly jumped. He flipped the paper over, folding it along the same creases, and tucked it back into his pocket. "Dammit, Sean!" he said a bit louder than he meant to. "Don't be such as an asshole."

Sean looked like Brian felt. The bags under his eyes and the dark circles told him that Sean had either not slept in days or had extended his little celebration a few days too many. Sean slid onto the bench across from Brian.

"Any news on my wife?" Sean asked.

Brian wondered what his real intent was. Was he genuinely concerned about Jane, or did he want Brian's information so he could find her and kill her himself? Either way, he decided it was best to keep Sean in the dark. "Nothing new." Brian watched Sean's face cloud. "Still following some leads."

Sean didn't bat an eye. "Leads? What kind of leads?"

As a cop, he had been trained to use his senses to follow clues. He could hear the strain in Sean's voice; his pitch increased when he talked. Brian knew what the man was digging for. Sean wanted to know if Mack had squealed on him. He shook his head. "Nothing you need to be concerned about."

Sean nearly foamed at the mouth. "She's my wife, you bastard. Of course, I'm going to be concerned." He noticed people staring at him when he looked up. He leaned closer to Enderly and pointed toward the window. "And by the way, why in the hell are you sitting here all nice and cozy when you should be out looking for her?"

The waitress set a tray of food on the table next to the booth. "A man's gotta eat," he told him. "Care to join me?" Brian pointed to the food in front of him.

Sean waited for the waitress to leave. He held his hand out, palm up, in front of Brian. "Let me see that paper you were looking at."

"Seriously? You think I'd give it to you? This is police business, not amateur hour." Brian rolled his eyes as he broke an egg yolk, cut a chunk of pancake, and swabbed up the thick yellow liquid.

"Screw you, Enderly!" Sean sputtered.

He set his fork down. "I can assure you of one thing, Sean."

"Yeah, what's that?"

Brian leaned toward Sean and, in a theater whisper, promised, "Whoever's responsible for Jane's disappearance, when we find her, alive or..." he swallowed hard, "well, that person's going to pay the price. So you just better hope to God it's not you, *Hartung*."

Sean sat upright. It was evident he was shocked to hear Brian use his real last name. Enderly could see the hamster wheels spinning inside Sean's head, but he said nothing. Brian continued to eat, watching Sean between bites. Finally, without a word, Sean slid from the booth and headed out the door.

Enderly grinned as he chewed. He'd given Sean just enough to worry about. He'd have to wait to see how this played out.

Brian noticed John Henry shuffling down the sidewalk on the other side of the street, still in his FBI disguise. He signaled for the waitress. When she arrived, he ordered a second breakfast and asked for a favor. Then he went out to retrieve the old drifter off the street.

When he returned, his food had been moved to a corner booth, as far from the front door as possible. Brian finished his breakfast while John waited for his meal.

The two men whispered as they spoke about the case. Enderly unfolded the sheet of paper and pushed it toward the drifter. Their conversation lasted until John had finished eating. Then Brian slid out of the booth and, for show, handed the old man a twenty-dollar bill. "Use this for food," he said. "Take care of yourself." He turned and walked toward the cash register to pay the bill while John pocketed the cash.

An elderly woman stopped him. "Chief Enderly. I saw what you did for that poor wayfarer." She reached out and touched his arm. "You're such a good person. I bet your mama would be so proud of you."

Brian shyly grinned. "Thank you, ma'am," he said. "I'd sure like to think so."

CHAPTER 27

Sean wandered through the house. He'd hired a cleaning service a week before but canceled them the following day. He'd tried to go back to work immediately after Jane disappeared, but by the middle of the third week, they forced him to take a leave. *Lacked focus, overly sensitive, jumpy,* they told him; time away was *expected, necessary for him to regain control of his emotions, to deal with his grief.* They told him to return when he was ready. When would that be? How long would it take to get over losing your sister a second time—or your wife?

He plopped down onto the couch. Who did he miss more? Jane or Emily? His wife or his sister? Which one had hurt him more? Emily had left him, had caused his mother's suicide, and had ruined his father, but she was young and didn't know what she was doing. But when Jane left him, she abandoned their marriage, took away his sense of family. And worst of all, his control of everything he'd worked so hard to hold on to.

Music streamed in the background. It was almost always on now—day and night. It was comforting, safe. It felt like someone else was in the house. Sean hated being alone; he had hated it since the day Emily disappeared.

The house was too quiet, stiflingly so. He weighed going

back to work, but it wouldn't be any better than when they had insisted he leave. Jane or Emily or whoever the hell she was had ruined everything for him. He saw them as two different people and yet, from time to time, they overlapped, and he couldn't separate them. Lately, he found himself saying Emily more often than Jane. Sean worried he was losing his grip on reality.

And, to make matters worse, Brian had called him by his given name—the one he had tried to hide for the past twenty-some years. How did he know? What else did he know? It frightened Sean, but what did it matter? He had changed his name to hide from no one except the Sterlings and Harrison Carter. They would have recognized the name *Hartung*.

The TV turned on and off and then on again as Sean fiddled with the remote control. The music continued to play the entire time. He watched a show he had never seen before, without the sound, without closed captioning, without actually *seeing* it. Before it was over, he clicked it off and threw the remote across the room. It bounced off a wall and broke apart, launching the batteries and cover in different directions.

Sean tipped his head back onto the couch cushion and stared at the rough ceiling. A sound that didn't sound human pierced the room. Over and over, he struck the sofa as he continued to wail. His legs had lost their ability to support him, and Sean crashed to the floor when he tried to stand. Within minutes, his yelling was replaced with torrential sobbing. His chest heaved and his body shook. An hour passed, and then another, and Sean was still on the floor. His crying had stopped because he had lost the ability to emotionally feel anything.

He wiped his face on the sleeve of his cashmere sweater. Snot streaks marred the fine woven burgundy threads. A month before, he would have cared, but no longer. He leaned against the couch and wondered what his life had become. With Jane gone, his boys no longer called or came to see him. It was rare they even responded to a text. His colleagues had grown silent; they didn't know what to say to him anymore, how to comfort him. Even his father had left him, not because he wanted to but because it was his time. He had no one. For the first time in his life, he understood what his mother must have felt when she hung herself after Emily disappeared. The one person his mother had wanted more than anyone else, including him, was gone. "You should have wanted me, Mom," he whispered from his place on the floor. "I should have been enough."

But like he lost his mother, Sean had lost Emily. The difference was *he* had survived. Now that he'd lost her again, he wasn't sure he would.

Finally upright, Sean felt weak; his legs shook. Real food hadn't passed through his lips in days. He'd been buried in a bottle, just as his father had done. That morning, he had tried to eat; he'd gone to Fat Pat's, but Chief Enderly had been at the restaurant, and he couldn't stay. After Brian called him *Hartung*, he was sure the cop could read his mind—knew exactly what he had done.

Slowly, he wandered into the bathroom and turned the shower on as hot as he could stand. He never touched the bar of soap or the bottle of shampoo. The punishment of the steamy water beat against his skin, turning it bright red. When the hot water ran out, he stood in the cold stream for a good five minutes before turning it off. He barely touched himself with a towel before he tugged on a pair of jeans and a t-shirt.

He had to get out of this house. One more minute and he was sure he would burst. The Steak and Ale had the two things he needed: food and beer. He pushed his belt through the loops of his jeans and angrily shoved his arms into the sleeves of his North Face jacket. Finding his cellphone between the couch cushions, he tucked it into his front pocket.

The door between the garage and the house hadn't been closed all the way. Sean wondered how it had gotten open in the first place. He pressed the garage door opener, climbed into his car, and started it just as his phone rang. It wasn't a number in his contacts, but he felt the need to answer.

"Sean Hart," he said in his attorney voice, a bit raspier than usual.

The caller's deep voice boomed through his car speaker. "Wren Brigham. Heard you might have some, um…work you want done."

Sean poked at the button on the garage door opener; he heard it groan as it started to close. He killed the car and pushed the button on his phone, transferring the call from the car speaker to his cell. The last thing he needed was for someone to overhear this conversation. His heart jumped in his chest. "I think you have the wrong number," he said.

"Don't screw with me, Hart. I don't like people who yank my chain." Sean squirmed. "So, let's talk about that hit you want."

Sean's hands were shaking as he pressed the red button on his phone and blocked the number. He sat in his car, frozen with fear. Scared didn't even begin to describe how he felt. As a lawyer, he'd been threatened before, but this went far beyond anything from his past. It was clear this Brigham guy didn't like to be toyed with.

His cell rang again, displaying a different number, but Sean refused to answer. He waited to see if the caller left a message. A couple of minutes passed before the voicemail indicator lit up.

I'm going to call you back in two minutes. If you know what's good for you, you'd better damn well answer. Sean could barely breathe.

The phone rang a third time. Again, the same angry voice burned across the line. "Hart, that wasn't a smart move. I don't take kindly to sissy-asses." The caller was silent for a few seconds before he continued. "Now, let's talk about that deed you want done."

Sean climbed out of his car. He grabbed a fistful of his hair as he paced the cement floor next to his BMW. This guy wasn't going away even if he blocked calls all night long. His voice cracked when he spoke. "I, ah, changed my mind."

"Really?" Sean cringed at the booming voice. "That's too bad. I was looking forward to making some money. Sort of need it after... Well, you know."

"I, I can still send you money," Sean offered, willing to do anything to get rid of him.

"How much?" Wren asked.

Sean's brain spun through numbers.

"How much?" he asked again, much louder.

"Ah, say five thousand?"

"Well, well, well. Five thousand big ones for doing nothing. Can hardly beat that deal. I'll get back to you, Sean ol' boy. Keep your checkbook open. I might need a little more convincing." Sean heard him laugh. "Don't forget, Hart, I know exactly where you sleep at night."

Sean's heart thudded; he could both feel it and hear it. Too afraid to hang up, he waited for Brigham to exit the call first. When the phone went dead, he pressed a few buttons and blocked that number too, but within seconds, unblocked it. This Brigham guy said he would call back. He didn't want to piss him off any more than he already had.

As he walked back into the house, his phone rang a fourth time. The number didn't show. He was afraid to answer, but he was more afraid not to. Finally, after the third ring, he picked up. "Hello," he choked out.

"Sean." The voice was larger than life, but it was one he recognized. "Just wanted to check in and see if you're okay after this morning's little—I suppose you could call it *a run-in* with me at the diner."

Sean blew out the breath he'd sucked in when the phone rang. Brian couldn't save him from Wren Brigham. If he knew, he'd know Sean had been snooping around for someone to do him a…favor. And then it'd all be over. "You don't scare me, Enderly," he said, trying to sound tougher than he felt.

Brian laughed. "Good to know. Some guys are scared shitless by someone like me. I mean, my voice alone is enough to frighten folks." A few moments of silence filled the air before Brian finished. "Glad we had this talk. Oh, and Hartung, don't do something stupid."

The phone went dead.

That sonofabitch knows, Sean thought. What was he going to do?

CHAPTER 28

It had been weeks since Jane's disappearance. Did she know they shared the same father? Had she always known? Was Jane running from him, or was there someone else who had discovered some dirty secret his sister had kept hidden?

Either way, time was running out. Harrison Carter wasn't going to live forever. He was edging closer to the other side every day. Drew had no idea where Jane was, but he had to make sure she was dead before his father met his maker.

He dropped into his leather desk chair and gave his newly renovated office the once-over. After his tirade, he'd spent the night cleaning up, tossing out everything he'd broken. The only thing he had kept was this magnificent desk of his father's. He had covered his office windows with large sheets of paper that displayed the message *Under Construction*. For the next week, he worked in the open workspace as designers reimaged his office. Truth be told, he enjoyed not being locked away behind those four walls. He didn't feel so alone.

His concern was not the space—or even the work he needed to do. He was focused on finding Jane or, at the very least, knowing she was already dead—at someone else's hands. Not one penny of his father's estate could go to her. It would take every cent to pull the company out of the hole he had dug.

Facing his window, Drew crossed his arms and stared out at the city. "You're out there, Jane. I know it," he said. "I feel it. But where are you? And more importantly, who's helping you?"

Turning back, Drew opened his desk drawer and grabbed Jane's file, the one he'd found among his father's things. He paged through it but couldn't find what he was looking for. Why would he? Jane would have never listed her parents as an emergency contact. Why would he have thought differently?

He plucked his cellphone from his suit coat pocket and entered a Google search for Vivian Sterling. After a few minutes, he recorded both her and Doug's cell numbers on a pad of paper. It wasn't Doug he needed to speak to.

Carefully, he entered the number, checking it before he pressed *send*.

"Hello?" Viv's voice came across as more of a question than a greeting.

"Mrs. Sterling, this is Drew Carter from Hallman and Carter."

"Yes?" Again, there was uncertainty.

"Viv, may I call you Viv?" Drew asked.

"Yes," was all she said. He was certain she knew why he was calling.

"You see, I was going through some of my father's things, and, well, I came across something I was hoping you could help me with." He mentally patted himself on the back for gaining the upper hand so early in their conversation. "Would you be able to meet me sometime today or tomorrow?"

For a moment, Drew thought Jane's mother may have hung up.

"I'm at home in Duluth. What does this have to do with, Mr. Carter?" she asked indignantly. "What do you need to know?"

"Call me Drew," he told her, smiling to himself. "Will you be returning to Cedar Point this week?"

Silence once again seeped across the line. "Just a minute," she said. He heard remnants of a muffled conversation in the background. He couldn't make out many of the words but assumed she was talking to Doug. "I'm planning to drive back to Cedar Point tomorrow morning. I could meet you after lunch," she affirmed.

Drew raised a fist in front of his chest in victory. He was careful to keep the *win* in his voice hidden. "That'll work. Will your husband be joining you?" he asked.

"No. I'll be coming alone."

"That sounds perfect," Drew said. "I'll meet you at the main entrance to H & C at one o'clock. Does that time work for you?"

"One o'clock," she agreed.

Drew scribbled Viv's number on the inside of the folder. He closed the file and tried to put it back into his desk drawer, but it wouldn't drop into place. With one hand, he spread the files apart. At the bottom of the drawer was the white mask—the one he had worn when he tossed the rock through Enderly's window at the station. He was positive that Brian had been looking at him when he took his crazy bow before running through the field that night. He knew his threat wouldn't scare off the police, but it may have been enough to slow them down—divert their attention in another direction. If Enderly found Jane before Drew did, H & C was as good as gone.

He jerked the mask out of the drawer and tucked it into his briefcase. Just like Jane, it had to go.

***

In a classic black pantsuit, white satin blouse, and a pair of peek-a-boo toe side-scallop pumps, Vivian Sterling, a self-professed member of the elite, walked into Hallman and Carter. The time was exactly 1:00 p.m. True to his word, Drew met her at the door. Little did she know he had been waiting for her since noon. He hadn't wanted anyone else to intercept her and sideline his meeting. Before she even stepped foot into the lobby, he shook her hand, took her by the elbow and guided her toward the elevator. Once upstairs, he introduced her to his secretary simply as Jane's mother.

"Oh, Mrs. Sterling, I am so sorry. This must be such a hard time for you and your family. Jane was wonderful. Everyone loved her," the woman gushed.

"Thank you," Viv said. "I appreciate your sentiment."

Drew smiled at Viv and his secretary. "I thought it might do Mrs. Sterling some good to hear all the wonderful things Jane did for Hallman and Carter," Drew told her.

"Of course." His secretary waved one arm outward toward the open space. "Please feel free to talk to anyone. We all loved Jane."

"Thank you," Viv said, portraying the epitome of the perfect mother. "As did I, ah, I mean *we*," she corrected herself.

With a hand on her back, Drew steered Viv into his office. "Hold my calls," he commanded before closing his door.

He pointed to his ultra-modern couch and chair—both around the corner from the door, out of sight of his secretary's prying eyes. "Can I get you a drink? Wine? Something harder? Water, perhaps?"

"No, nothing," Viv said, shaking her head.

Drew poured himself a whiskey and set it on the table across from her. He unbuttoned his jacket and lifted the front of his trousers before he sat down. The folder was already on the low, stone coffee table that filled the space between them. "Do you know why I asked you here?" he inquired.

Viv watched his face. Drew sensed her curiosity. "I assume it was for the reason you stated to your secretary," she said.

"Really?" Drew took a drink from his glass. "So, you would have driven all this way just to hear me talk about how wonderful your daughter was? Please!" He took another swallow of whiskey. "Especially since you've hated her since the day she was born. I'm not that naïve, Viv."

The two engaged in a stare-down. Neither spoke nor looked away for the longest time. "How about you just tell me what

263

you know and cut the crap?" Viv told him.

Drew snorted. "You're one tough broad. Hardcore all the way, aren't you? You're nothing like your daughter...or my *half-sister*, are you?" The words floated between them. He waited for Viv to respond, but she said nothing; her face held no expression. He opened the folder and read the part of the will about half of Harrison's money going to his daughter, *Jane Hart*.

Viv grinned. "Well, how delightful! I'm sure she'll be thrilled with a windfall like that."

He was losing patience. "Well, I guess that's true—if she isn't already dead." Picking up his drink, he walked toward his desk and leaned against it. "Because, you see, if she's dead, I inherit the entire estate. Every. Last. Penny." He grinned. "It says so in the will." He repeatedly poked a finger into the pages he held.

Viv's shoulders drooped, her erect posture falling away. "What exactly are you saying? Did you kill my daughter?"

Drew laughed out loud. "Want that drink now, Viv?" he asked. He didn't wait for her to answer. He moved toward the counter and poured her a whiskey and set it on the table directly in front of her. "Drink up. You're going to need it." He watched her pick up the heavy tumbler and take a sip. She closed her eyes as she held the whiskey in her mouth. When she swallowed, her entire face looked pained. Drew was pleased. "More of a wine person, are you?" he taunted smugly.

Viv held the drink in the palm of one hand and balanced it with the other. "Did you kill my daughter?" she asked again.

"Your daughter? My sister? Interesting question, isn't it?" He again sat on the sofa opposite her. "I suppose the honest thing to say would be no." He pressed his lips together and the corners of his mouth turned downward. "Or maybe, *not yet* would be a better answer."

Viv suddenly rose; her drink sloshed over the top of the glass. "I don't know what kind of a game you're playing, but I intend to call the police the minute I walk out that door."

"Oooh, I'm so scared," Drew teased. "Our illustrious chief of police is a bumbling idiot. He doesn't know his head from his ass." Drew retrieved a napkin and handed it to Viv. He watched her daub the wet spot on the front of her slacks. "You know, Viv. I'm a businessman. I make deals. It's what I do. So, perhaps you and I could make a little business deal."

Viv took another sip of her drink and sat back down. "What are you proposing?" she asked.

Drew also sat down. "First of all, who else knows Jane and I share the same father?"

"No one." She absently wiped at the front of her pants again. "I thought Harrison would take that knowledge to his grave."

"Did my mother know? Is that why she left my father?" Drew asked.

"No. Your mother had her own issues. They had nothing to do with you or your father—or me, for that matter."

For one brief second, Drew felt relief. If he could believe Viv, his mother hadn't left because of him. But, at the moment, that was neither here nor there. He scooted to the front edge of the couch. "Does your husband know about Jane's paternity?"

"Of course not. A secret like that would destroy our marriage." She locked eyes with Drew. "You're not planning to tell him, are you?"

Drew leaned back on the couch; he crossed his legs and stretched his arms out along the top of the cushions. "If we strike a deal, the fewer people that know, the better."

Viv nodded. "So don't keep me in suspense," she told him. "I'm anxious to hear about this deal of yours."

Drew, unable to sit still, got up and strolled to the bar and poured himself another drink; he knew it was a mistake, but he needed the courage it provided. He held the bottle into the air, silently asking Viv if she wanted more. She shook her head no. He set his glass on the table and walked to the door. The click of the deadbolt nearly echoed in the entry to his office. He smiled to himself before he returned to the couch.

"So, you know I stand to inherit millions and millions of dollars when Two dies."

"Excuse me," Viv said. "Two?"

Drew laughed. "Two, as in Harrison *the second*. Two," he said again.

Viv nodded in understanding.

"If you help me find Jane before Two dies, I'll give you two million of it." He watched as Viv gasped.

"Two million?" she asked. "Just for letting you know where Jane is?" Her hands started to shake, both from excitement and fear. "First of all, how am I supposed to find her? The police haven't been able to." She glared at Drew as she slid forward on the chair. "Secondly, if your father's leaving you as much as you indicate, then I want more." Her stare was uncompromising.

Drew nearly spit a mouthful of whiskey at her. "Wow! You're a greedy old bag, aren't you?" Drew said. "Okay, five mill." He angrily pointed a finger in her direction. "But if you push me on this, you could end up following your daughter six feet down."

Viv sucked in a sharp breath. "So that's it? Five million just for letting you know where Jane is?" Drew nodded. "What happens if Jane has already…passed?" she asked.

"Are you asking if you still get the money?" Drew snorted. "Think about it, Viv. You know too much. I don't have a prayer if you go to the cops, do I?" He raised his eyebrows and glared at her. "If I don't pay you off, either way… well, you've got the goods on me."

Viv picked up the glass and downed the rest of the golden liquid, this time without a grimace. She stood up and stuck her hand toward Drew. He shook it, signaling their agreement. "Good doing business with you, Mr. Carter." She smiled as she walked toward his office door. "I'll be in touch."

CHAPTER 29

Jane Hart

I had been alone for so long I was riding the edge of becoming unhinged. One more day of sanity may have been all I had left. Talking to myself and answering my own questions had me believing I was nearing Sean's level of craziness. Often, I spoke out loud, just to hear my voice; I needed to make sure it still worked. Even so, I longed to hear someone else's voice too, to feel someone's arms around me, to know I was loved. My boys were my everything. It was Cole and Luke I longed for more than anyone else. The ache I felt for them often woke me in the middle of the night.

John Henry had warned me I could trust no one. He claimed it wasn't safe to let anyone know my whereabouts, not even my sons. But a mother knows, and I knew Cole and Luke were on my side. They always had been.

I grabbed a sweater and a handful of shirts and jeans from Sheila's closet, tightly rolled them together, and shoved them into my backpack. The folders and envelopes I took from Sean's safe went back into the plastic sack and inside the string bag. I tugged it closed to keep them corralled.

Once I was packed, I planted myself on the window seat in the guestroom and peered through a tiny opening in the wide wooden blinds, watching for cars. The road had been silent for nearly ten minutes by the time I finally worked up the courage to make my escape. I threw both bags on the passenger's side floor and climbed into the Haydens' car. I pushed the garage door button and whispered a prayer. The door moaned as it opened. The noise was amplified as it rang in my ears. I quickly backed out and let the door close. Once on the road, a rush of air escaped from my lungs. My chest felt tight. The prickly sensation I felt over my entire body would not subside.

After twenty-six years, the gravel road was as familiar as a worn pair of jeans, yet my pulse raced as I maneuvered the car over the washboard ruts and through the soft sand. If I hit the highway without seeing another vehicle, I knew I was free and clear. But that was not to be. At the stop sign, a patrol car raced toward me. I prayed it would pass, but the blinkers flashed on, indicating a turn down my road. I cranked my head in the opposite direction, searching for imaginary traffic that might travel the highway in the middle of the day. Before the squad even made the turn, I pulled out, not making eye contact, not giving them enough time to grab my plate number.

My heart pounded in my chest as I drove the ten minutes into town. Having the boys live on a dead-end street was my saving grace. The uncut cornfields surrounding their narrow road made me grateful for the extended fall. Still, I kept my face tilted downward, peering over the top of my sunglasses. I scanned the yard and street before I crawled out of the car and ran to the porch. Their key was tucked inside a flowerpot on the front porch. I dug through the dirt until I found it, wiped it on the front of my jeans, and let myself inside.

Hoss, Luke's Newfoundland, greeted me with a foot on each shoulder. "Get down, Hoss." I gave him a shove and rubbed his head before bending down to hug him; I was thankful to have even that small interaction with a living, breathing animal. I pushed the sliding door open and let him into the backyard. The wooden fence kept Hoss from barking at people or animals or the fictitious things he thought he saw off in the distance, but it also protected anyone from noticing him—or me.

Once Hoss was outside, I went into the garage and pushed the tools and workout equipment toward the walls, making enough room to squeeze Bill and Sheila's car inside. Cautiously, I opened the door. I eased the car into the narrow space and pressed the button on the wall. When the double-wide door banged against the cement floor, I took a deep breath and started to cry. An overwhelming feeling washed over me. I couldn't wait to hold my sons.

For the first time in weeks, I felt nearly normal. I let Hoss in and talked to him as I opened the fridge. It was filled with real food, fresh food, not just what came from a can or a box. I spun around and laughed out loud. I helped myself to a piece of cold pizza. It was curled on the edges and dried out, but I hadn't tasted anything that good since before I had disappeared. I opened a bottle of beer and tipped my head back. It tasted better than I remembered. Grabbing a second slice, I went in search of a computer.

I had given Cole and Luke laptops for Christmas. Here, I wouldn't have to watch my searches. Undoubtedly, the boys would be looking for information about me. If anyone were monitoring their activity, they wouldn't think twice about it. The time of day might be suspect, but I had to take a chance. Cole's laptop was closed, and I had no idea what his password was. Luke's was open. When I touched the trackpad, the screen sprang to life. With Hoss snuggled at my feet, I spent the next two hours googling myself. Some of the same articles I had seen before popped up; I didn't waste time rereading them. But there were new ones also: the bullet through the window at the KDIG Radio Station, Sean's interview with one of the Alexandria Stations, and several short news clips.

The hair on the back of my neck stood on end when I heard the front door open. I was almost positive it was one of the boys, but I couldn't be sure. My heart raced as I held my breath.

"Ho-oss?" Cole melodically called. My shoulders fell in relief. His voice moved closer to Luke's room as he searched for the dog. "Where in the hell are you? You always meet me at..." Cole froze when he came around the corner and saw me. "Mom? Oh my god! Mom! It's you."

Before I could even get off the chair, he had wrapped his arms around my neck in the same way he had when he was a small boy. "I can't believe it! I can't believe you're here and you're safe." He planted a palm on each of my shoulders and held me at arm's length. His eyes grew glassy. "Are you okay? Where were you? What happened? Why did you leave?" He leaned back. "And what happened to your hair?" The questions were machine-gunned at me, one right after the other.

I pulled him into a tight hug. "One question at a time, honey." I just wanted to hold him. "But let's get something to drink first."

I was only a couple steps behind Cole on the way to the kitchen. Twice, he looked backward, checking to make sure I hadn't been a figment of his imagination. He snatched two beers from the fridge and handed me one. "Nope," I wagged a finger back and forth. "Already had one. I'll take a soda." Cole pulled a Diet Coke from the fridge and handed it to me. "Are you boys drinking diet soda now? My mother didn't allow me to drink anything else. It was diet or water."

"No," Cole said sheepishly. "Grandma made us dinner a few weeks ago; she was the one who brought the case of Diet Coke."

"*Grandma?* As in my mother?" I was shocked.

Cole grimaced. "Yeah, Mom. There's a lot of things you don't know." He walked to my side of the island and wrapped an arm over my shoulder. "It's so good to see you. Does Dad know you're okay?"

I cleared my throat. "Well, Cole, there's a lot of things you don't know either. But can we wait until Luke gets home? I'd prefer to go through this just once."

For the next half hour, I caught up with Cole: work, gaming, potential girlfriends, and everything in between. The grin on my face never slipped. At times, I didn't even hear what he told me. I was too absorbed in being happy, just spending time with my son.

The front door opened again, and Luke walked into the entry. "Do you ever pick up the mail, asshole?" he called from the foyer.

"Well," Cole smiled at me, "I didn't get the mail, but I did pick up a special delivery package." His smile grew as he waited for his brother to break the corner.

Like Cole, Luke froze when he saw me. "What the f-?" His face slipped into an apology. "Oops! Sorry, Mom!" He ran toward me. "No, I'm not. This surprise deserves the f-word." Luke grabbed me around the waist and swung me in a circle. "How are you? Where were you? Why are you back? Does Dad know you're here?"

The three of us laughed as he set my feet back on the floor. I stuck my hand out and caught myself as I dizzily toppled onto the couch. Luke dropped down next to me. "What happened to your hair?" he asked as he gently touched it.

"Wow!" I laughed. "I didn't think you boys would even notice."

"It's, ah, different," he said, making a face at Cole.

I reached up and touched it in the same place Luke had. "I've sort of gotten used to it." Shifting my eyes from one to the other, I began to cry. "I missed both of you boys so much." They weren't boys; they were grown men, but all I saw was their tiny newborn faces, their pudgy little muddy hands, the two of them tossing their football in the yard. I took Luke's hand. "But, like I told your brother, one question at a time. There's a lot we need to talk about tonight."

"Did you cancel tonight?" Luke asked his brother. "Mom's home! Video games don't even compare."

Cole grinned. "Didn't think about it. I'll do it now."

"Stop!" I blurted before Cole left the room. "No one, and I mean no one, can know I'm here." I waited to make sure they understood. "Not your father or your friends or the police. And definitely not your grandmother."

Luke whispered to his brother. "She knows about Grandma?"

Cole shook his head. "It's one of the things we need to talk about." Then he disappeared to his side of the house.

Hoss jumped up on the couch between Luke and me. He turned in a circle, knocking us both sideways before he lay down with his head in my lap and his hindquarters in Luke's. "Seriously, Hoss! She's my mom." He laughed as he slid to the corner of the couch.

By the time Cole returned, Luke and I were in the kitchen making dinner—or rather a smorgasbord of this and that. Luke tossed a mixed pan of fries and tater tots into the oven while I sliced up some cheese. Cole rummaged through the cupboard until he found a can of tomato soup to add to the mix. When the fries were about halfway done, Luke tossed the rest of the uneaten pizza on the hot pizza stone and shoved it into the oven. It was the worst combination of foods ever, but being with my sons, it far outranked anything I had tasted recently.

The boys sat at the island while I did the dishes, reminiscent of the days of their youth. I loved seeing their faces, watching them laugh and bicker. There was no place I'd rather be.

When the kitchen was clean, which has always been a relative statement with my boys, I grabbed the string bag and set it beside me on the floor next to the couch. "So, tell me about Vivian Sterling and how she came to be *Grandma*—especially since I never allowed you to see her." The curiosity was killing me.

Luke shook his head. "It wasn't us, Mom. We didn't want it. Just remember that when you hear the story."

I nodded. "Okay. So, holding you responsible is out of the question?" I quipped.

"Do you remember when we used to go on those camping trips with Dad? *Boys' time,* he called it." Cole glanced at his brother as he continued to talk. I nodded. "Well, we never actually went camping."

"Wait! I'm confused," I said as I pulled my leg from beneath me. "If you didn't go camping, where did you go?"

"To Duluth." Luke looked down at the floor. "Before Grandma and Grandpa moved up there, they would meet us at a hotel on Lake Superior. We stayed with them while Dad disappeared for a day or two."

I touched Luke's arm. "Where did he go?"

"We never knew. We still don't," Cole said. "All Dad told us was that if we ever let you know we were spending time with Grandma and Grandpa Sterling, or that we didn't go camping, you would leave us, and we'd never see you again."

"Oh, boys," I whimpered, looking from one to the other. I wanted to cry for them. "I would never have left you."

Cole raised his shoulders and tipped his head to the side. A pained expression drifted across his face. "Well, Mom, you kind of just did."

Tears rolled down my cheeks as I jumped up. I grabbed them both and pulled them into a three-way hug. "I'm so sorry, so very sorry. I never meant to hurt either one of you." We stood huddled in the middle of the living room as I kissed their cheeks over and over. Finally, I pulled away. "So, now it's my turn," I whispered. "I have a lot to share with you. It might help you understand why I had to leave."

I removed the plastic grocery sack from the string bag and emptied the stack of folders and envelopes onto the couch next to me.

"What's all that?" Luke asked.

I held my breath for a moment as I considered what I was

about to reveal. "It's my life," I finally told them.

Long into the night, I shared the stories and photographs and newspaper clippings. I explained about my kidnapping and my life as Emily, their father's sister. I revealed what my childhood had been like at the hands of Doug and Viv, and how I met their father—a meeting I had now come to know was a setup by Sean. Then, unable to protect them from the truth, I described the years of abuse I suffered at the hands of their father, showed them the scars. When they wanted to know why I hadn't left him, I told them the truth. I had stayed to protect them. Finally, I told them about John Henry, why I had to leave, and where I had been for the past month. When there was nothing left to say and nothing left to ask, we sat in silence.

"Dad's not exactly who we thought he was, is he?" Luke finally asked.

I locked my fingers with his. "Luke, even though your dad's pretty messed up, he has always loved you boys. He still does. There's nothing that can take that away. This was never about the two of you."

"But he controlled everything about you, Mom. Doesn't that make you angry?" Cole asked.

I nodded. "Yeah, it does. But that was between him and me. It had nothing to do with you boys." Luke yawned. "Tell you what," I said as I patted Luke's leg, "we'll talk more tomorrow night after you get home from work. For now, we could all use some sleep." I watched them walk toward opposite ends of the house. "I love you, boys," I called. Instead of just saying it, they both returned and clung to me like they didn't want to let go. I hadn't known until that moment just how loved I was.

CHAPTER 30

Viv Sterling had six grandchildren. Lily and Laurel each had two daughters. Three of the four lived out of state; the fourth had married a border guard and lived so close to the Canadian border, she could throw a rock into the neighboring country. Viv's granddaughters were all so busy with their own children, they rarely found time to visit their grandparents.

With the girls out of the picture, she focused on Cole and Luke. Unbeknownst to Jane, they had been part of her life since they were small. Yes, she had lied to Brian Enderly when he asked her about seeing them, but what difference did it make? Their father had little time for them. He couldn't be bothered with anything other than work or visiting his father when he came to Duluth. And as for their mother, she wasn't worthy of a couple of fine boys like Cole and Luke. Jane may have been her biological daughter, but it was evident she hadn't inherited the refinement of a Sterling woman. And her looks? Those and her unsophistication had definitely been inherited from the Carters.

Harrison Carter II and his son Drew were a matched set. As far as Viv was concerned, insanity ran in their family. In college, when Doug introduced her to his best friend from high school, she had liked Harrison. But it didn't take long before she saw him for who he really was—a conniving womanizer. When Doug's back was turned, Harrison had his hands all over her. She couldn't bring herself to tell Doug what he was really like. Ruining their friendship wasn't something she wanted to do. So, she vowed to keep her distance.

Then one day during the boys' senior year of college, something changed. Weakened by a moment of passion, Viv gave in to Harrison's advances. She relished the excitement of someone new showering her with attention, but when Doug suddenly walked in, she slapped Harrison across the face and pushed him away, yelling at him to get away from her. That moment ended the longstanding friendship between Doug and Harrison.

Viv and Doug married after he completed his pharmaceutical degree. They were in love and happy. Life seemed perfect. Then the twins came along, a perfectly matched set. The joy she felt was beyond anything she could have imagined. Their son, JJ, was born a couple of years later, and instead of becoming overwhelmed by another mouth to feed and a greater demand on their time, she and Doug were overjoyed with their picture-perfect family. Money was tight between college loans and Viv not working, but there wasn't a day that passed that she didn't consider herself the luckiest woman in the world.

But then JJ was killed, and everything fell apart. She knew Doug blamed her for their son's death. He never once said those words out loud, but he retreated so far inward, it was impossible to believe any different. Why shouldn't he hate her? She had imploded their lives when JJ died under her watch. She and Doug no longer made eye contact. They never touched and rarely spoke more than a few words. Everyone and everything took a backseat to their grieving.

Then one day, Viv ran into Harrison in front of the grocery store. They talked for a few moments before she went inside to begin her auto-pilot mission of grocery shopping. The next day, he called her and asked her to join him for coffee in a neighboring town. She agreed to the meeting—and dozens of others that lasted nearly a year: in hotel rooms, after hours in his office, and other places they could steal away for an hour or so without raising suspicion of their spouses.

She dreamed of leaving Doug, of falling happily into Harrison's arms and forgetting all about the perfect family she once had. But then she discovered she was pregnant, and one thing became clear—leaving her husband meant she would become an outcast in the same town that had envied their perfect family and had wrapped their arms around her when her son died. A *floozie or a tramp* was how people would see her. So, she ended her relationship with Harrison—never admitting she was with child. She immediately threw herself back into her marriage to a man who never had a clue his wife had spent the last year in the arms of another.

Viv and Doug hadn't shared a bed since JJ died nearly a

year before. She always slept in her son's bed, lying awake into the early morning hours, reliving her time with Harrison.

Plans spun in her head, and she searched for a way to recapture her life as a Sterling. One evening, she farmed the girls out for a sleepover and set her husband up for a reunion. Doug had no idea his wife was playing him.

Lying in bed, drawing swirls on her husband's bare chest as he cradled her in his arms after a night of lovemaking, Viv brokered a trip to Disney World; *a new beginning,* she called it. By the end of the following week, the four of them were on a plane headed off on a new adventure.

On the last day of the trip, Viv spent much of her time in the bathroom regurgitating nearly anything she had eaten during the previous seven days. *The flu bug* was what she told Doug and the girls. But morning sickness had hit hard.

Once home, Viv hid her queasiness from her husband. Fortunately, it was summer; the girls slept in or found ways to entertain themselves while she kneeled on the floor with her head hung into the porcelain bowl. By evening, all was fine.

The morning sickness was nearing its end when she told Doug about *their* baby. He was thrilled, positive it was a gift from their son. She knew he hoped for another boy, but to be perfectly honest, she didn't want either. This baby had been a mistake, a reminder of her infidelity.

Doug was patient with her when she didn't appear to be as over the moon as he was. He tried to explain that the baby would heal their family, make them whole again. But he also understood her apprehension, caused by her fear of losing another child.

Viv fudged the due date, reminding her husband, a pharmacist, a trained medical professional, that babies don't always come on time. Some arrive early and some late. Some just don't need to *cook* as long, she told him. So, when she went into labor three weeks before she was due, Doug never questioned the early arrival. Jane weighed in at six pounds, five ounces, and appeared to be perfectly healthy.

Viv refused to hold her daughter. Just looking at the baby made her stomach churn. From the moment Jane was born, Viv saw Harrison, yet she convinced Doug that the infant had his chin and ears. She knew Doug was concerned about her inability to bond, but he didn't push her. So, when she left the hospital at the end of the first day without Jane, he blamed it on depression—the fear of history repeating itself.

The day after Doug returned her to the hospital, Harrison unexpectedly appeared in the doorway of her hospital room, haphazardly holding a bedraggled bouquet. Before visiting Viv, he had stopped at the nursery. "She's mine," was all he said. When Viv didn't deny it, he dumped the flowers in the trashcan near the door and walked out of the room. She didn't see him or hear from him again until a letter arrived in the mail the following week.

Harrison had set up an account for his daughter's care. The

account was in Viv's name. Each month, he deposited an exorbitant amount of money into it. His business had grown faster than expected and he wanted to make sure his daughter would be taken care of in his absence. Being the sole keeper of their finances, she hid the secret account from her husband.

Viv begged Harrison not to breathe a word of Jane's paternity to anyone, including Doug. After days of pleading, he finally agreed. Out of respect for his family, he remained silent even when Jane went missing. But upon her return, he was overjoyed. For the next sixteen years, Harrison Carter II, worshipped his daughter from afar while Viv hated Jane's very existence.

***

Once she had a taste of the good life, money became everything to Viv. Her lifestyle had to be glamorous and coveted. So, the money Drew offered her to turn over her daughter's whereabouts, or at least ensure she was dead, caused pure ice to course through her veins. It was easy money— especially at a time when they were penniless. She would continue to hide it from her husband. Besides, five million dollars would last her a long time; she was old. How much longer would she live anyway? How long would Doug live? If she needed to, she would make sure it wasn't long.

CHAPTER 31

Cole wanted nothing more than to eat one of his mother's amazing dinners like the ones she used to make when he lived at home: lasagna, fried chicken, or swiss steak. Thinking about her food on his way home from work made his mouth water. It was childish, and he knew that, but the one meal he wanted more than any other was tater tot hotdish. For as long as he could recall, it had been his birthday meal. He craved it the way other people wanted steak or ribs. When he moved out, she had given him the recipe, but it never tasted the same.

On his way home from work, he stopped at the grocery store and picked up every item on the list his mother had handed to him that morning. He had no idea what she did with half of the foods she wrote down—things like kale and turnips. Knowing her, she probably pureed it and snuck it into recipes like she did when he and Luke were small. Except for a few basic dishes, neither of them ever learned to cook. He loaded his cart with doubles of everything. By the time he was finished shopping, he was convinced there was enough food for at least a month.

"Hey, Cole," Jenny said as she rang up each item and tossed them down the conveyor belt toward the bagging area. "What are you doing with all this food?" she asked. "I've never seen you or Luke buy fresh fruit or veggies before."

Cole cringed. He'd dated Jenny briefly a couple of years before; it hadn't ended well, and she hadn't given up on him. Before he unloaded his cart, he checked the register. The little old lady who never spoke had been standing there. Where had she gone?

"Where's the old clerk?" he asked as he tucked the grocery list into the pocket of his suit coat and started bagging the food and placing it into his cart.

"She went on break. Lucky for me, huh?" She giggled like a schoolgirl. Cole distinctly remembered one of the things he most disliked about her—she had never grown up. "Are you going to Jason's party tonight?"

Cole had forgotten about the party. "Nah, Luke and I are meeting up with some online gamers. We're having a little competition."

"Ah, that's too bad." Jenny set her hand on Cole's shoulder and slowly ran it down his arm as he swiped his card and entered his pin. "I was sort of hoping you'd come," she pouted.

"Sorry," he said as he quickly bagged the last of his groceries. "Maybe next time." As he walked away, he whispered, "You Klingon." That was the other thing he disliked about her. She wouldn't leave him alone.

***

Cole arrived home seconds after his brother. Luke had parked where Cole usually did. "Hey, butthead, get back here and help me with the groceries," he called to Luke.

Luke walked back to the car, whining and complaining the whole way.

"Fine! Next time, you buy the groceries and I'll haul them in."

Luke mimicked his brother, spewing made-up words as he followed Cole into the house.

Jane got up from the couch and helped them put the groceries away. "What do you boys want for dinner tonight?" she asked.

"Do you even have to ask?" Cole shook his head.

"Tater tot hotdish!" Luke called from down the hall. "We want tater tot hotdish every night until we get tired of it."

Jane looked at Cole and laughed. "Is he serious? What do you want, Cole?"

"Ah, tater tot hotdish, Mom. Luke and I already discussed this."

"Okay, I'm on it," she said as she watched her son head to his side of the house to change out of his suit.

Dinner lasted almost an hour. As Jane washed the dishes and loaded the dishwasher, the boys sat at the table, plainly suffering from a food coma.

"What'd you do today, Mom?" Luke asked when his mother returned to the table for a second load.

"I scrubbed your bathroom." She wrapped an arm around Luke's neck and bent close to his ear. "Do we need to have the stand-up or sit down to pee discussion we had when you were three?" Cole burst out laughing. "Cole, don't laugh at your brother; your bathroom was twice as bad."

Within seconds, the boys were wrestling on the dining room floor, teasing and taunting one another. It ended when Jane yelled, "Cole Taylor and Luke Brandon! Stop it right now!"

"Yes, Mother," they said in unison as they picked themselves off the floor, righting the chairs they'd knocked over in their fray.

Jane laughed. "You two will never grow up, will you?" Simultaneously, they shrugged and headed into the gaming room while she finished cleaning up.

***

Neither Cole nor Luke heard the doorbell ring above the booming surround sound of the video games. Their mother suddenly appeared in the doorway; her face had gone white. Suddenly, the bell rang again. They all froze. "Maybe they'll go away," Luke said quietly.

Cole slugged his brother. "Brilliant, dumb-ass. The entire house is lit up."

The bell rang again and again until it pulsed into one long bell. Jane's shoulders shot upward in a question.

"Go into my room and shut the door, Mom," Luke told her. "We'll get rid of whoever it is." Without question, their mother raced from the room and into Luke's bedroom, quietly shutting the door behind her.

Cole drew a deep breath and blew it out through his pursed

lips before opening the door. Jenny and another girl he recognized but couldn't recall her name blew past him and into the house. Luke corralled them in the hallway. "Jenny. Lola," he greeted, pressing a hip into one wall and leaning his hand against the opposite side. "What are you ladies doing here?"

Jenny pulled an open bottle of beer from her purse and pressed her finger to her lips. "Shhh," she drunkenly sprayed. "Jason's party was a bust." She giggled. "So we snuck out to come party with you two."

Cole grabbed her by the shoulders and steered her back down the hallway. "Sorry. We're in the middle of a gaming tournament; we don't have time to hang out."

Lola, obviously the less impaired of the two, quietly followed Cole. "Are you okay to drive?" Luke asked her.

She nodded. "I'm good. I haven't had much to drink." She took over pushing Jenny toward the door. "Come on, girl. We have to go," she told her.

"But I don't wanna go," Jenny drunkenly whined. "I came to see Cole." She turned around and touched Cole's face. He instinctively pulled back. "I love you, Cole," she murmured.

"Come on, Jen. They're busy. We need to go," Lola insisted as she wrapped an arm over her friend's shoulder and fought to pull her forward. "You can talk to Cole some other time."

Jenny stood upright. She grabbed the wall to keep from tipping over. "You're such a bitch!" she shouted at Lola. Then she laughed. "Shhh," Jenny said again, looking right at her friend. "Don't tell Lola I called her a bitch."

Jenny's eyes glanced toward the hooks in the entryway. "What's that?" she asked, staring directly at Cole. "That's a girl's sweater," she stammered. She looked confused. "Why do you have a girl's sweater in your house, Cole. Are you cheating on me?" She tried to slap his cheek, but she missed.

Cole could feel his face grow warm. "It's, ah, one my mom left here." It came out more like a question than a statement.

"Is your mom back?" Lola asked Luke.

He swallowed hard, "No. She, um, left it over the summer."

"Oh." Lola turned Jenny toward the door. "Come on, Jenny. We have to go."

"Are you okay getting her home?" Luke asked again.

"We'll be fine." Lola nodded toward Luke and pulled the door open.

"Grandma?" Cole said, shocked to see her standing on the other side of the door.

"What's going on here?" Viv asked as she studied the two girls before pointing at Jenny. "It appears this one tied one on a little early."

Lola pushed Jenny past Viv and toward the car as the three of them watched.

Viv shut the door and hung her jacket on the row of hooks near the woman's sweater, but she said nothing, nor did it appear she even noticed it. "Anyway, I thought I'd make dinner for you two boys. I know it's late, but I also know you basically live on junk food. So, since I'm in town for the night, I thought a good home-cooked meal might be welcomed," she said as she headed toward the kitchen.

Luke maneuvered himself in front of her just as he had with the girls. "Grandma, we already ate." While he distracted her, Cole grabbed the sweater from the hook and shoved it into the bench seat below the coat hooks.

"What did you have? Pizza? Again?" she asked as she ducked under Luke's arm.

"Well, ah, no, actually. We made tater tot hotdish," Cole told her as he came up the hallway.

"With veggies," Luke added.

"Hotdish? That's not a meal," she said. "That sounds like something your mother would have thrown together." She raised her eyebrows in disdain. "But since you insist you ate, how about if I make you something you can heat up tomorrow night?" She opened the fridge and looked at the boys suspiciously. "What's with all the food?"

Cole glared at his brother. "Luke's been taking a cooking class and he's been practicing."

Viv swung the refrigerator door shut, "Well, Luke, if you cooked for that one girl I met at the door, I doubt very much she'll even remember it by morning."

Luke laughed. "That was *Cole's* old girlfriend. She's a real winner."

Viv looked at Cole. "Past tense, I hope? *Was* your

girlfriend?"

Cole nodded. "Yeah. I saw the error of my ways with that one. She, of course, hasn't given up quite so easily—hence the reason for the visit."

"Ah," Viv said. "Well, then, you boys have food covered." She looked around. "How about if I do a little cleaning?"

"We hired a cleaning service, Grandma," Luke spewed. He swung his arm out to the side. "See? They were here today."

Viv scanned three open rooms. "Well, then, it looks like you boys don't need me after all." Her lips turned upward into a sad smile.

"We need you, but, ah, everything you want to do for us has already been done," Cole told her.

"Okay, then, I suppose…" She stopped talking. "Would you boys mind if I used your bathroom before I go?" she asked.

Luke pointed to the one near the front door. "It's down the hall. You walked past it."

Viv whispered, "I know, but I, ah, need a little more privacy. I might be a bit," she said. "It's just terrible getting old. Someday you boys will understand."

"You can use Cole's bathroom, Grandma." Luke pointed to Cole's end of the house. As he walked her down the hallway, he signaled for his brother to let their mom know what was happening.

Cole raced toward Luke's room and threw the door open, but his mother was not there. He gently tapped on the closet door before opening it. His mother's face was as white as a ghost; she was shaking uncontrollably. Cole wrapped his arms around her and whispered into her ear, "Grandma's here. Stay put. We're trying to get rid of her. I'll let you know when she's gone." He pushed his mother backward. "Okay?" he mouthed. Jane nodded, stepped farther into the closet, and pulled the door shut.

Cole leaned his head against the closet door. He couldn't believe this was happening. After several deep breaths, he returned to the kitchen. His brother was already there, but their grandmother was not. "Is she gone?" he whispered.

Luke shook his head no. "Bathroom," he mouthed.

Cole nodded. The two stood in silence, waiting for their grandmother to return. Several minutes later, Viv walked in. "Thank you, boys." She slowly looked around the house. "Luke, I'd sure like to see your side of the house. May I? The last time I was here, I was only in the main part." Viv looked around the living room, dining room, and kitchen. Finally, she poked her head into the gaming room before heading toward Luke's end.

"It looks just like Cole's," he said. He suddenly felt too warm. He wiped the back of his neck with his hand.

"Yeah, except that Luke is a lot messier," Cole said as he stepped in front of his grandmother. "You don't want to go in there," he insisted.

Viv stared at Cole. "But I do. You boys are as different as

night and day. I'm sure it looks quite different. Besides, you said the cleaner was here today, so how bad can it be?" She pushed her way past Cole and walked through Luke's workspace and into his bedroom.

Cole felt his heart beating in his throat. He imagined Luke felt the same. "Okay, Grandma. This is it. It looks just like my room, doesn't it?" he said loudly, hoping his mother would know they were close.

"Yes, it does. The colors are different, but otherwise, they're almost identical." Viv clapped her hands together. "You boys did a wonderful job remodeling this old house. Your grandfather would be very proud of you." She faced the closet door but turned toward the boys. "Oh, that reminds me, Cole. Your suit coat was hanging on your chair. I was going to hang it up, but it had a spot on the front, so I cleaned out the pockets and threw it in the dry-cleaning box in your closet."

"Thanks, Grandma." Cole felt extremely uncomfortable knowing she had been going through his things. He slowly worked his way between his grandmother and the closet. "Let's…"

"I'm curious. Is Luke's closet the same as yours?" she asked as she grabbed the handle of the door and swung it open. Cole and Luke held their breath as she looked left and then right. She looked up and down. Their grandma bent over and snatched a piece of thread from the floor on the right-hand side. She stood up and held the white thread toward Luke. "Doesn't look like your cleaner vacuumed your closet, Luke. I'd let them know you expect them to do the job you pay for."

Their grandmother smiled and tossed the thread in Luke's garbage can. "I should get back to the Moonlight. I promised your grandfather I would call him before he falls asleep."

Viv sauntered to the front door and slipped on her jacket. She kissed each of her grandsons on the cheek and opened the door to leave, but before she stepped out, she held one finger in the air, shaking it at them as she spoke. "I know you boys miss your mother, but remember, everything happens for a reason. Sometimes the thing you want to happen the least ends up being the best after all."

Then she stepped into the night and disappeared down the street.

CHAPTER 32

Viv pulled into the lot of Living Waters Memory Care. She drove into a space on the far end, in what she believed to be overflow parking. The security lights barely reached the small lot, leaving her in the shadows of the large trees that grew along the edge of the property.

She checked her watch and scanned the grounds around her. He was late, and not just a few minutes either. It was closing in on fifteen minutes past the time they had agreed to meet. As she reached down to grab her phone from her purse, the passenger's side door opened and Drew climbed in.

"Drive," he commanded.

"Where?" she asked as she started the car.

"I don't give a shit. Just put the car in gear and drive away from here. Just don't go back toward town."

It was clear he was upset. He shivered as he rubbed both arms at the same time. She pointed to the temperature control for his side of the car. "I'm not cold. I'm pissed off," he grumbled.

She watched him from the corner of her eye as she drove toward the exit and clicked on her blinker.

"Left! Go left!" he barked. "I told you, not toward town."

Viv bumped the blinker downward and pulled onto the

nearly empty road. Drew stared out the window, looking toward the starry sky. "The moon's so bright," she said, making small talk. "I can't believe how beautiful it..."

"Shut up!" he yelled. "Just shut the hell up." He turned back toward his window as she drove in silence, still keeping a watchful eye on him.

They reached the next town before Drew spoke again. "Two is bad," he said.

"Harrison?" Viv asked, clarifying who he was referring to.

"Yes! My father," he snapped. "Who the hell did you think I was talking about?"

Viv ignored his rant as she drove down the main street of the small town. She placed her hand on top of Drew's. "I'm sorry," she said, sincerely meaning it.

He pulled his hand away and glared at her. "Are you? Are you really? Because it seems to me you effed-up my father's life and then just walked away." He watched the road as they continued out of town on the same highway that brought them into the tiny village less than a minute before. "He loved you. And you screwed him over, not just in college, but again when your life fell apart—after your son died."

Viv swallowed hard. "JJ. His name was JJ." She looked at Drew when she said it. "I loved that little boy so much," she said softly. It was one of the first times she had spoken about her son since his accident. She had always been afraid that if she so much as whispered his name, it would open a floodgate of memories, and she would never be able to stuff it all back inside. No, losing control wasn't an option.

"I. Don't. Care," he snorted. "I don't care if you did or if you didn't love that kid. He probably got off easy. Because honestly, you're kind of a crappy mother to love one kid and not another. Don't you think?"

Her heart felt as if it had been ripped in two, but she couldn't argue with him; he was right. "I suppose that's true." She dimmed her lights as she met an approaching car. "I didn't know how to be a good mother to Jane. She was a constant reminder of, well, my infidelity." She sighed loudly as she glanced toward Drew. "Even so, I loved your father. But…"

"But what?" Drew demanded. "What?"

"Just…nothing," she said. "I loved Doug too. And leaving him meant leaving Lily and Laurel. I just couldn't do it."

"Huh!" Drew snorted. "But you could leave Jane?"

"Drew," she said, glancing between the road and him. "For what it's worth, I still love your father."

"Really, Viv? You have a piss-poor way of showing it. Do you know that for the last two hours, I listened to my dad repeatedly call *your* name? Not my mother's. Not my name. He just kept yelling for you."

Her eyes widened. "Oh, my God! I hope you explained to the staff that it was a different Vivian. Those people know me out here."

Drew glared at her before releasing a loud, raucous laugh.

"Really? That's what you're worried about?" He spit on the floor of her car. "You're a piece of work, aren't you? A first-class piece of shit."

They drove in silence for another five minutes or so. Drew appeared to be searching for something, but Viv couldn't be sure. "Slow down!" he shrieked. "Here! Turn here." He pointed to what appeared to be an old logging road. Even from the side, she could tell it was deeply rutted and covered in tall grass.

"I'm not taking my car down that road," Viv told him as she shook her head. "I can pull off up ahead."

"I said *turn here*. If you want your damn money, you'd better do as I say." Drew glanced into the side mirror. "I don't want anyone to see us. You don't have to go down very far, just past the top of that hill."

Reluctantly, Viv turned onto the path and slowly guided the car over the deep ruts. Tree branches brushed along the side of the vehicle as she passed through the narrow opening. When she broke the hill, she killed the lights but left the motor running.

"Well? You wanted to talk, so talk," he said, staring at Viv's moonlit face.

She tugged her purse from near his feet and set it on her lap, laying her arms across the top. "I know where she is."

Even in the dim moonlight, Viv could see the excitement in Drew's eyes. "Where?" He shifted in his seat. "Where is she?" he practically screeched.

Drew's breathing grew labored; his breaths were louder than they had been just minutes before. She was sure he was hyperventilating. "Are you okay? You seem to be…"

"Where is she?" he said louder.

Viv stared down at her purse. She was about to give away her daughter, her grandsons' mother. Was it worth the money? Could she live with herself if she told Drew where Jane was? He'd just accused her of being a terrible mother. If she told him, it would only confirm what he thought of her.

She turned toward him, shifting in her seat so she almost faced him. "So, it's five million, correct?"

"That's what I said," Drew huffed. "Now, where is she?"

"And I will receive the money, when?" She knew Drew's patience had grown thin, but she wasn't stupid. If she didn't work out the details before she told him, he could easily screw her over.

Drew took a deep breath. "The minute Two dies, I will put the money in an account in your name. It'll be an offshore account. More private, less traceable."

Viv sat quietly for a moment. She again asked herself if she was making the right choice. But the way she saw it, it came down to two things: her way of living or her daughter's life. Viv had always been decidedly clear in her choices. Her needs and wants came before anyone else's. It had been true with Doug and Harrison. It was true with her children and grandchildren. Like a beacon, the words of her own mother always flashed before her: *No one is as important as you are.*

"Okay." She nodded. "She's staying with her sons, Cole and Luke. They live in a big house on Mitchell Way on the edge of Cedar Point. It's surrounded by cornfields. The house next door is empty, as is the first one near the intersection." Drew looked straight ahead. A crooked smile continued to grow. "Their house number is 209." She reached into her purse and handed him a small piece of paper with her grandsons' address on it.

Drew turned sideways in his seat. "How do I know you're not playing me?" His smile was gone. "How do I know you don't have the cops sitting at this place waiting to arrest me?" He watched Viv. "What proof do you have?"

Viv smiled. She pulled a second sheet of paper from her purse and handed it to Drew. "Here," she told him.

Drew tipped it toward the window. The moonlight illuminated the words. "This is a damn grocery list." He grabbed her by the arm and squeezed. "Don't you dare screw with me, old woman," he said as he waved the paper in her face.

She jerked her arm away. "Of course, it's a grocery list. Don't you recognize the handwriting? It's very distinct. I've never seen writing like that anywhere else."

Drew looked at it again. "It's Jane's writing. But how does this prove where she is?"

"Last night I paid a visit to my grandsons. There was a woman's sweater hanging by the door. It disappeared while I was in the house."

"It could have been a girlfriend's sweater," Drew said.

"It wasn't the style a young girl would wear. Besides, the house was clean, and the refrigerator was filled with food—food two bachelors would never buy." She watched Drew's face to see if he was following her. Deep lines creased his forehead as his eyes flitted across the dashboard, trying to connect the dots. Finally, she connected them for him. "I thought it was odd, so I excused myself to go to the bathroom and I snooped around. I found this list in Cole's suit coat pocket. I saw much of the same food that was on the list in the fridge."

"So?"

She couldn't believe how dumb he was. "Don't you see, it had to have been a current list." Again, she waited for him to catch up to her, but he didn't seem to be following. "Anyway, it could have been just a freaky coincidence, but something didn't seem right. So not seeing Jane anywhere in Cole's bedroom, I asked to see Luke's."

"Are you nuts? You told them you were looking for their mother?" Drew's eyes were wild. His look frightened her, but she kept talking.

"Of course not. I told them I wanted to see his room, see their remodeling job. They didn't appear to want me there, but no one says no to their grandmother." She smiled. "Once I looked around, I opened the closet, and when I did, you could have heard a pin drop; those boys held their breath. I have to admit, when I saw no sign of Jane, I was gravely disappointed.

But then I bent down to pick a thread off the floor, and I saw the foot of someone hiding behind a pair of Luke's work coveralls."

Drew smiled. "So you saw her?"

"Well, yes, her foot anyway," Viv clarified.

Drew's eyebrows furrowed. "How do you know it was Jane? It could have been some stupid girl your grandson was trying to hide, maybe the same one the sweater belonged to."

Viv shook her head in disbelief. No wonder he'd already run his father's company into the ground; he couldn't find his head from his ass. She took a deep breath. "I thought you might ask that." Viv shifted in her seat. "I know it was Jane's foot because, when she was a teenager, she had an accident that left her with a scar from her little toe to damn near her ankle. I saw the scar."

Drew leaned back in his seat. He laughed out loud. "We've got her. We've got the little bitch." He looked at Viv. "My worries are finally over."

"Mine too," she whispered.

Drew pulled a pack of cigarettes from his jacket pocket. "Smoke?" he asked.

"Not in this car," she told him. "It's a lease."

"Outside, then," Drew said as he opened his door and stepped into the cool evening air. He tripped in the tangle of grass as he got out of the car. Viv didn't see him until he popped up in front of the vehicle. A devious smile grew on his face as he lit his cigarette.

Viv watched him take a long draw and blow a smoke ring. He lit a second and showed it to her through the windshield. *Oh, what the hell,* she thought. She climbed out of the car and carefully made her way to the front. She leaned her backside against the warm hood. Drew handed her the lit cigarette and the two smoked in silence.

He plucked two more from the pack, stuck them both between his lips, and lit them at the same time with the lighter he again pulled from his jacket pocket. He handed her one. As he did, his cigarette fell to the ground. "Shit," he said as he bent down to pick it up. But instead of grabbing the cigarette, he lifted a large rock with both hands and swung his arms to the side, striking Viv just above the temple. He watched her crumble to the ground. Blood oozed from the gash. "One down, one to go," he said as he laughed out loud.

He ground out both cigarettes. Stepping over Viv's body, he climbed into her car and backed up. As he eased the car to the top of the crest, he watched her in the headlights. "That was for my dad, bitch!" he said. "You had it coming."

Drew drove Viv's car to the outskirts of town, near his home. Depravity settled over him as he turned onto a farm road, shut off the lights, and gunned the car into a cornfield that had yet to be harvested. He climbed out of the car and walked perpendicular to the road, through the rows of corn, toward his house, whistling the entire way. Drew had no doubts about his safety. The town was a hamlet, a cow-town, nothing more than a village really. They'd barely made it into the twentieth century, let alone the twenty-first. He had money. No one was coming after him.

He walked into his house and closed the door. Awkwardly, he pulled off his jacket and threw it to the floor, one sleeve inside out. The mansion was dark, but he refused to turn on the lights. Even with his confidence, his hands shook as he moved down the hallway. Holding them in front of him, he considered about the power they had. He had just killed someone. Never would he have believed he had it in him, but he had just taken out Viv. The corners of his lips curved ever so slightly upward as he thought about what was next. *They say the first is always the hardest.*

CHAPTER 33

Brian shoved the investigation board into the corner of his office; one of the small wheels caught and he grabbed the edge of the board before it toppled over. He had added and removed information more times than he could count. It made no sense anymore. As far as he was concerned, he was still focused on three suspects: Sean Hart, Vivian Sterling, and Drew Carter. They could be working together for all he knew. The only one he hadn't spoken to yet was Drew.

He impatiently paced the floor of his office, replaying interviews, reviewing notes, and thinking about Jane. Something inside of him told him they were close to solving this case. His stomach had been tied in knots for days and he had barely slept. He had that weird prickly sensation he used to get in law enforcement school when they were close to solving a case.

The door to the station opened and closed, but he didn't leave his office. Mauri stuck her head through his doorway. "Ah, Boss, you might want to come out here." She looked between him and the outer office a couple of times before he moved to the door to see what she was concerned about.

John Henry, the incognito old drifter, sat in a chair poking his finger through a hole in the side of one tennis shoe. Brian had to give it to him; the man could stay in character.

He backed into his office, grabbed Mauri's arm, and pulled her with him. "Listen, no matter what you see or hear, you say nothing—not to your husband, your family, or any other person you feel so inclined to talk to. Do you understand?"

Mauri smiled at him. "I take it you think I have a big mouth."

"Dammit! This is serious. Do you understand?" He still had not let go of her arm.

She nodded. "I've got it, Brian. I would never do anything to jeopardize a case. You know that."

He let go of her arm and sighed. "I know. I'm sorry." His shoulders sagged forward. "I'm just so stressed."

"It's okay, Boss. When this is all over, you can make it up to me."

"How?" he asked.

She laughed as she walked toward the drifter. "Second fridge filled with Pepsi."

"Ain't happening," he said from his doorway.

Mauri helped the old man up and led him into Brian's office. Once inside, she nodded at Brian and pulled the door closed.

"Have a seat, John." Brian pointed to the chair on the opposite side of his desk. John sat down and started to remove his hat and wig combo. "Wait," Brian told him. "Do you want anything to drink?"

"A cup of coffee would be great," he told him.

Brian buzzed Mauri. "Can you bring in a cup of coffee and a can of Coke?"

"Hold on a second. I think I overheard your secretary mention Pepsi. Right?" John asked.

Brian laughed at the irony. "Change that…"

"I heard," Mauri said.

Seconds later, she walked into Brian's office with two cans of soda. "A man after my own heart," she said to the drifter as she handed him the Pepsi. "If you can convince my boss to switch to Pepsi, I'll buy you dinner."

The drifter laughed. Brian loudly whispered, "Get out!" He pointed his chin toward the door.

"I'm going. I'm going. Geesh," Mauri grumbled.

Once the door was shut, the agent pulled off his hat and wig. John popped his teeth out and slipped them into his jacket pocket. "I hate these dentures most," he said. He picked up his soda and took a sip. "Dang, that tastes good. Drifters don't often get a soda break in the middle of the day." John laughed.

Brian joined the laughter. "I suppose not." He flipped a page in his yellow notepad and grabbed a pen. "I assume you have information for me. And it must be important, or you wouldn't have chanced coming to the station."

"Yeah, it is," he said. "Could be a huge piece of the puzzle in finding Mrs. Hart." He took another drink of his soda. "I assume you know a Harrison Andrew Carter the third. From what I can tell, he goes by Drew Carter."

Brian flinched at the name. He had been trying to get ahold of Drew Carter for days, but every time he showed up, Drew was missing in action. "Yeah, he runs Hallman and Carter. Took it over from his dad about five years ago, right around the time the old man started to fall apart." Brian stared at John. "He's not exactly someone I'd trust."

"That's the one. The guy's been running a small-scale Ponzi scheme. Of sorts," John added. "About a year after his dad stepped down, he started rounding up investors for some fabricated company called Perform Investments. His investors believed he had inside trader information that would earn them two-fold on their money. They all knew it was illegal, but their greed got the better of them."

"Sounds less like a Ponzi scheme to me, and because they all knew it was illegal—maybe a bit of a crime ring."

"Regardless, Carter's ass is in a sling."

"Sounds like it," Brian agreed.

John continued. "Thing is, the guy hasn't invested a dime of the money he's collected; he uses every penny to keep H & C afloat. It's obvious he's not a good businessman. A few months back, one of his investors started questioning why his payout was taking so much longer than he'd been told. When Carter didn't give him the answer he wanted to hear, he came to us—with the understanding he'd be protected, of course."

"So, the FBI is looking into Hallman and Carter." Brian nodded. "Makes sense. What do you need from my department?"

John scrunched his face. "Nothing." He squirmed. "I haven't exactly been candid with you though."

Brian looked confused. "When? What haven't you told me?"

"Remember when you hauled my ass out to that old trailer?" John asked. Brian nodded. "There were things I couldn't tell you then."

The chief leaned forward. "Well, suppose you talk now."

"The reason we were supposed to put Jane into protective custody had to do with Carter. I purposely led you to believe it was about her husband."

Brian stood up. "Are you kidding me? You've been sitting on this information while we've been busting our butts following leads that took us nowhere?" His face turned as red as his soda can. He felt like his neck had suddenly grown too large for his shirt collar, and he dug a finger inside and pulled it away from his throat. "You'd better start talking, then. I swear to God, I'm about ready to blow."

John held his palms toward Brian. "Whoa! I understand your frustration, but the information I had was strictly confidential. I couldn't share anything at the time. We were in the middle of our own investigation and, once we found out Mrs. Hart could be in danger, I went from digging around for information on Carter to trying to protect her. I've spent the last month trying to track her down." He took another drink and set the can on Brian's desk. "So, here's the deal." He cleared his throat. "As you know, when we investigate, we work from the inside. We've had a guy working in the finance department at H & C for almost two months now. He's been going through information each night after the staff leaves. At times, it was hard because Carter has no life. Sometimes he was there into the early morning hours." John wrapped his hand around the empty can. "When he started, he came across some information that made us believe Mrs. Hart might be in danger."

"Yeah, and what was that?" Brian angrily asked, his face warm with rage. "What information did he find?"

John squeezed the can, denting it in his hand. "It was a will, Harrison the second's will. The old man is loaded well beyond what he has in the company. He has investments that are bordering on half a billion dollars. But the thing is, he's not leaving all of it to Drew."

Brian didn't look surprised. "So? People leave money to friends or organizations all the time. It's not that unusual."

"Well, in this case, it is unusual—not because of who it is, but because of *who it is*," John told him, repeating the exact phrase with a different emphasis.

"What the hell does that mean?" Brian was furious.

"His fortune, including H & C, is to be split between *both* of his children." He watched Brian's questioning face.

"How's that possible? I've known Drew my entire life. There was never another kid in his family. He was an only child."

"That's what everyone thought," John told him. "According to the will, the money is to be split equally between the two siblings unless one of them is deceased *before* the old man dies. In that case, the other one inherits it all."

Brian picked up his soda and leaned back in his chair. You're starting to piss me off," he said. "Just tell me, how does this concern us? What does this have to do with Jane?" He poured the last of the Coke into his mouth.

"Drew's sibling is… *Jane Hart*."

The soda can fell into Brian's lap, bounced off his leg, and rolled onto the floor. "What?" he tried to ask as he choked on the mouthful of Coke.

"Shocker, right?" John asked. "So, the old man is on his deathbed and one of his children is missing. I'd like to say we've solved your case, but Jane's still missing."

Brian didn't pick up the soda can. He tried to grasp the fact that Doug wasn't Jane's father. Did Doug know?

"Brian? Hey, Brian." John snapped his fingers, trying to garner the chief's attention. "Brian?"

Enderly leaned forward in his chair, his arms crossed on his desk. "Let me get this straight. Drew and Jane are siblings?" He was so angry he could barely get his words out. "And Harrison Carter the second left his estate to be split between the two of them—providing one of them hasn't died before he does. The old man's close to dying and Jane's missing. So, if she's dead,

Drew gets everything."

John nodded wildly. "That about sums it up."

Brian stood up, hovering dangerously close to John. "And the FBI has known about this for weeks and never said one word to me about it?" He jabbed a finger into his own chest.

John leaned back in his chair, away from Brian. "I couldn't. You know that. That's how the FBI works." He stood up and moved to the opposite side of the room.

"What you just told me changes everything. I was positive it was Viv Sterling who wanted to do Jane in." He shook his head. "Drew was only a blip on my radar because of a Key Employee life insurance policy he bought on Jane."

"What? Our guy never mentioned that," John said.

Brian glared at John. "Maybe it was confidential FBI information, and he couldn't tell you." He sneered.

"Listen." John stepped forward. "We're going to have to work together if we want to find Jane."

Brian conceded; besides being angry, there was nothing he could do about the time he'd already wasted following inconsequential leads. "Holy shit! I can't even comprehend this." Brian said as he walked past John to the investigation board. He pointed to Viv. "If Jane was Harrison's daughter, it makes sense why Viv treated her the way she did."

There was a quick rap on the door before Mauri stuck her head in. "Holy shit!" she exclaimed. She couldn't take her eyes off John. He had entered as the town's latest drifter and now, he sat before her as a handsome gentleman with perfect teeth.

"Popular phrase today," he said with a laugh.

"Mauri, remember that conversation we had earlier?" Brian warned her.

"I do. I've got it." She closed her lips, twisted the imaginary key, and tossed it over her shoulder.

"Did you need something?" Brian asked.

"What?" She continued to stare at John. "Oh, yeah. Doug Sterling called. He's in Duluth, but he said Viv came down here a couple of days ago and he hasn't been able to get ahold of her since that first night."

"Lovers spat?" Brian asked.

"Don't think so." Mauri pursed her lips. "He called the Moonlight. Viv went out near dark and hasn't returned."

"Sonofabitch!" Brian said as he swung his fist through the air. "Mauri, get everyone in here ASAP. We've got a hell of a lot of work to do. Call Doug and tell him we'll call him when we know something. And…"

"Yes, I can work late tonight," she said as she closed the door to his office.

CHAPTER 34

When John Henry, the drifter, removed his disguise in Brian's office that afternoon, he simply ceased to exist. From that moment on, he became John Wallick, FBI agent.

Within thirty minutes, every squad car was parked at the station. Several FBI vehicles rolled into the lot as well. John and Brian tag-teamed their meeting, filling everyone in on the developments of the last few hours, as well as reviewing everything they already knew.

 Mauri ordered sandwich makings from the grocery store. She expertly tracked each squad as they were dispatched to various locations in their search for Viv. She'd updated the whiteboard with new information, questions, and data. By 1:00 a.m., they finally called it. The darkness hindered their search.

"Five hours," Brian told them. "I want everyone back here by 6:00 a.m."

He locked the door and walked Mauri to her car. "Thanks for everything you did today," he paused, "and tonight."

Mauri smiled at him. "Sure thing, Boss." Brian watched her until she was safely on her way before he climbed into his squad and headed home.

Numerous thoughts pelted him as he drove through the sleepy town. He should have turned left on Carver Street;

instead, when the light turned green, he cranked the wheel to the right. Even though no railroad ran through the town, the west side had always been referred to *the right side of the tracks*. The houses were more extravagant than the ones to the east. They housed people like the Carters, people who loved to be on display. Jane had grown up just a street over.

As he neared the edge of town, Brian turned down Engler. Many of the homes were lit up, most already decorated for Halloween. Ghosts swayed in the breeze.

Drew's house was pretentious. A sizeable wrought-iron fence ran around the perimeter of the yard. The personalized gate arched upward; the name *Carter* was displayed across the front. The house was the largest in the town. Even nestled among the other homes in the area, it looked out of place. Drew's father had built it for the woman who walked out on him and left Harrison and Drew high and dry.

Brian pulled over and cut his lights. He stared at the house and wondered if the woman Harrison had married and the woman he loved was the same person. Had Harrison always been in love with Viv? Was that why his wife had left?

The two Carter men had shared the mansion, as it was known around Cedar Point, until Drew left for college. Harrison employed a full-time housekeeper and cook as well as a live-in nanny until Drew could drive. From that point on, besides the help, Harrison had been the only resident of the house until he moved to Living Waters when his dementia took away his ability to care for himself. Once he was settled into the facility, Drew moved from a small house on the other side of town into this monstrosity. Living there by himself must have been tremendously lonely; everywhere he looked had to be a reminder of just how alone he was. Brian could relate. But the size of this house had to make it so much worse.

The place was quiet. The lights were off—both inside and out. Brian pulled back onto the street and slowly drove past. Making a U-turn at the end of the block, he parked and watched the house from the other direction. He thought he saw the curtain flutter, but he wasn't sure. Was Drew watching him? He leaned his arms across the top of his steering wheel and rested his chin on the back of one wrist. He continued his surveillance of the house but saw nothing. Finally, he turned on his lights and headed home.

Brian's house was cold. The programmable thermostat had turned down several hours before. He looked at his watch: 2:49 a.m. In another couple of hours, his thermostat would kick back in and begin its recovery mode. After a trip to the bathroom, he tossed his clothes onto the floor and crawled into his unmade bed. The moon cast ribbons of golden light through his gridded windows panes.

He rolled over and closed his eyes, but sleep didn't come. Resigning himself to the fact that it was going to be another sleepless night, he rolled to his back and folded his hands across his stomach. The day replayed in his mind repeatedly, but every time he got to the part about Jane and Drew sharing the same father, the reel broke. Jane was missing. Drew needed money. Viv couldn't be found. He repeated it over and over, trying to make sense of it.

Sometime around 5:00 a.m., he finally drifted off to sleep.

CHAPTER 35

Drew saw Brian's squad car sitting on the street outside his house. How much did the cop know? Had he found out about Viv? Had he been following him?

After Brian drove away, Drew walked through the dark house and into his father's study. A rack of pool cues hung on one wall of the massive room. He reached under the frame, pressed a button, and stepped back. The wall slowly opened, revealing a passageway into a hidden room. Drew stepped into the room and pressed a button on the wall. The wall quietly closed. The room was devoid of all light; it was what people meant when they used the phrase *pitch-black*. He had needed to close the door before he could turn on the lights in case anyone outside was still watching. Running his hand along the wall, he flipped the switch. He shielded his eyes from the bright overhead light, blinking several times until his eyes adjusted. It was the first actual light he'd seen since he left his father's side many hours before.

Drew sat down at his father's desk and removed the top drawer. He dumped the sparse contents on the mahogany top. On the bottom of the drawer, a piece of black electrical tape housed the key he needed. He peeled back the tape and squeezed the cold metal key between his fingers hard enough to leave a slight imprint. He shoved the fake thermostat cover to one side, pushed the key into the hole, and pulled the wooden door open. An array of guns gleamed in a glass case; light reflected off the metal and the glass.

He had been raised with guns; he had been trained in how to use them, but more importantly, how to respect them. They weren't toys. His father had taken him hunting since before he was old enough to carry a real gun. The two sat in duck blinds and deer stands for hours every weekend in the fall. With a toy gun in his hands, he had walked through fields, flushing out grouse for his father to shoot. He imitated his dad, pretending he had killed the birds that fell around him. Guns had always intrigued him, especially the ones in his dad's gun case. He knew which ones were registered and which ones weren't— which ones couldn't be traced back to him or his father.

A Colt Single Action Army revolver caught his eye. That gun had been his favorite since the day his father told him about it. He slid the glass door on the gun case to one side and gingerly touched it with the tips of his fingers. *Now that's a gun!* he thought. But the barrel was too long. It was a showpiece, nothing more. Next to it was a .44 Magnum. Drew lifted it from its holder and held it in his hand. The metal felt cold against his warm skin. It also felt familiar. The hole through the window at KDIG radio had been his doing. He held the gun, got a feel for it again—just like his father had taught him. It was the perfect choice. It wasn't registered.

Drew pointed the gun toward an imaginary target; he wrapped both palms against the stock of the gun, steadying his aim. This was the gun that would fix everything he'd screwed up in the past several years. But this gun, while repairing one thing, would destroy another. If his father were more aware, he would hate him for killing Jane, but then again, his father was a ruthless businessman. Would Two have sacrificed his daughter for the company? Drew had to believe he would.

He opened another cabinet and found the box of bullets he needed. One was all it would take. After all, he was an expert shot. But he wasn't going to chance it; he pulled the six bullets he needed to fill the chamber. Drew loaded the gun and checked the safety before flipping off the lights and pressing the button to open the secret passageway. Once back in Two's office, he stood in the dark until his night vision returned.

His work satchel had been left in his car at Living Waters, so he grabbed a cheap green canvas hunting bag and tucked the gun inside. Drew peeked out the window again. Enderly hadn't returned. Leaving wasn't a problem, providing he left under the cover of the night. Where to wait out the time until Jane's sons had both left for work was the issue.

An enormous, attached garage ran perpendicular to the house. It was filled with expensive cars, each lined up in front of one of six doors. Selling even half the cars would have helped his financial woes—at least for a few months, but until Two died, Drew's hands were tied. Until he was the owner of the entire estate, and Jane was out of the picture, he couldn't do diddly-squat.

A narrow door separated the first garage from the second. The other side held a handful of more traditional cars, including a thirty-five-year-old Toyota Camry, a vehicle that would blend into the small town unnoticed. It was dated, but it didn't have a scratch on it. The mileage was low because it had rarely been driven. That was the car his father gave his mother not long before she left. When she left, she had taken the car with her. However, out of spite, his father had refused to let her keep it. Their prenuptial agreement allowed her nothing, and Harrison made sure that was exactly what she got.

Before his spiral into dementia, Two drove each car several times a year. He kept the tabs up to date. Since his dad's move to the home, Drew kept up the charade of pretending someone was ever going to drive these cars. But a currently licensed car would be easier to sell than one with old plates.

The Camry was the last car his father had ever driven. On that night, Drew spent hours trying to reach him. He was doing his *sonly* duties—checking in on his elderly father. Finally, after almost two hours of not making contact, he set out to search for his dad. Two had gotten lost on the other side of town, not far from where Jane's boys lived. Harrison had no idea where he was or how to get home. When Drew found him, he was sobbing in the front seat of the Camry. He crawled in and sat with his old man, trying to assure him he was all right. Harrison didn't want to talk about what had happened; he wanted to talk about everything else, and being a good son, Drew obliged him. One of their conversations was about loves won and those lost. Drew assumed he was talking about his mother when he talked about the love of his life, but now he understood it wasn't his mother at all. It was Viv Sterling.

That night, after he had gotten his father settled into bed, Drew sat in Two's study and cried. He knew their time together would be short; he felt it. There would come a day when his father no longer knew his name, wouldn't even recognize him. Something inside of him broke that night, something so profound and so miniscule that even he didn't notice it right away.

Drew set the canvas bag with the pistol on the passenger's seat of the Camry and opened the garage door. He drove down the long dark driveway, through the gate, and onto the street. Once he hit the main drag, he headed out of town in the same direction he and Viv had traveled. He peered into the cornfield where he had left her car, but it had been swallowed by the tall stalks. According to his calculations, Viv had been dead for almost six hours. In another six, her daughter would be as well.

It was still dark when he reached the road where they would eventually find Viv. He checked for car lights in front of and behind him before slowing down. He glanced down the road as he drove past, but he wasn't sure why. Morbid curiosity, perhaps? Maybe it was just an *attaboy* moment.

Drew was now a murderer. If anyone ever found out, he'd be just like those people on the documentaries they showed on TV. People would know his name; they would say it with disgust, spit it out of their mouths. They would hate him, wonder how he got to be so ruthless that he could kill not one but two people. In one way, he found it too grotesque to even think about, but in another, it excited him. He was playing God.

With a good six hours to kill, Drew kept driving. He was nearly three hours from Cedar Point before stopping for fuel. He flipped the hood of his sweatshirt up before climbing out to pump gas. The card Drew inserted into the pump was inscribed *Harrison A. Carter*. It just didn't belong to him; this Harrison was his father. If the police tracked Drew's credit cards, searched where his whereabouts on the day Jane died, they would find nothing. A wicked grin stretched across his face as he watched the numbers flash by.

Main Street of the small town boasted only one restaurant: The Little Red Hen. After parking his car on the street in the back of the building, he walked around to the front. He held the menu in front of his face when he ordered. When the waitress brough his food and the check, he turned toward the window. He kept his head low, his face pointed at his food as he gobbled down his last meal before he finished off his sister. When he was done, he threw a twenty-dollar bill on the table and headed back to his car. *Easiest ten-dollar tip she ever made*, he thought.

"This is the beginning of the end," he said out loud as he

turned onto the road headed back toward Cedar Point. His mind twisted and turned; thoughts floated in and out like airplanes taking off and landing. Not once had he wondered if he was doing the right thing; it was all about making sure he did the wrong thing right. He wasn't about to screw this up.

Around 9:00 a.m., he twisted the dial of the archaic radio to the *on* position and pressed the AM radio button. He searched for news as he turned the knob; instead, all he got was static. But the silence was deafening when he turned it off.

Almost two hours after leaving the restaurant, he knew he was nearing the logging road where he'd killed Viv. From the other direction, he could find it easily. Many deals had been made on that road in the past few years. But he'd never had to locate it from this side of Cedar Point.

As he hit the top of a steep hill, he saw a barrage of flashing lights almost a mile ahead. He slowed the car and pulled onto the gravel shoulder. "Dammit!" he yelled as he slammed the palms of his hands against the thin steering wheel. "Dammit all to hell!" His mind raced. Was that the logging road? Had they already found Viv? Were they stopping traffic? Were they looking for him?

No cars were coming, so he spun the wheel hard to the left, hit the gas, and headed in the direction he had just come from. He had to find a back road, a way to get back into Cedar Point without taking the main highway. He was focused on the dilemma of a new route when a siren screamed behind him.

Instinctively, he pulled to the side as the ambulance raced by. His heart thudded in his chest as a patrol car followed; a string of *what-ifs* spun through his brain.

"Siri, route me to Cedar Point, Minnesota," he told his phone. His voice shook and he had to repeat his directive before she understood. She immediately gave him directions, telling him to turn around and go back the way he had been headed. He canceled Siri and drove to the next town and turned right on the highway. From there, he asked for a new route.

CHAPTER 36

Sean stared at the photograph of his wife. "Emily," he said out loud as he tenderly touched her face. "I love you so much." He no longer spoke in past tense. He no longer called her *Jane*. At some point during the past two days, Jane had disappeared, and Emily had taken her place. The girl and the woman had become one—his sister. Sean knew it was Emily who had saved him from his mother's sickness and his father's drinking. He needed her; he didn't need Jane—so, in Sean's mind, Jane simply ceased to exist.

Sean picked up the whiskey bottle and filled his glass more than half full. He hadn't eaten or showered in days. He was so far gone that he couldn't comprehend the extreme roughness of his unshaven face or that the smell that permeated the room was from him. The only thing Sean knew was that he wanted his sister. He wanted Emily.

She had come back to him once; no, that wasn't right. He had found her; he forced her to return. But when she came back, she wanted to leave him. She told him she didn't love him. He knew that wasn't true. Emily loved him and needed him as much as he needed her.

Sometimes his sister made him mad. When she was small, before she disappeared, he had been so nice to her. But that hadn't worked; she left anyway. When she came back to him, he changed his tactics. He had needed to be firm, let her know he was in charge, and she couldn't leave him again. That was why he hurt her sometimes, to punish her. She had to learn how to behave.

Anger swelled inside of Sean as he thought about her disappearance again. At first, it was a tiny ripple, but they quickly expanded until they grew into massive waves of rage. In his mind, he saw a flipbook of photos from the time Emily was little until the day she disappeared the second time.

The threads of his fury wove themselves into a hard knot inside his stomach and he felt them spill over, filling every inch of his body. He squeezed the framed photo of his sister so hard the glass snapped beneath the pressure of his thumbs. He dropped it to the floor and ground his bare heel into it. "Bitch!" he screamed. "Bitch! If you think you can leave me, you'd better think again!" Tiny slivers embedded into his foot, but he felt nothing.

Bloody heel prints stained the carpet and the wood floor as he walked to the kitchen. When he reached the island, he leaned both hands against the edge and stared at the shattered frame and marred photo lying on the floor in front of the couch. An intense wave of remorse flooded through him, and he raced into the living room, picked up the photo, and hugged it to his chest. "I'm so sorry, Emily. I love you. I didn't mean to hurt you. You're my sister."

His emotions whiplashed again, this time erupting into uncontrollable fits of rage. The framed picture sailed across the room and smashed into the marble fireplace. In his frenzy, he stomped through the house, destroying every photo of Jane— *his Emily*. Broken glass littered nearly every inch from the den to the bedroom.

Standing in the middle of the grisly mess, Sean screamed, "Emily! Emily, get in here now! Pick this up! He pulled on his hair and stomped his feet, driving additional fragments of glass into his soles. "I said, get in here and clean this up!" When Emily didn't appear, he screamed again. "You'll be sorry when I find you!"

Blood oozed from the wounds. He was so consumed with other emotions, he didn't feel the pain. The only hurt he felt was from the agony of having Emily leave him—again. Sean fell onto the couch, pulled a pillow over his face, and screamed, kicking his feet like a toddler. Blood spattered in all directions. Finally, he rolled to his side and held the pillow to his chest.

The original broken photo rested on the floor in front of the fireplace. "Emily, I miss you," he cried. He rolled off the couch and crawled toward the picture. Glass crunched beneath him. Sean held the frame to his chest. Tears rolled down his face as he carried *Jane's* picture back to the couch. Laying it on top of the pillow, he gently rocked the cushion back and forth. Then, between sobs, in his rough, cracked voice, he sang a lullaby, the same one he sang to Emily when she was just a baby. *"Rock-a-*

bye, baby, on the tree top. When the wind blows, the cradle will rock. When the bough breaks, the cradle will fall, and down will go baby, cradle and all."

Sean suddenly stopped rocking. "Down will go baby…" he growled in a low, black-hearted voice. Once again, he picked up the broken framed photo and hurled it across the room. The corner of the heavy wooden frame crashed into the wall, poking a hole in the sheetrock before falling face down onto the carpeted floor. "Down will go baby," he whispered loudly. "Down will go baby!" he yelled.

The family portrait of him and Jane and the boys still hung above the mantel. He hadn't thought of his sons in days. The longer he stared at the picture, the angrier he got. Cole and Luke belong to Emily. They belonged to him. They were *his* boys.

Again, he traipsed through the broken glass, making his way to the mudroom. He was aware enough to put on his shoes, but he was cognizant of little else. The key fob was in his pants pocket; when he pushed the starter, the car sprang to life immediately. Anxious to reclaim his sons, he slammed the car in reverse, but the garage door hadn't opened all the way and it scraped the top of his car. Sean didn't even notice.

Everything he did was on autopilot. All he knew was that he had to save his sons before that bitch, Emily, turned them against him.

CHAPTER 37

It was nearly 11:00 a.m. when Drew drove into town. The lunch crowd hadn't hit the streets yet, so it appeared desolate. He pulled off Main Street and traveled a parallel side street to the outskirts of Cedar Point. A few moments later, he was parked between the cornfield and Jane's sons' yard, the ancient Camry hidden from sight.

With the green bag draped across his back, he grabbed a low tree branch and pulled himself into the huge elm tree that grew next to the fence. Tentatively, he stepped on the top of the wooden frame before dropping into the yard. He removed the gun from his bag and tucked it into the waistband of his jeans, against the small of his back. Without a sound, he pressed himself against the house and slowly crept toward the sliding glass door. A deep bark came from inside; Drew froze.

"Okay, okay, Hoss. Hold on. I'm coming." There was no doubt about it; the voice belonged to Jane.

Drew leaned against the siding and waited. He reached for the gun and held it in both hands, just like his father had taught him. The safety was off, and he had two fingers on the trigger. When the door opened, the dog leaped at him, and he shot. Hoss dropped to the ground, a whining heap on the stone patio.

Drew's eyes met Jane's as he ran toward her. He stuck his

foot in the track of the door to block it from closing. Jane shoved him and tried to slam the door, but he threw his weight into it and held it open. She raced toward the front door as Drew sent off a warning shot into the wall above her head. She froze.

"Well, well, well," he said. "If it isn't the elusive Jane Hart." He kept the gun pointed at her as she tried to inch away. "Stop moving," he commanded. "You're not going anywhere until I say you are." He grabbed her arm and flung her onto the couch.

"Drew," she whined, "why are you doing this? What have I ever done to you?"

Nervous laughter erupted from Drew as he held the gun in both hands, still aimed at her. "Well, let's start with just being born."

"What?" Jane's voice quivered. "I don't understand."

He walked from one end of the couch to the other, never taking the gun off her. "For someone so smart, you really are pretty dumb." He lifted the bottom of her hair and let it fall. "Dumb blonde, they say. Don't they?" he scoffed. "Is that your natural color? It would be fitting."

Jane didn't respond. With her eyes, she searched the room for something to use as a weapon.

"You're not getting out of here, so stop looking," Drew remarked.

"Why are you doing this? Why? I thought we were friends," Jane whined.

Drew shrugged. "Well, Jane, it looks like we're more than

friends." He waited for that message to sink in.

"What are you talking about?"

"Apparently, your mom and my dad did the dirty about nine months before you were born. You're not a Sterling after all; you never were. You're a Carter, just like me."

Jane's face fell. Drew watched her put the pieces together. "You're my brother?" she asked in a loud whisper.

Drew brought the gun to the side of her head. "Well, you figured that one out quickly," he said, laughing.

She felt the pressure of the barrel against her temple. "Please, Drew," she begged. "I'll give you whatever you want. Please, don't do this."

He swept the end of the pistol sideways across her face, leaving a thin line that began to ooze red droplets. "There's only one way you can give me what I want," he said. The lines in his forehead grew deeper and his eyebrows pressed inward. "Death, Jane. That's all I need from you. That's it."

"Help!" Jane screamed as she tried to distance herself from Drew. "Help!"

He backhanded her across the face, knocking her to the floor. "Shut the hell up or I'll kill you right where you sit." Roughly lifting her by the arm, he threw her back onto the couch. "Now, Jane," he said very condescendingly, "I really don't want to kill you here, but I will if I have to. I'd rather take you somewhere else—where your boys won't have to clean up what's left of their mother."

The gun bobbed up and down as he pulled the straps of the old backpack off his shoulders. He threw a blindfold at her. "Put this on and tie it tightly." His heart had gone dark; any spark of decency had long been extinguished, beginning the moment he discovered his father's dirty little secret. Drew felt nothing when Jane begged for mercy, nothing when she cried out loud. All he saw were dollar signs and looking like a hero to his dad.

"Please, Drew. Stop!" Jane begged. "I won't say a word to anyone. I promise."

A sinister laugh cut across the room. "Are you kidding? You've got Enderly on speed dial. You've loved him since we were kids. Everyone knew it." He raised an eyebrow. "I wouldn't trust you to feed my pet fish." He picked up the blindfold again and pitched it into her lap. "Now put the damn thing on or I'll blow your effing head off right here."

Jane whimpered as she tied the thick scarf behind her head. Her hands shook, and it took her longer than Drew felt warranted. "Hurry the hell up."

Once her blindfold was tied, he set the gun down and grabbed a long rope from his bag. He tightly bound her hands together. Jane winced, but it only made him laugh. "Suffering builds character," he told her.

He jerked her to her feet and shoved the gun into the small of her back. "Walk, bitch," he said.

Jane held her roped hands in front of her, feeling her way with her feet as he impatiently pushed her forward. "Where are you taking me?" she wept.

"It won't matter anyway, so just shut the hell up." He pressed the gun deeper into her back. She arched her shoulders to keep it from digging in.

Drew guided her from behind, twisting the gun in the opposite direction he wanted her to go. Once outside, she heard Hoss's whining. "Hoss? Are you okay, boy?"

"Not a word," Drew told her. "I'll finish him off if I hear one more word out of you."

He unlocked the gate and forced her through the opening. Jane was dragging her feet through the grass. "Get moving." Drew shoved her in the passenger's side and slammed the door. Just in case she tried to do anything dumb, he kept the gun pointed at her as he passed in front of the car.

He started the old Camry and backed it out from the side of the house. Shifting into drive, he sped along the road that ran in front of the house and headed toward the main drag. Drew was so focused on Jane that he didn't notice the black BMW sitting at an intersection he passed through.

CHAPTER 38

The Camry slowly passed in front of Sean's BMW. The woman with the blindfold in the passenger's seat looked familiar. Even with the cloth covering her eyes, he was sure it was Emily. But the hair color was wrong. His sister's hair had always been a mess of brown curls, not blond like this woman's.

Sean should have turned right toward his sons' house, but instead, he turned his car to the left. He followed the Camry north, just past the outskirts of town where it turned onto a paved road.

The highway was the main thoroughfare leading to several smaller lakes and restaurants just outside of Cedar Point. The townspeople traveled it in droves in the evening when they headed to The Hook, Wine, and Sinker or The Lookout Super Club. Fishermen drove the road in the early morning and again in the evening as they headed to the Neenah chain of lakes. Before all those places, a long-abandoned gravel pit was cut into a tall bank on the right-hand side, not more than a hundred yards from the main road.

The Camry turned into the pit. Almost instantly, the car tipped to the right as the passenger's side wheels were sucked into a pothole of loose sand. The driver rocked the vehicle, quickly shifting between forward and reverse until it popped back onto the road and stopped. Still in a drunken stupor, Sean maneuvered his BMW past the gravel pit and onto a side road about seventy-five feet away.

He had to know if the woman was Emily. And if it was his sister, why did this man have her blindfolded? Sean pulled his pistol from beneath his seat and climbed out of his car. Emily needed him, and he would do anything to protect her—anything. Tree branches snapped as Sean stumbled through the woods to get a better look. No one seemed to notice.

Sean couldn't see the man's face when he climbed out of the car, but the sunlight glinted off something he held in his hand. *Did the man have a gun?* He switched his weapon from his left hand to his right. The man walked to the woman's side of the car and jerked the door open. Roughly, he grabbed her by a rope tied around her wrists and pulled her out of the car. The top of her head hit the doorframe and the woman screamed. She tried to pull her blindfold down, but the man told her to leave it alone or he'd kill her.

When the woman turned, Sean got a clear view of her face, at least the part that wasn't covered by the narrow band of material. It was Emily. His heart raced; it pulsed in his ears as excitement mixed with fear. Why was this man punishing his sister? Sean was the only one who could punish her. It was his job to make her pay for leaving.

The man slammed Emily's door and shoved her from behind; she stumbled and fell onto the eroding road, unable to catch herself because her hands were bound together. "Asshole," Sean said out loud, but still, no one looked his way.

"Get up, Jane! Get your ass off the ground," the man screamed at her.

The man had called her Jane, but that wasn't right. It made no sense to Sean why he would call his sister by that name. "It's Emily. Her name is Emily!" he yelled as a car with a missing muffler approached. But, again, no one looked in his direction.

The rusty old car slowed in front of him. He could see the driver's face, but she did not see him through the trees. She looked petrified as she punched numbers into her phone as she sped away.

The man and Emily moved closer to Sean but didn't see him through the thicket. The man looked familiar, but he couldn't place him.

Sean watched him push his sister up the hill toward the top of the old gravel pit. Emily didn't want to go; he could tell. He heard her sobbing, begging the man to release her. She told him she would do anything. His sister fell again and screamed out in pain. The man jerked her up by the elbow. "Leave her alone," Sean whispered. "She's just a little girl."

He stumbled through the brush, moving closer to the hill leading to the top of the gravel pit. A few cars raced along the road, past the three of them, but no one stopped. No one paid attention to Sean or the man and his sister as they climbed toward the crest of the hill.

Sean moved out of the brush and into the opening below the incline. He started to climb but had to fight his instability from a week of drinking. Several times he caught himself from nearly tumbling backward. The gun flopped around in his hand as he continued his ascent. Emily was crying, still begging the man to let her go, but he just kept yelling at his sister.

"It's the will, Jane. It's the will," the man said to her. "Harrison left you half of everything. If I have it all, I can save his damn company."

Emily sobbed; Sean could hear her more clearly now as he moved closer. "You can have it all, Drew. You can have every single penny. I don't want it. Just please, don't do this."

None of it made sense to Sean. Multiple days of alcohol had frayed his thoughts; it had taken away his ability to reason. Within the last thirty-six hours, his sense of reality had vanished. Emily was his past and his present. Somewhere, he had lost Jane; he didn't even recognize her name.

"It's too late, Jane. I can't trust you." The man laughed. "Just think of this as sibling rivalry. You're not afraid of a little brother-sister competition, are you?" He shrugged. "I mean, you must have experienced it with your perfect sisters, didn't you?" Drew laughed.

"Help! Help me!" Emily screamed. "Help!"

The man Emily called Drew laughed louder. "Just shut up, will you? No one can hear you, and you're just pissing me off." He slapped her across the face. Emily lifted her knotted hands to her cheek.

Sean seethed with anger as he continued to climb precariously, frequently stopping to adjust his footing. *No one could hit his sister. Not his mother or father. No one except him.*

"Do you think the people in those cars care about you? Hell, they can't even see you up here." Drew smiled. "Besides, they already think you're dead. You've been missing for a month as it is."

The man put a hand on each of Emily's shoulders and slowly walked her backward as she sobbed. "I mean, that's why I brought you here to the old gravel pit. They won't find your body until spring, and by then, it might be damn hard to tell *when* you died. Perfect play on my part, don't you think?"

"Drew, please," Emily begged.

The man stepped away several feet and pointed his gun directly at Emily. "Don't step back, Jane, or it's all over."

Sean heard the click of the gun as the man carefully aimed. "Bye-bye, Sis," he said.

"She's *my* sister!" Sean screamed as he raised his gun and emptied it into the man. When Sean heard only a click, he threw it down and clumsily stumbled the last few steps up the hill. The man lay face down; one hand hung over the edge of the bank. Dark red spots appeared in ever-widening circles across the back of his sweatshirt.

Sean couldn't find his sister. "Emily!" he screamed as he raced around the top of the sandy hill. "Emily!" He dropped to his knees at the edge of the bank, wailing uncontrollably. Suddenly, he looked down and saw her tiny body, awkwardly lying at the bottom of the pit, on a mound of sand. "Emily," he cried. "Please don't leave me! Not again. Not ever again."

A hand touched his shoulder. "You're okay, Sean. It's going to be okay." The man gently helped him to his feet, pulling him away from the crumbling edge of the pit. "Come with me," Deputy Porter told him.

Officer Serrano knelt next to the man lying on the ground, the one Sean had filled full of bullets. Sean saw him shake his head toward the man holding him up, but he didn't understand.

In his psychotic and drunken state, Sean didn't recognize either man; he didn't know why they were dressed alike or why the one man was pulling him away from his sister. He pointed to the cliff, trying to make him understand. "That's my sister down there," he wept. "That's my sister, Emily."

"I know, Sean. It's okay. We'll take care of your... your sister. But first, we're going to get you some help. Okay?"

CHAPTER 39

Jane Hart

I had no idea where I was, but I knew if I stepped backward, I would fall off the edge of the cliff Drew had warned me about; I could feel the sand eroding beneath my feet. There was no way to know if what he told me about Harrison was the truth. Was I a Carter? How could that be? Nothing made sense to me anymore: my parents selling me as an infant, living as Sean's sister for two years, finding out that Doug wasn't my father, and being kidnapped by a psychotic killer who claimed to be my brother. And if that were true, would Drew really rather kill me than share his inheritance?

I begged him to let me go, pleaded with him, but it was like bargaining with the devil; there was no way I was going to win. I promised him he could have every penny his father left to me in his will. It could all be his. The only things I wanted was to hold my sons again, know my future grandchildren, and leave Sean and his unhealthy obsession with his imaginary sister, Emily.

As I stood where Drew left me, unable to see what was happening, my sense of hearing was on high alert. I had heard the sirens in the distance minutes before. Holding on, keeping Drew talking, was my only hope. But then I heard a commotion.

Several shots were fired, but none of them hit me. With my bound hands, I pushed the blindfold from my face and tried to step forward, but the sand gave way beneath me, and I fell. Everything suddenly switched to slow motion, and I was acutely aware of the sensation of falling, like in a dream. My eyes were open as I dropped through the cool autumn air. With my arms tied, it felt awkward. I braced myself for the impact, but it never came.

Instead of feeling the crash, I felt this incredible sensation of immense…love. There was no other way to describe it. It was so far beyond the love I shared with my boys. It was warm and bright and mind-numbing. The gray of the day had faded away, and the sunshine on my face was like nothing I had ever known and, instead of falling, I suddenly had this feeling I was floating.

Somehow as I drifted toward the ground, I separated from my body. I saw everything: Sean crying in the arms of Deputy Porter, Officer Serrano kneeling over Drew's lifeless body, and Brian on his knees next to me in the sand. Tears filled his eyes as he touched my neck. I wanted to reach out and tell him I was going to be okay, but my hands wouldn't move.

Then, suddenly, Brian was gone, and I watched myself stand up and walk toward the woods on the other side of the gravel pit. My grandmother stepped out of the trees. Mesmerized by her appearance, I wanted nothing more than to touch her. Her skin was translucent, and she had an iridescent glow that made her look even more beautiful than I remembered. I couldn't wait to hold her, but I couldn't run. My eyes were focused only on her, and I prayed she wouldn't disappear before I could reach her.

As I got close, I grew incredibly shy, afraid to put my hand in hers. I had never seen anyone look the way she did. She almost floated to me. She wrapped her arms around me, holding me in a hug so warm it made me want to cry. Her touch was gentle and soft and felt like warm sunshine. I didn't want her to let go; I wanted to stay there forever.

A small boy with the same brilliant light around him stepped toward me. He threw his arms around my waist as Grandma Betty let go. "I've always loved you," he said. "From the moment you breathed life." I hugged him back. His love flowed through me. With his arms still tightly wrapped around me, he tilted his head backward and smiled up at me. "I have wanted to hug you forever, Jane. I wanted to know my sister," he said.

Over the top of the boy's head, I stared at my grandmother. I mouthed the name JJ, and she nodded. I dropped to my knees and held him in my arms, hugging him more tightly than I should have. There was such joy in that moment; it felt like my heart was going to explode. Finally, I stood up and wrapped one arm around my grandmother and rested the other over my brother's shoulder. I stepped toward the woods behind them, leading us toward the beautiful trees—colors so vibrant, I couldn't even begin to describe them.

There was nothing I wanted more than to walk into that forest, to live among the colors that exuded only joy. But suddenly, JJ stopped walking. He moved in front of me and tugged on my shirt. I dropped to my knees. "I love you," he said. At that moment, I knew true love.

"I love you too, JJ." I tried to hug him, but he locked his elbows and pressed his hands against me to keep me from getting close.

For the first time since I laid eyes on him, his smile disappeared. "It's not time, Jane. You can't come with us. You have to go back."

Violently, I shook my head. "No. I don't want to go back," I looked up at Grandma Betty, but her smile had vanished also.

"I'm afraid you have to, honey," she said. "You have so much more to do. So much love to give. There are people who still need you."

JJ threw his arms around my neck. "Someday, Jane. Someday you will see us again. I promise," he whispered into my ear. He stepped backward and took Grandma Betty's hand.

"Please don't go," I cried. "Please don't leave me."

"You'll be okay, honey," Grandma said as she laid a warm hand against my cheek. "Just know that we love you and are always near you."

Tears rolled down my face as I watched the two of them walk toward the woods. I wanted to chase them, but my feet were pressed deep into the sand, and I couldn't move. The longing to follow them and not being able to was torturous.

I cried as they slowly faded, their bodies becoming more transparent the deeper they walked into the forest. Then, just before they disappeared, JJ looked at me over his shoulder and waved.

From that moment, until I woke up in the hospital nearly a week later, I remember nothing.

A thunderous round of applause brought me into the moment. Rows of people were on their feet as they clapped and cheered. Whenever I told my story, I'd lose myself in it. I am always back standing with my grandmother and my brother, watching them walk away.

EPILOGUE

Jane Hart

Two Years Later

I spun my ring around on my finger as I walked down the hall toward Sean's room in the psychiatric care unit. At the request of his doctor, I had visited him nearly once a month for the past two years. Each time was more difficult than the last, and I wasn't sure how much longer I could commit. After each visit with Sean, I spent the next two sessions with my own therapist, learning how to breathe again.

"He's anxious to see you today," the doctor said as she unlocked the door. "We talked about you just this morning." I took a deep breath before I stepped inside.

"Emily!" Sean yelled as he clumsily ran toward me and threw his arms around me. "I missed you. Where have you been?" he asked in a childish voice that had developed since his breakdown.

"Hi, Sean," I said. "How are you?" I unlocked his arms from around my neck and sat in a chair on one side of a table. Sean sat on the other, swinging his feet like a small child.

"Sean, remember, this isn't Emily," the doctor reminded him. "She looks a lot like your sister, but this lady's name is Jane."

"Jane, Jane, Jane," he sang as he smiled at her. Then his face fell as he looked at the doctor. "I don't know anybody named Jane," he said.

I rushed toward the door and pulled on the handle, but it was locked. "I can't," I sobbed. "I can't do this anymore." I pounded my fists on the steel door as the doctor reached around me to unlock it.

"Bye, Emily," Sean called, waving at me. "When you come back, I'll read you *Beauty and the Beast*." I looked over my shoulder at him. The irony of the story was lost in his child-like mind.

Once outside, I took a deep breath and blew it out. "I can't do this anymore, Dr. Mansford. I know you're trying to help him, but these visits are destroying me," I explained.

"I understand, Jane. I feel like we take two steps forward and one step back with each one. It's taking much longer than I had hoped. We have to find a way to help Sean process the trauma he suffered from his dysfunctional family life."

"*His* dysfunctional family life?" I glared at her. I couldn't believe she had just said that to me—the person who had had her entire life puppet mastered by others.

"We all deal with our pasts differently." She looked back into the room. Her foot held the door slightly ajar. "Do you want to tell him goodbye? Do *you* need closure?" she asked.

I looked through the thick glass window at the man who used to be my husband, the one with whom I shared two incredible sons. His lips moved as he spoke to no one. I shook my head as I rested my hand against the cool glass, continuing to watch. "No. We said our goodbyes a long time ago."

***

Brian met me at the door with a glass of wine. He tenderly kissed my cheek. "How'd it go?" he asked.

I took a sip as I gently played with a handful of my straight brown hair. "I'm not going back," I said. "It's too hard and I don't see the point." Brian's nod was slight, but I knew he understood. "Sean and I were never meant to be. Not when we were children and not as adults."

Brian wrapped his arms around me from behind. "Did you get a chance to tell him?"

I shook my head. "No. He wouldn't understand anyway. He still sees me as his sister. At least for now, that's the world he's living in." I turned toward Brian and rested my cheek against his chest. "I just need to move forward."

Brian kissed the top of my head and tightened his arms around me. "You're right, Mrs. Enderly. You're one hundred percent right. Let's make that happen."

I was getting used to my new name. It had only been a month since Brian and I had gotten married, but it still shocked me when people called me Mrs. Enderly—in town or at H & C.

"I need to go back to work this afternoon, at least for a while," I said. "The auditor's report came in and I have an initial meeting set up with the finance team."

Brian smiled. "What time will you be home? The boys and Doug will be here around 7:00. And we better dog-proof the house because Hoss is joining them." We both laughed. "Do you want me to make anything special for dinner?"

"You decide. Ordering Pizza would be just fine," I laughed. I kissed him passionately, my lips lingering much longer than they should have if I planned to make it to work. I finally pulled away, grabbed my purse, and walked toward the door. It wasn't the house I had shared with Sean; it wasn't on the lake, but on a large lot in town, close to my boys. Between two years of intensive therapy sessions and designing our new place, I was exhausted. However, working with the builders and designers had been therapeutic and gave me something positive to focus on. The house isn't big or pretentious, but I know it will always be filled with happy memories.

During that first year, I went to the office a couple of hours once or twice a week, just to acclimate myself to H & C again. I suffer from severe post-traumatic stress disorder; I'm sure I always will. One of the parking garage attendants meets me at my car and walks me into the building each day, and when I leave, another picks me up at the door and returns me to my car. I don't know if I'll ever be able to make that walk alone.

"By the way," Brian said, interrupting my thoughts, "They're transferring your mom to a prison in Milwaukee. I didn't know if you wanted to see her before she goes."

I watched the dust particles float in the ray of light that

shone through the sidelights of the front door. Somehow, Viv had survived her ordeal with Drew, but that hadn't kept her from being incarcerated for what would likely be the remainder of her life.

"I think…" I honestly didn't know what I thought at that point. "You know, we've thrown our relationship down on that mat so many times over the past two years. She and I have wrestled with the past and fought about it over and over again. I don't think there's anything left to say." I nodded my head slowly. "Just like with Sean, I think it's time to let it go."

Brian smiled. "It's your call, Hon."

I disarmed the alarm and grabbed the front door handle, but I didn't pull it open. "You know what?" I asked as I turned back toward Brian. "My entire life was built on lies that other people told. No one was honest with me for one second. But…" I smiled at my husband, "for the first time in my life, I feel like people see me. I feel like I'm a real person."

Brian stepped toward me and wrapped me in his arms again. "For what it's worth, Jane, I see you."

My heart skipped a beat. "I know, Brian. You always did."

***

Brian watched Jane drive down the street until her car vanished from sight. He pushed the door shut just as his cell phone rang. "Well, well, well, Mauri. Did you miss me on my day off?" He laughed.

"You wish." Brian heard her clear her throat. "Hey, Boss,"

she said softly.

"Why are you whispering?" Brian closed the door behind him and walked toward the kitchen. "You're the loudest person I know."

"There's, ah, someone here to see you."

"On my day off? Who in the hell is it?" he grumbled.

"I think it might be better if you just come down here," Mauri suggested.

"Oh, for crying out loud, who is it?"

"Well, it's, ah, a woman, and she says her name is…"

Brian waited through the pause. "*Wren Brigham.*" The line went silent. "Brian? Hey, Boss? Boss? Are you okay?"

"Who did you say?" Brian asked quietly, positive he had misheard.

"I know, right? The woman said she was born *Wren Brigham* but was adopted shortly after her birth. She thinks you might be her brother."

Brian choked. *How is that even possible?* "I'll, ah, be there as soon as I can," he mumbled as the room spun around him.

If this woman was his sister, could his mother be alive also? If he had learned anything in the past two years, it was that nothing was impossible. *Nothing.*

He drew a deep breath and stumbled toward the door. His dad had some explaining to do.

From the first time I picked up a chubby Crayola crayon, I have been writing stories. I always wanted to be an author, but my mom told me I should get a job that made actual money. So, after four years of college and $2,500 in student loans—it was a long time ago—I spent thirty-six years honing my writing skills. Clearly, I am a slow learner. During most of that time, I taught middle school, because I fall in about the same place on the quirkiness scale as they do, and trained teachers to help students personalize their learning.

I was an award-winning Minnesota teacher. Some of my awards include the 2006 Fox 9 Top Teacher, 2010 Eastern Carver County Teacher of the Year, and 2011 Minnesota Teacher of the Year—Top 10 finalist. I also present at educational conferences across the United States as well as freelance for educational companies.

I hold a master's degree in education, but, while I loved teaching, I jumped ship three years ago and retired to a small Minneapolis suburb. I now have time to spend with my husband, Mitch, a retired principal, my son, Brandon, and my daughter, Taylor, who both still come home to see what's cooking in my pots and pans, my Parti Yorkie, Harper, and my two grand pets: Baxter, a Wheaten Terrier, and Guinevere, a tabby cat.

We spend a great deal of time at our cabin in Northern Minnesota, where I lose at waterskiing, but win at Cornhole. We enjoy boating, ATVing, and entertaining our massive group of families and friends. Of course, there is never a lack of food due to the fact I was raised by the Food Devil herself.

My husband has a gold personality, planner, and I have an orange personality, spontaneous. That makes us the perfect pair. We love to travel. He likes to plan, and I don't ask where we are going until we get on the plane.

Between all the family shenanigans and laughter, I spend time spinning tales—stories that entertain, inform, and teach. So, stay tuned. There will be many more to come.